DEAD AT THE START

Rowan McFarlane Detective Mysteries

ANGELA C NURSE

A Note from the Author

Please note this book is written by a British author and is set in Scotland. All spellings are the British and Scots versions.

A couple of helpful notes;

Blue42 is not real.

Whilst Strathcarron and Kyle of Lochalsh are real and very beautiful places, I have used some creative licence when it comes to describing the places within them.

Chapter 1

I stretched back in the tweed armchair next to the fire. The small hotel's lounge bar felt full, even though it was mostly locals out this evening. I watched as Alana burled about the makeshift dance floor as the band played on the small stage, it was a nice way to see in the New Year.

I was glad I'd taken Ellie up on her invite to come and visit. The last few days in her cottage just outside the high-land village of Strathcarron had been the perfect tonic to the last couple of years. And for once it was nice to let my mind wander and relax.

Ellie slumped down in a chair next to mine, 'Alana has much more energy than me, I'm beat.' Her face was a rosy pink from the exertion of the dance. 'You not going to at least get up for one reel?' She asked.

'No chance, I have two left feet and the last thing we need is me colliding into someone and sending a whole pile of folk crashing to the ground,' I laughed. 'Alana looks like she's having a good time, though.' I watched as she danced happily with an array of partners and wondered how it was my daughter had such chameleon like social skills, she certainly hadn't got them from me.

It was 2am when I pulled the bed covers up tight to keep me warm, I drifted into such a deep, deep sleep that it took me a couple of moments to realise that the distressed voice I could hear was real and coming from Ellie.

I rushed out of my room, almost colliding with Alana at the top of the stairs. The front door was open, the cold breeze filled the house. Halfway down the stairs I caught sight of Ellie's bright pink dressing gown. The light from inside the cottage a contrast to the still dark morning sky.

'Ellie are you alright?' I called out.

She turned, her face streaked with yesterday's unre-moved makeup. 'Thank God you're awake Rowan.'

I took the last two steps in one and was by her side in only a couple of movements. At the door was a young man that Ellie had introduced us to on the first day we'd arrived as the local PC. 'What's going on?' I asked.

'Callum wanted to know if we remember seeing Brodie last night,' Ellie said.

'Why?'

'The family he's staying with said he didn't come back from the hotel, so Mr Fraser went out looking for him, he found his rental car at the side of the road with a burst tyre, but no sign of Brodie anywhere. Mr Fraser thought that Brodie must've decided to walk the rest of the way so he drove about looking for him in case he got lost but couldn't find him. Then he chapped up Jock from the hotel and the two men went out on foot...' Callum trailed off

'What is it, what did they find?'

'His jacket, the sleeve was torn and bloody and that's when they called it in. I was the nearest and it'll take some while before I'll get any help from the main station at the

Kyle, so they've told me to go door to door for now on the assumption that he's likely lost his balance, fallen and taken shelter in someone's out buildings.'

'What time did Mr Fraser realise he was missing?' I asked.

'About 5.30am, he got up to go and check on the animals, it's a small holding he's got these days…' Callum trailed off realising he was getting distracted. 'Anyway, Brodie's bedroom door was open and his bed hadn't been slept in.'

'I saw him at about 12.30am,' Alana's voice came from behind me. 'We had a dance and he offered to buy me a drink, I just had a coke, but he was on the whisky. I didn't know he was driving back though otherwise I'd have said something, mum had the car and we could've given him a lift, he wasn't in a fit state to drive.'

'You weren't to know,' Callum said. 'I was there too, and I didn't notice. Any chance you can remember when he left?'

Alana wrapped her hoody around her body, 'we headed off about quarter past 1 and I think he'd left by then.'

'Did you see him talking to anyone else?' Callum asked.

'Sorry, I wasn't paying that much attention to where everyone was.'

'He was on the phone to someone not long after he bought Alana that drink,' I said. 'I had to go to the loo, and he was stood in the hallway by the toilets, it was a bit quieter there.'

'I don't suppose you know who he was talking to?' Callum asked.

I closed my eyes trying to bring up the scene from my memory, 'he sounded annoyed, he said something like, "he'll have to wait, I can't do it now" and something about it not being his fault. He was still in the hallway when I came back out, leaning on the wall, he looked stressed out. I asked him if he was okay, he didn't seem to hear me, like he was lost in his own world. I asked him again and he replied everything was fine, just family stuff.'

'Do you think he was talking to a family member then?'

I shrugged, 'no idea.'

'Okay. Can I get a look in your shed Ellie, just in case.'

'Of course, I'll turn the outside light on for you if you like?' It was still early morning, the day was going to be one of those grey overcast affairs where it felt as though the sun never truly rose. The back of Ellie's garden where the shed stood shadowed by the cottage itself was even more gloomy.

'If you wouldn't mind,' Callum said.

'Actually, it would be best not to, we've no idea what state Brodie is in, turning on the lights might frighten him,' I interrupted.

'I didn't think of that, you make a good point.'

'You know if you need help figuring out what's happened Rowan could help you, remember I told you she's a private detective,' Ellie said.

Callum gave me a pitying smile, 'that's okay, this is a bit more than finding a lost kitten, no offence, leave it to the police, we know what we're doing.'

I bit my lip but said nothing, Ellie visibly cringed for me. 'When you get home you should probably Google her, and then apologise for being such a patronising twit and hopefully, under the circumstances she'll accept.

Callum frowned briefly, giving Ellie a sideways glance unsure whether to take her seriously, likely thinking she was just blowing my horn and inflating my achievements. This wasn't the time to start a crime solving pissing contest, more important things were at stake than my reputation.

'Is this your first missing persons case?' I asked wondering what experience PC Sinclair had of hard police work.

'Not really, we get people going missing quite regularly,' he replied.

'Do you mean hillwalkers?'

Callum nodded, 'even experienced hikers can get caught off guard sometimes.'

'But mountain rescue looks for them, don't they?' I replied.

'True, I don't think Brodie is missing though, just sheltering somewhere from the cold, anyway I'll let you get warmed up.' Callum turned and headed in the direction of the large garden.

Ellie closed the door rather than watch Callum search the garden, whilst I considered what would make a young injured man hide in a shed in the freezing cold rather than knock on our door and ask for help.

Chapter 2

It's none of my business I told myself on repeat as I stood in the shower. Me and Alana would be home in a few days, and I'd promised her a holiday. By the time I arrived in the kitchen where Ellie was preparing bacon rolls and hot chocolate for breakfast, I'd promised myself I wouldn't get involved.

'What do you think's happened to Brodie?' Ellie asked, pushing a plate of food towards me.

'Probably nothing, just like Callum said, I expect that he'll already be safe and sound back at the Frasers' sleeping off a hangover.' I took a bite of my roll, enjoying the thick rashers of bacon and tomato ketchup.

'Liar,' Alana said taking a sip of her hot chocolate.

'I agree, you suspect something's happened, don't you?' Ellie said.

'I'm on holiday, and you heard Callum, he doesn't want my help, he'll have a team of people on it if Brodie doesn't turn up.'

'When has someone not wanting your help ever stopped you?' Alana said.

I stuck my tongue out at her. 'How long has Brodie been staying with the Frasers?'

'He arrived late September, they needed a bit of help around the place because Ali Fraser, their son, went to New Zealand last year, they thought he was going to be back by the end of summer, but he'd got himself a job and a boyfriend so extended his trip. Mr Fraser advertised on Workaway – it's a website where people who want to travel can come and stay with you and in exchanged for board and food they agree to work.'

'He had a bit of an accent, do you know where he's from?'

'Canada, he's been working his way around Europe,' Ellie said.

'He told me he was heading to Germany next week, that's why he'd hired the car, there were some places he'd not visited on Skye that he still wanted to see, he'd been borrowing Mrs Fraser's car but it failed it's MOT the week before Christmas,' Alana said.

'I thought you only danced with him the once?'

'I did but I was chatting with him earlier in the evening when we first arrived at the hotel, that was when you and Ellie were talking to that bloke that runs the outdoor place, the one with the axe throwing,' Alana replied.

'Duncan,' Ellie and I said in unison.

'Probably, I haven't talked to him yet.'

We'd only been at Ellie's for a couple of days, arriving late on the 29th of December. The Hogmanay celebration was where we'd had the opportunity to be introduced to more people from the village and surrounding area.

'Did he tell you anything else?' I asked.

'Just that he was going to be sorry to be leaving, I asked him why he was going then, and he said he was meeting up with friends from when he'd worked in Berlin and then we talked about some of the places he'd been. I remember thinking that he'd been to so many places and I've barely been out of the country.'

'Did you know him well?' I asked Ellie.

'A bit, I mean it's hard not to get to know all about your neighbours when there's so few of you. The Frasers have been here since time began and as far as I know they used to have a lot more farming land but it was split between Grant Fraser, who has the small holding and his brother Henry,' she replied.

'Where does Henry live?' I asked.

'He lives in the big farmhouse, you probably saw it when you drove here, he doesn't come down to the village much, tends to keep himself to himself. His wife comes down though and so does their son. They were at the Hogmanay celebrations.'

'Was there any animosity between the Fraser brothers?' I asked.

'No, at least not that I know of, I'm still an outsider here so it's possible that I wouldn't know about it but from what I can gather by talking to Eileen, Grant's wife, they didn't want the farm and despite Grant being the older brother they came to a compromise that suited them both. Eileen and Grant have half a dozen yurts at the edge of their land that they rent out for glamping and they stock the local croft box with eggs from their hens and local baking, tablet, that kind of thing, it's so popular the locals sometimes have it emptied before the tourists get a look-in during the summer months. This is the type of place where honesty boxes are respected, whatever's happened to

Brodie I can't see it having anything to do with the Frasers.' Ellie said.

'You're probably right, anyway, it's nothing to do with me – what's our plans for the day,' I said trying to change the subject.

'To be honest I thought we would stay in, light the fire, maybe watch a couple of DVDs, it's freezing out and nothing's going to be open on New Year's day,' Ellie said.

I was glad of the suggestion, I was still tired after last night and I couldn't get Brodie out of my head. Callum said that his car had come off the road with a burst tyre, and I could see how that might've happened, but why not call for help, admittedly mobile phone signal wasn't always the best here but he surely wouldn't have had to go far to get enough to phone Grant Fraser.

Ellie and Alana had selected a suitably festive film and we sat around in our PJs watching. After about twenty minutes I noticed Ellie's head lollop to the side, her breathing slow and steady, a slight snuffle of a snore every so often. I smiled at Alana.

'Think I might grab my laptop and do a bit of Uni work if that's okay,' Alana said.

'Sure, could you grab mine at the same time.'

We turned off the television and pulled a crocheted blanket over Ellie, leaving her to rest as Alana and I sat on stools at the breakfast bar in the kitchen.

I checked my emails, I'd put a notice on my website saying I wouldn't be available until the 20th of January, we were going to be at Ellie's until the 10th and then I wanted to have some time free of distraction to get Alana settled again in Dundee. She'd moved out of halls at the end of last term and had secured herself a room in a student flat share for the next term, filling the space of a student doing a term abroad. I glanced up to look at her. She was looking at her screen deep in concentration.

With nothing new in my inbox, I started Googling the area we were staying in, the first 3 pages of the search were, as I expected, all about tourist attractions around the area, there was a lot of hill walking to be done and Skye wasn't far away either. I widened my search to cover a broader geographical area and still nothing out of the ordinary, there had been hillwalkers going missing, getting lost and needing rescued as was par for the course in most of Scotland.

These were tight knit communities where, by and large, people supported and looked after one another, but like many island and coastal communities, drugs occasionally infiltrated their peace and caused problems with the young and old alike. About six months ago there were a few head-lines about a group of students staying on Skye who all needed airlifted to a nearby hospital because of a reaction to a new synthetic recreational drug. None of this was surprising, scratch the surface of any town, no matter how tranquil, and some trouble will have occurred at some point.

I tried searching further back in time, a lot of my investi-gations had involved historical cases which had led to me having subscriptions for a couple of newspaper archive services. After an hour of searching the only story that had piqued my interest was the case of missing Flora Dunn in 1998. The 48 year old woman was divorced, originally from Kyle of Lochalsh, but at the time of her disappearance she'd been living and working in Portree on Skye. She'd been seen at the hotel bar in Strathcarron the day before she went missing. She'd turned up three weeks later in Canada. I sat back and stared at my screen, it was a long time ago, but hadn't Alana said that Brodie was from Canada.

Chapter 3

Canada, apparently, had a population of 38 million, with strong ties to Scotland, hundreds if not thousands of Canadians must travel to Scotland every year to discover their ancestry. There was no reason to think one missing person 20 plus years ago would be connected to another now.

I was still staring at my screen when I became aware of Alana watching me, her head no longer engrossed in her own work, instead she was frowning at me, sitting with her arms crossed.

'What are you up to?' She asked.

'Nothing.'

'Nope, don't buy it, you've got that look on your face.'

'What look?'

'The one you get at the start of an investigation or when you've just uncovered an important piece of evidence. You've started looking into Brodie's disappearance, haven't you?'

'No, well not really…a little bit maybe.'

'I knew you couldn't leave it alone, you think Callum's

wrong don't you, that there's more to his disappearance than it looks?'

'Unless they find him today, otherwise yes, I think something is going on. Where abouts in Canada did Brodie say he was from?'

'Nova Scotia, he said that his family heritage traced back to this area, I remember laughing because so many people across the world have heritage that traces back to Scotland.'

'Is that why he came here then?'

Alana shrugged, 'I don't know, it was a party, the music was loud and we only had a bit of a chat.'

Our conversation was interrupted by a knock at the door, with Ellie still sleeping in the living room I answered it. Callum looked tired and cold, his nose was red and his eyes watered in the chilly breeze.

'I just came by to let you know that there's still been no sign of Brodie.'

'I'm sorry to hear that, I take it you've sent his coat off to get tested to see if it's his blood?'

'Aye, but it'll not get picked up until tomorrow, it can be hard enough getting forensics done here but on New Year's day you've no chance. There's a DI coming in a couple of days with a small team, but for now they've started their investigation with online interviews and I'm to go look at his room at the Frasers place.'

'That's good,' I replied. He'd made it very clear that he wasn't interested in my help, I didn't offer it again.

'I Googled you, you know,' Callum said.

'Okay,' I never really knew what to say when people said this to me, of course I'd looked myself up to see what others would find and it was okay, I'd had a few big successes in my career.

'It says that you've been a police consultant a couple of times.'

'That's right.'

'How come?' He asked.

I looked at him shivering involuntarily, 'do you want to come in and get a coffee or something, you look freezing.'

He took a moment to think before he said, 'if that would be okay.'

I moved backwards out of the way to let him inside, happy to be closing the door behind him. 'Go through to the kitchen, Ellie's having a wee sleep in the living room.'

Alana had been one step ahead, overhearing our conversation at the door she'd already got the kettle on.

'You were going to tell me how you came to be a police consultant,' Callum said once he was holding his hot mug.

'I'm really good at what I do, I've built up a good relationship with DCI George Johnston, he trusts me and knows that I'm worth having on a team.' It was a brief but honest answer, a detailed one would've required too much time and too much personal information.

'Because you found that girl, Sally Mitchell?'

'That's part of it.'

'And what's the rest, your sparkling personality?' He chuckled to himself.

'Must be,' I agreed. It had been a long time since someone mocking my lack of social graces had offended me.

'Why did you decide to become a police officer?' Alana asked. Callum wasn't much older than her.

'I knew I didn't want to go to university, my uncle was in the police, and I spoke to him about it and the more I thought about it, the more I thought it was the right thing for me.'

'And were you right, do you like it?' Alana asked.

'I do, although I don't want to stay rural forever, it's fine for now but I'll never progress to detective out here.'

Alana smiled, people with ambition tended to impress her, 'is your uncle a detective?'

'He's a DS but planning on doing his inspectors exam this year.'

'Whereabouts does he work?'

Callum's cheeks flushed a deep pink, 'he used to work in Shetland, but he was transferred to work a big murder case a few years ago, now he's in Fife.'

I narrowed my eyes and looked at him, frowning. 'Your uncle is DS Richard Hargreaves, isn't he?'

Callum looked away for a moment, 'yeah he is, but I swear I didn't know who you were when we spoke earlier, Uncle Richie doesn't talk about his work like that, it was only when I saw the stuff online about you and then I called him, and he told me all about you.'

I'd always liked Richard, he's honest and straightforward with a very dry sense of humour. 'he's a nice bloke, I like him.'

'He said some pretty complimentary things about you as well...listen I know that I was a bit of a dick this morning, but I wondered if you fancied tagging along when I go to search Brodie's room. The truth is you've got more experience than I have, and I could use a second pair of eyes, it would need to be unofficial, obviously...I mean there wouldn't be any payment or anything.'

'I'd be happy to help.' Ordinarily I wouldn't work for free, but my desire to be involved in this case outweighed the needs of my bank account and frankly that wasn't looking too shabby, I'd been paid in full on a big case at the end of last year and that would keep us ticking along for a while.

'Great, thank you.' He finished the last of his coffee, 'could we head over there now? I'd like to get a look around before it gets to lunch.'

'Let me grab my bag.' When we were packing to come on holiday I'd thought about not bringing my work bag with me, but I'd reasoned that it had all my camera stuff in it and where was the harm in having everything else I usually carried.'

A few moments later I was ready to go. 'Can you let Ellie know where I've gone when she wakes up,' I said to Alana.

'Of course, send me a text when you're done and I'll make some lunch, I can make something up for you as well if you'd like,' she said looking at Callum.

'That would be brilliant thanks, otherwise my lunch is likely to be a pot noodle,' he replied.

I pulled my collar up as we made the dash from the cottage door to the car through the rain. Callum had a Land Rover Defender, inside it was basic, but at least if felt like it was capable of going anywhere through any weather Scotland chose to throw at it.

'When we get to the Frasers let me do the talking at first, folk around here can be a bit funny with strangers and we are asking them if we can snoop around their house.'

I agreed, I wasn't good at holding my tongue but after years of working with George and honing my detective skills I'd learnt that sometimes it was necessary.

The wind made the rain batter against the windscreen so violently that the wipers barely stood a chance at clearing it. I was pleased that the roads were relatively empty.

'There's talk of people getting together to form a search party,' Callum said.

'Is there much point in that?'

'If Brodie had wandered off and got lost he might've found a bothy or something to hunker down in.'

'In this weather it feels like a quick way to end up with more missing people.' The rain had brought a mist over the mountains that had made them all but disappear.

'Most of the locals know the landscape pretty well, but I get what you're saying.'

A few moments later Callum turned off the main road and drove us up a farm track until we reached a white stone house. A man I vaguely recognised from the Hogmanay celebrations came to the door as we exited the car.

'Morning Mr Fraser,' Callum said.

'What can we do for you?' Mr Fraser frowned, 'are you here on official business?'

'Aye, we've come to take a look at Brodie's room, mind I said to you I'd need to do that.'

Grant Fraser nodded, looking over Callum's shoulder towards me. 'You didn't tell me you were bringing company though.'

'You'll have met Rowan last night,' Callum said.

'Ellie's friend from Fife?'

I nodded.

'I don't see why you've brought her with you though, no offense.'

'She works as a civilian consultant for the police in Fife, Richie has worked with her a fair bit, we're lucky she's here, the guys in Fife think very highly of her.'

'You'd best come in.'

I was glad to be in out of the cold. Inside I could smell

burning wood and coal, the smell of a cooked breakfast lingered in the air.

'Take your coats and shoes off in the hallway, I'd rather you didn't spread muck up the stairs,' Grant said.

I complied of course, although I hated having to take my shoes off, if the situation turned nasty it put us at a definite disadvantage, feet were easily injured, the soles of mine still bore some scars of my dash across stones and gravel after being held captive a couple of years ago. I looked over at Callum's feet and wondered if he was regretting his choice of novelty Christmas socks now.

Grant led us to Brodie's room but didn't stay once we went inside. The room was devoid of any of the personal touches you'd normally find in a young man's bedroom, but then this wasn't Brodies home, it was the Fraser's guest room.

I took my camera out and began to take photographs.

'You seen something already?' Callum asked.

'No, I just like to take a lot of pictures, it helps me later when I start putting other parts of the puzzle together.'

Callum opened the drawers in the chest next to the bed. 'Looks like he hadn't packed up to leave yet, but then he wasn't due to head to Berlin for a few days, so I suppose that makes sense.'

I looked at the neatly folded and stacked items of clothing, 'doesn't that feel overtly tidy to you?' I asked.

'I'm a tidy person, so not really and could be Brodie is the same, or it could be that Mrs Fraser did his laundry and put it away for him.'

'I can see her doing his washing, but putting it away, I'm not sure about that. Perhaps if he was her son, but just someone you're effectively employing to help out around the place, I dunno it feels odd.' I took pictures of the open drawers.

In the bottom of the wardrobe were a pair of trainers and a pair of steel toe capped work boots, I suspected they'd been provided for him for working around the small holding. Hanging up were some jeans, a couple of shirts and a jacket. I felt in the pockets of the jacket, and found half a packet of chewing gum, a plastic lighter and a bank card.

'Did Brodie smoke?' I asked.

'Not that I ever saw?'

'What about cannabis?'

'Again, not that I saw, but he was hardly going to roll a joint in front of me was he.'

I put the items into a small evidence bag in case they proved important at a later stage before I felt my way through the jeans' pockets starting with the pair that looked like they were recently worn. The left pocket had a folded wedge of blue roll, the stuff that garages used to mop up spills, I presumed farmers used it in the same way. It was stuck together, and as I looked at it in more detail, I realised that the layers were glued together with dried blood.

'Did Grant mention anything about Brodie getting injured at all recently?' I asked.

'No why?'

I showed him the paper.

'This is a small holding, I'd be more surprised if he'd never got hurt,' Callum said.

I bagged it any way, despite Callum's protests that getting hurt was part and parcel of rural life. I reminded him that we couldn't be sure it was Brodie's blood, and it would be better to double check rather than make assumptions.

I was about ready to close up the wardrobe thinking it

had yielded all the information it was going to when the light from my torch caught on a small white bundle of paper screwed up in the corner behind his trainers. I crouched down to retrieve it, unfolding it carefully so as not to tear it.

At first glance it looked like it was just an old receipt from the co-op but when I turned it over there was a mobile phone number written in blue biro. I took a photograph of the number before securing the receipt.

'Do you recognise this number?' The 07 at the start of the number identified it as British.

'No, it could be anyone's though, someone he met abroad and intended on meeting up with when he was next in the UK.'

'I don't think so.'

'How come?'

'The receipt is dated 27th December, that's just a few days ago, why would he be writing a number of someone that he met months ago down now, in fact why write it down at all, if it was someone you wanted to keep in contact with surely you put their number straight into your phone.'

'We could try calling it.' Callum said.

'Maybe, but not now.'

'Why not?'

'Because we have no way of knowing what Brodie might've been involved in, you should see if you can trace it, but I suspect that it's a burner. And when you do call it you're going to want to do that somewhere you can easily record the conversation.'

'Why would he have a burner phone?' Callum asked.

'Just a hunch, but experience tells me that there's usually more going on beneath the surface of a person's life than meets the eye.'

'That makes sense.' He looked at me, 'I'm pretty sure I'm going to get my backside booted for involving you in this.'

'That all depends, I suppose.'

'Depends on what?'

'What the DI in charge of the investigation is like.'

He frowned but said nothing further, instead he went back to the search. In the bottom drawer he found three photographs, one was of Brodie and a man and woman that I thought were likely his parents, there was one of Brodie with a girl a few years younger than him, they shared enough similarities they were probably brother and sister, the third was of Brodie and a girl about the same age, a girl-friend perhaps. Unusual for anyone under about 40 to be carrying actual photographs, let alone someone who carried his life in a backpack, whoever they were they must be important.

'We should find out who this is,' I said pointing to the girl.

'That's Lauren Davidson,' Callum said. 'She was in my year at school.'

'In that case we should go talk to her.'

'We can't.'

'Why not?'

'She died a few years ago, accidental drug overdose at a nightclub, it was just before the Covid lockdown happened.'

'If she died in 2020 then Brodie has been lying to every-one, he had been here before. Where was the club?'

'It was in Glasgow, that's where she went to uni then afterwards she got a job there and stayed. Her parents were understandably devastated, Lauren was their only child, they swore blind that there was no way Lauren would've taken drugs, she was born with a hole in her heart, she had to have surgery as a baby and her parents were super careful with her because of that.'

'Could she have been rebelling, away from home, living her own life away from the watchful controlling eyes of mum and dad?'

'I doubt it, I wouldn't have called them controlling, they were careful sure, but Lauren still got involved in everything at school, went on trips and all that, they were proud of her when she got into Glasgow to study graphic design.'

'You agree with them then, it would've been completely out of character for her to have taken drugs?'

'I was shocked when I found out that was the cause of death for sure.'

'The police in Glasgow didn't think there was anything suspicious about it?'

'There were two other deaths from that same night and a bunch of people were hospitalised, and most of them admitted buying drugs at the club, so I think they didn't see anything suspicious with her specifically. I know her mum tried to get them to open a separate investigation into Lauren's death, but it didn't happen.'

Chapter 4

'Any chance of you taking me to where his car was found?' I asked as we left the Frasers' small holding.

'If you want.'

We drove mostly in silence, I wasn't sure if it was because Callum was starting to regret his decision to invite me to search Brodie's room.

He pulled off the road, driving the Land Rover on to the verge. 'It was just here.'

I got out the car and looked around at the spot, taking photographs of the road in both directions. It wasn't a stretch of the imagination to think that his car might've picked up something that burst his tyre, but if that had been an accident, something unpredictable, where was he now?

'Where's his car?' I asked, I'd expected to see it abandoned on the road with police tape around it.

'It's been taken away, you can't leave a car on the edge of a road like this otherwise you're likely to cause more accidents.' Callum replied.

'How far would you say it is from here to the hotel?' I asked.

'About a mile.'

'And from the Frasers?'

'Less than half a mile, I think that's why Grant thought he'd most likely got out and walked.'

I looked at my phone, I had signal, not a lot but enough to call for help, so why hadn't he. 'Do you have signal?'

'Aye, but you won't get all networks here, we've got a couple of masts nearby but if you're not on the right network then signal's a nightmare so Brodie might not have.'

'He'd been here a while though, hadn't he?'

Callum nodded.

'If you were staying somewhere for a while and you weren't on the right network, wouldn't you get yourself a sim card for one that would let you use your phone? I saw the shop in the village sells them.'

'I suppose that would make sense.'

'Then if Brodie could've called someone, why didn't he?'

'Maybe he was embarrassed, didn't want Grant to know he'd burst his tyre.'

'Why would he care, it's not the same as phoning your dad and telling him, not like he was going to get into trouble, it was a hire car why would Grant care about it.'

'Maybe he just didn't want to wake the Frasers in the middle of the night, he'd have known that even though it was New Year's Day that Grant would be up at the crack of dawn anyway, like he always was.'

'Perhaps, but are you telling me that in all the time he stayed here he didn't make any friends? There was no one he could've called to get help?'

'It was Hogmanay though, most of his friends would've been half cut and no use to him. And he wouldn't have wanted to call me, not if he'd been drinking and then got behind the wheel.'

'If he got out of the car with the intention of walking the rest of the way back, where did he go? As long as you stick to the road there's not much room for getting lost, at least not until you're much closer to the small holding and he must've known that area well, certainly well enough not to take a wrong turn and get lost.'

'If he was drunk though he might not have stayed to the road, he might've wandered off anywhere.'

'Did you speak to the guy behind the bar at the hotel yet?'

'No, I'm going to see him later this afternoon, why?'

'You going to ask him how many drinks he served Brodie?'

'Is there any need, Alana said he was drunk and then he ordered another drink.'

'She said he seemed drunk, that doesn't mean he was drunk, someone could've slipped something into his drink.'

'Why would anyone do that? You think someone at the hotel last night was out to get him?'

'I've no idea, but I'd want to know how much he'd actually had to drink last night. Where was his coat found?' I asked changing the subject, Callum was nice but a bit clueless when it came to the finer points of investigation.

He pointed back up the road we'd driven down, 'a bit further along and off to the side.'

'Do you have any photos?' I asked.

'I took a couple on my phone.'

I walked over to him so I could have a look, get my bearings. He handed me the phone and I flipped back and forth over the pictures looking up to place them in the land-scape. 'Did you find any sign of blood anywhere between the car and where his jacket was found?'

'Nothing obvious.'

'What about in the car?'

'No blood.'

I strolled back down the road to where Brodie's hire car had been discovered, Callum followed. 'He pulled the car off the road here?' I said looking at Callum, he nodded in agreement. 'He probably got out, had a look at the tyre, realised that it was burst…' I paused. 'Wasn't there a spare?'

'No, it didn't have one, just a can of that foam you can use to get you home, the tyres were run flats, but the hole in the side of his tyre would've made it impossible to do anything on the roadside himself.'

'Okay, he gets out of the car, realises it's not going to drive him anywhere and thinks he'll walk the rest of the way instead of calling anyone for help, which I still find surpris-ing, but anyway, in the few minutes it would've taken him to get along here,' I continued walking the route I suspected Brodie would've taken, 'something happened to injure him to the extent that blood soaked through the sleeve of his jacket, which for some reason he took off and threw on the ground.'

'He probably took it off to look at his wound,' Callum said.

'It was bloody freezing last night, without his jacket he would've been painfully cold. If he didn't make it to shelter, he would've got hypothermia by now and if he did make it to shelter then why has no one found him?'

'What are you suggesting?'

I looked around, this was a road that ran through the hills, heather and gorse bushes punctuated the ground, but if you wandered off there were several ways you could've gone. In the warmer summer months this area would be inundated with tourists, hill walkers in their brightly coloured jackets would appear like little pins, but not today, today it looked empty and foreboding.

'It doesn't add up. Where is he? I think it's time to start investigating the possibility of a third-party being involved.'

Chapter 5

I text Alana to let her know we were on the way back. By the time Callum pulled up outside Ellie's cottage my fingers were white with cold and I'd lost the feeling in my toes. Alana reminded Callum about her offer of lunch, but he insisted that he had to get back to work, saying that it had all taken longer than he expected, then there was a mumbled promise about keeping me informed of any developments, but I suspected that when the DI arrived tomorrow that I would be very much on the side lines.

'You manage to scare Callum off already?' Ellie asked, she'd woken up from her sleep whilst I was out and Alana had filled her in on all the details.

'I think he's worried about getting into trouble with the DI, that and the fact that I keep poking holes in all his theories,' I replied. Alana and Ellie had made soup for lunch, nothing fancy, Heinz tomato out of a tin, and it was divine.

'What do you think's happened to him then?' Ellie asked.

I shook my head slowly, absent mindedly dunking a

chunk of white bread in my bowl until it became so satu-
rated with the orange-red liquid the end fell off. 'I don't
know, but he certainly didn't just wander off into the night
by himself.'

'There's a group of farmers out looking for him now,
checking the further away bothies in case he took shelter
there and isn't keeping well,' Ellie said.

'They'll not find him, not alive anyway.'

'You think he's dead?' Alana asked. I noticed a look of
sadness flit across her face.

'Not necessarily, I think if they find him on this search
he'll be dead, either because he's been murdered and his
body dumped or because I'm wrong and he did wander off
after his car came off the road and he's died from his
injuries or hypothermia.'

'You're not usually wrong about these things though…'
Alana paused, 'and if they don't find him?'

'Then there's a couple of options, best case scenario a
good Samaritan saw him walking along the road injured
and a bit out of it and picked him up and took him to the
nearest hospital and there's just been a mix up in communication and in a day or so we'll find out that he's been tucked
up with nurses taking care of him.'

'Worst case?' Alana asked.

'Then he's got himself involved in something much
more dangerous than he realised it would be and now he's
paying the price for it.'

'He's only been here a short while how could he have
got himself involved in anything criminal?' Ellie said.

'When Callum and I were searching his room we found
some photographs, seems like he had a younger sister, but
there was also one with a girl, Lauren Davidson, that was
taken somewhere in Scotland, Callum was at school with

Lauren and she died in February 2020 at a nightclub in Glasgow, accidental drugs overdose, apparently. So, when Brodie said he'd never been to Scotland before he was lying and if I can find out why he lied about that then I'd be a heck of a lot closer to understanding what happened last night.'

'Why don't you ask his family?' Alana asked.

'Because I'm pretty sure Callum and his DI wouldn't appreciate me giving Brodie's family a call, on this occasion I'm going to have to sit back and only get involved where I've been invited.'

'What if the family *did* invite you, then there wouldn't be much the police could do about it,' Alana said.

'How would the family even know who I am?'

'You've heard of social media, right?' Alana said sarcastically.

I frowned at her, 'and?'

'Do you want to investigate this case?' She asked.

'Obviously.'

'Then leave it with me.'

'Why what are you going to do.'

She tapped the side of her nose, and for a moment I considered whether my cavalier approach to rule breaking had been much more of a bad influence on Alana than I'd realised, then I reminded myself that she would never do anything to deliberately put any of us in danger or that could cause harm to Brodie's family.

'Well,' Ellie said breaking the moment of silence, 'this wasn't exactly what I had in mind when I suggested you come up for New Year to visit,' she laughed to herself. 'I'd thought that you might've been able to take a break from investigating and instead I've landed you right in the middle of one.'

She'd said it with a smile, but I could tell there had been concern behind her words, perhaps she was remembering visiting me in a worse for wear state when I'd been trying to find her friend Harmony. Maybe she had held on to some guilt that I had been badly hurt, it hadn't been her fault of course, I'd made a series of foolish judgement calls during that case, and I'd learnt my lesson since.

'How is Harmony?' I asked.

Ellie blushed as though she thought I might've been reading her thoughts. 'She sold the apartment, did I tell you that?'

I shook my head

'As soon as the Covid restrictions were lifted she put it on the market, it sold pretty quickly, she had to paint over her mural – I was sad to see that go. She bought one of those little campervans, had it spec'd with all the mod cons and now she's travelling around Europe.'

'That's good.' I was pleased to hear that Harmony hadn't slotted back into her old, rigid life, that she'd had the courage to let go and do something different.

'Her dad went out to meet her in Italy and they spent a couple of weeks there.'

I understood complicated parental relationships and I hadn't been sure if Harmony would ever be able to mend the bridges there, but I was glad that she had.

'I suppose she might have to come back one day, but I don't think it'll be any time soon.'

I felt a moment of jealousy, the lure of travelling was strong, but then I thought about how that had turned out for Brodie, he should have been having the time of his life travelling through Europe, instead he was missing or perhaps worse. I wondered if there was a way to contact the Work Away organisation to find out where else he'd worked and with who, in case it shed any light on why he came here.

After lunch the cottage had a bit of a subdued atmosphere with both Alana and I itching to open our laptops and get on, but both of us aware that it would be very rude to ignore our host.

A few moments passed in which no one spoke, then Ellie said, 'I'll be making a start on dinner preparations soon, we're having roast pork and I thought I'd make a tiramisu for dessert, so I'm going to be busy most of the afternoon if you two want to work at the table.'

'Do you need any help?' Alana asked.

'Honestly I can see you're both desperate to start work and if it might help find Brodie then I'm all for it.'

We sat at opposite ends of the old wooden table. I did a quick check, Halifax in Nova Scotia was four hours behind the UK. Depending on how late a night Flora Dunn had bringing in the New Year she might be up and about now. I'd found her on social media earlier and now composed a message that I hoped would be enticing enough for her to feel that it was worth her while.

> Hi Flora, My name is Rowan McFarlane, I'm a private detective and I'm currently investigating a missing person in Strathcarron, Highlands, Scotland. The young man that's missing is from Halifax, Canada. I know that you're from around this area and I'd like to talk to you about the circumstances that took you to Canada.

Perhaps she'd take one look at the message and think I was utterly bonkers to be trying to draw any parallels between her disappearance and this one. In my experience though, curiosity wins out over scepticism with this sort of message, especially when a quick Google search can confirm I am exactly who and what I say I am.

Now I turned my attention to Lauren Davidson, starting with her death and working backwards. There had been a lot of media interest at the time of the story.

Death On The Dancefloor

NIGHTLIFE found itself at the centre of another health and safety scandal as the whole place was cordoned off and teams of people in hazmat suits sealed the area following the death of 3 patrons and the hospitalisation of a further 30.

Local residents were evacuated in the early hours of 15th February 2020 after loved up revellers began dropping like flies on the dance floor. Concerned that this was some kind of biological attack, the streets around NIGHTLIFE were cleared and businesses were not allowed to open.

An emergency care zone was created in the church across the road to allow the remaining 600 patrons to be observed and treated where necessary.

Cordons came down in the late afternoon on Saturday as the area was deemed uncontaminated. The police have yet to announce the cause of such widespread illness and death.

NIGHTLIFE had only recently reopened following a 6 month closure due to failing an adhoc fire inspection. Jane Rutherglen, owner of the club, said that they are devastated that this has happened, and their thoughts go out to the families of all those affected.

Further research taught me that the Valentines night 'love in' had been intended to be the clubs big re-opening comeback. Lauren had been amongst 3 young women to die that night, a further 3 had been seriously ill in hospital with 4 dying from related complications in the following few weeks. With 7 dead a lot of questions were asked about the safety of the club. When it was determined the club had capacity for 480 guests, with it being 32% over capacity it was permanently closed.

The initial concern had been that some sort of biological poison had been released through the ventilation system. As the toxicology reports started coming back from the hospitalised victims it became clear that they were suffering from a drug overdose. Later some of the affected people admitted buying drugs that night and the doorman Roderick 'Rod' Harris was arrested for supplying the drugs.

When criticised for how long it took to identify the substance and treat the affected people, the health board stated that they were dealing with a brand new synthetic drug, called Blue 24, which contained amongst other things Rohypnol, it had taken time to identify all of the various properties of the drug to allow the patients to be treated safely.

The police admitted that they had not seen any other cases of this drug and the papers were full of fear for the safety of those inclined to take recreational drugs. Of those that made a full recovery only 5 admitted buying the drug. Everyone else said that all they'd knowingly consumed that night was alcohol.

Had Lauren had her drink spiked? She'd been dead before the ambulance had arrived at Nightlife, along with 2 other young women. One of them, Emily Patterson, was only 17.

With lockdown happening only a month later the drug seemed to go away as quickly as it had surfaced, I couldn't find any information on where abouts in the drug sales food chain Rod Harris had been.

Harris had been sentenced to 14 years in prison, this was his first criminal offence and in his defence he stated that he got into debt with a loan shark in order to pay off his younger brothers gambling debts. When he began to struggle to make the payments his family started to receive death threats. He'd then been approached about selling the drugs at the door of Nightlife and had seen it as a way out of his problems. Harris, who had been in the Army, said he regretted his actions and was deeply sorry for the loss of life the drugs had caused.

With Harris behind bars and no mentions of the drug that had killed Lauren in the media for quite some time there didn't seem to be much point in delving into the matter too much more.

Chapter 6

Callum called round with an update later in the evening to let us know that the search party had found no trace of Brodie. Ellie had invited him in, but he'd declined saying he wanted to go home and get some rest, the DI had called a meeting for 8am the next day.

'What would you like to do tomorrow?' Ellie asked.

'Did you have anything in mind?'

'I dunno, the plan had been for the two of you to have a relaxing time, maybe take a drive across to Skye or something?'

'That sounds nice,' I replied, although honestly as much as I'd like to visit Skye, I'd much prefer to be getting my teeth stuck into finding Brodie.

It had felt like a very long day, from the early morning knock on the door by Callum to the delightful roast pork dinner lovingly handmade by Ellie. It was only half past nine, but I could feel my eyelids drooping.

'Not to be an old fuddy duddy but I'm shattered, if it's all one to you I'm going to head to bed,' I said.

Most nights it took me a little while to fall asleep as my brain went through the events of the day and thought about next actions, not tonight though. At 8.30am there was a tap on the bedroom door followed by Alana and the smell of coffee entering.

'Thanks sweetheart,' I said taking the mug. 'Did you sleep alright?'

'Fine,' she paused. 'Do you think Ellie would be upset if we didn't go to Skye today?'

'Why, are you not feeling well?'

'No, I'm fine, it's just remember when I said yesterday about Brodie's family asking you to look for him?'

I nodded.

'Well I found his sister Lilly on social media yesterday afternoon and the police must've already been in contact with the family because she had photos of Brodie all over her pages asking anyone to get into contact if they'd seen him, so I reached out to her in a private message, told her who you were – gave her the link to your website and said right now your hands are tied because you can't interfere with a police investigation, but I suggested that you'd be very willing to help if they wanted to engage your services. We chatted for a bit, she's a couple of years younger than me and her and Brodie are really close, she was meant to be joining him in Berlin in a couple of weeks, she said they had been speaking every day until two days after Christmas and she hasn't heard from him since, he's not responding to messages or answering her calls. She'd already told her parents she was worried, Lilly said her dad phoned Grant Fraser to check everything was alright and he said that Brodie had been working hard and that he'd remind him to check in with his family.'

I said nothing for a few moments, why did the 27th of

December ring a bell, I took a sip of coffee and remembered the till receipt I'd found in Brodie's wardrobe, the one with the telephone number written on the back. I was sure that was from the 27th. I handed Alana my mug and sprang out of bed to look for my camera, I brought the picture up on the display screen on the back of the camera and zoomed in. I was right, 2 bottles of Irn Bru, a Crunchie and a Kit-Kat and on the back a mobile number, one that he must've needed but for some reason didn't want stored in his mobile phone.

'Something happened on the 27th, Brodie had to have bumped into someone that scared him or that made him feel like it wasn't safe to keep on talking to his sister. I wonder if the shop has CCTV.'

'You'll have the chance to discuss that with his family later, Lilly came back to me last night, she said she'd spoken to her parents and they wanted a meeting with you over video chat, today at 11am – it'll be 8am their time.'

I smiled at my daughter, 'thank you. You know forensic anthropology's gain is private detection's loss.'

'I'll still be investigating, just with more science and I'll probably see more dead bodies than you.'

'I'm sure I'll be picking your brains for a long time.'

'Do you want me to speak to Ellie, seeing as it was me that made the arrangement?' Alana said.

'Speak to me about what?' Ellie appeared in the doorway to the bedroom. She looked at me then Alana, then back at me. 'What's happening? Has there been a development that I wasn't aware of?'

'Kind of,' I said and then explained about Brodie's sister and the meeting at 11am.

Ellie had come fully into the room now and was sitting on the end of the bed next to Alana. 'How can I help?'

'You're not disappointed?' I asked.

'No, finding Brodie has to come first. Besides this way you'll definitely owe me another visit and we can do all the touristy things then, maybe when the weather is a bit warmer too.'

'Thank you. I won't know what the plan of action is until I've spoken to Brodie's family, but it would be really helpful if I knew more about the people living here, so if you could write me a list of all the people that were here on or around the 27th of December and draw me a rough map showing where everything is, that would be great.'

'I can do that.'

'I'll get us some breakfast, porridge alright for everyone?' Alana asked.

'Perfect, I'm going to grab a quick shower and make myself presentable.'

Before any of us had the chance to move, my phone began buzzing, 'it's Sonya,' I said to Alana as I answered.

'Happy New Year,' I said.

'You too,'

'Everything alright?' I asked.

'I'm looking for a favour actually,' Sonya replied.

'Shoot, if I can help I will, we're up in the highlands still though…' I trailed off.

'Yeah, I know and that's where the favour comes in,' Sonya paused. 'I'm not sure if you're aware a young man has gone missing near where you're staying.'

'Brodie.'

'Yes, I don't know if you know, but they found his jacket and it had some blood staining on it?'

'Callum, the local police officer, told us.' I could see Ellie and Alana looking at me trying to follow the conversation.

'The blood was fast tracked and then sent to me after

traces of a synthetic street drug named Blue42 was found in it…'

'That was the stuff that killed all those people in Glasgow just before lockdown,' I interrupted.

'How do you know about that? Never mind, you can explain later, but I've been doing a lot of work on drug pathology, and I was part of the team involved in that case so because of that I've been invited up to help the local DI on this case and that's where the favour comes in, I was wondering if your friend Ellie had any room for me. The police are going to be working out of the local hotel and they've taken up all the rooms there, plus I want to be somewhere I can get peace to think properly.'

'You must be desperate if you think living in a house with me will give you peace,' I laughed. 'Give me a moment and I'll check.'

I quickly explained the situation to Ellie and Alana.

'I could sleep in here with you and Sonya could have the room I'm in,' Alana said looking at Ellie for confirmation.

'That's fine with me as long as you two don't mind bunking together, the more the merrier,' Ellie said.

'Not sure how much of that you heard, but you're welcome to stay here.'

'Thank Ellie in advance for me, I've a couple of things I need to tie up here so I won't leave until tomorrow morning, I'm hoping to be there in the afternoon, I'll get my briefing with the DI and then head over to you, and you can fill me in on everything you know when I get there.'

'Great, looking forward to seeing you.'

Chapter 7

Alana moved her things into my room and by the time I'd had my shower, Ellie had changed the bed linen and Alana had made breakfast, which left me with plenty of time to write a list of questions for Brodie's family.

I sat at the table in the kitchen to talk to them. I recognised the girl immediately from the photo I'd seen the previous day.

'Hi, you must be Lilly,' I said.

She nodded, 'this is my mum and dad,' Lilly indicated towards the couple sitting next to her. It was difficult to see them properly with everyone squished onto the one screen.

'I'm not sure how much Alana explained.'

'We looked you up,' Lilly said.

'That's good, do you have any questions?'

'You think you can find my son?'

'It's not black and white Mr…'

'Call me Graham.'

'I don't like to make promises I can't keep, so what I

would say to you Graham is that I will do everything I can to find out what's happened to your son.'

'I'm not sure why we need you when the police are looking into it, are you telling me the police in Scotland are incompetent?'

'Not at all, in my experience of working alongside them they're excellent and will do everything within their abilities to find Brodie.'

'Then why do we need you?'

'You don't necessarily *need* me, but the benefit of being a private detective is that I don't have to deal with as much red tape or toeing the line of my boss, that type of thing. I'm not a police officer, I don't think like one, I know what it's like to want answers, real answers, not carefully constructed responses. Lilly said you'd looked me up and that's great, you can see from my website the sort of success I've had.'

'We did, and I was impressed,' he cocked his head to one side, 'not as impressed as Lilly, but you certainly seem to have made a name for yourself. My concern is that typically it seems you're dealing with historic cases, no one's life is at risk while you take your time over an investigation.' Graham said.

I took a moment to consider my response, in the early days I would've been offended by his remark, I'd have felt a fleeting angry sensation, these days though, I let comments like that pass over me.

'In 2020 I was hired to find a woman who went missing, it turned out she'd been kidnapped by her very violent ex-husband, that wasn't an historic case.' I didn't want to add that my first major case was finding out who murdered my own father.

Graham turned and looked at his wife, Lilly was

watching them both. 'What do you think Muriel?' Graham said.

'What harm can it do, we have the money and surely the more people looking for Brodie the more chance we have of bringing him home.' Her voice cracked as she said the last bit and I noted that she hadn't said 'alive,' did she think it was too late for that or was she afraid to tempt fate.

'Okay,' Graham said turning back to face the camera and me. 'How do we do this?'

'This morning I'm going to ask you some questions, see if I can get a better understanding of Brodie as a person and what he was doing in Scotland, that sort of thing, then we'll talk through what you already know and see if I have anything to add. I'll let you know what I'll be doing next, and I'll ask that you speak to the police and tell them that you've engaged my services and that you would like them to feed information through me and keep me involved.'

Ordinarily that last part wouldn't have been necessary – I could've gone to George and told him the situation and he would've grumbled and complained but ultimately, he'd have included me in his investigation and me him, but I didn't know what the local DI was going to be like and I would deal with the fact they'd likely be pissed off at me for getting in their way at a later date.

'What would you like to know?' Muriel asked.

'What made Brodie want to come to Scotland?'

'I'm sure you hear this all the time, but we have ances-tors there, and not just the ones from hundreds of years back, my cousin was originally from out that way and she's always talked so fondly about where she grew up and she would tell Brodie and Lilly stories about the village, he'd always wanted to go.'

'Had he been to Scotland before?'

'Yes, January 2020 – he was planning on staying a year or so, but then the pandemic happened, and we didn't know how long it would go on, I was scared so I asked him to cut his trip short and get home,' Muriel said. 'And it turned out to be a good decision, he got home before things got too crazy, whilst there were still flights, he had to take a bit of a convoluted journey, but he got here.'

'Do you know where he was staying when he was here last time?'

'He had a couple of weeks in Edinburgh and then he went to Glasgow, that's where he was before he came home, he didn't make it north that time.'

'Did he have friends in Glasgow?'

'Not before he left home, but I know he liked it there, he was really disappointed to leave and then just after he got home, he was really off with everyone, kept saying he shouldn't have come home, that he should have stayed in Scotland during the pandemic, that it had been a waste of time coming back. I was really upset by his attitude, it wasn't like him, he was such a quiet, even tempered young man. And I know what you're thinking, that all mothers think their sons are angels, but honestly I'm not just saying it because…' Muriel trailed off and looked to her husband. Graham wrapped his arm around his wife.

'I assumed he'd met a girl and was kicking off because, perhaps without him there she might move on, or that he'd discovered she already had,' Graham said.

I noticed Lilly's eyes flick towards her parents and then away, careful not to make eye contact with me. What was she hiding, it was possible that her brother had confided in her where he hadn't wanted to with his parents. I made a mental note to try and arrange a chat with her one on one.

'How long did he behave like that for?'

'A few weeks, a month maybe and then he found his way back to his old self.'

'This time when he went travelling, he decided to see some of Europe as well, do you know why that was?'

'When he was in high school, he did an exchange with a German lad, Emil. Emil stayed with us for four weeks and then Brodie went to stay with his family in Berlin for four weeks, they got on so well that they stayed in contact all this time and then Emil invited him to go to Germany and work his way around Europe for a few months and that's when he came up with the plan to go back to Scotland for a while in the process.'

'Any reason he picked Strathcarron?'

'That's where Flora is from,' Muriel said.

'Flora Dunn?' I asked remembering the article I'd read about a local lass running away and appearing with family in Canada.

Muriel frowned. 'How do you know Flora?'

'I read about her in the papers after Brodie went missing.'

'That's old news and Flora had her reasons for leaving,' Muriel said.

'What were they?'

'I don't see what this has to do with Brodie,' Muriel replied.

'I don't like coincidences, and if I'm to do my job properly I need to have full disclosure from you,' I glanced at Lilly hoping that she would understand that I knew she'd been holding back earlier.

'What harm can it do to tell the woman?' Graham said to his wife.

'Flora ran away because her parents, more her father, wanted her to marry a friend of his, she was young and he was considerably older and she didn't want to, it caused quite a rift in the family. She tried to leave and work on Skye, but it wasn't far enough away. Her father booked the church, got the wedding licences and told her point blank she would marry this man. The next day she sold everything she had, borrowed some money from her boss and got a one-way ticket here. She never did forgive him for making her leave her home.'

'Does Flora still have family in Strathcarron?'

'A sister, I think, she was only a year younger than Flora and not so stubborn and strong willed, less than six months after Flora arrived here, she received a piece of wedding cake and a wedding photo of her sister and the man her father had wanted her to marry.'

'Are they still in the area?'

'I really don't know, Flora doesn't really speak about her family much and I've never wanted to push it.'

'As far as you know Brodie was happy here and there wasn't anything bothering him?'

'You'd be better talking to Lilly, her and Brodie spoke more frequently, but we all became a bit worried when he stopped checking in just after Christmas,' Graham said.

'Is that when you spoke to Grant Fraser?'

'He said he'd remind Brodie to call and check in but there was nothing to worry about, he apologised saying that he was probably working him too hard.'

'And did he, check in?'

'No, we thought we'd hear from him yesterday to wish us happy New Year, but nothing, and then we got contact from the police...I'm sure you can imagine that wasn't the start to the New Year any of us were hoping for.'

'When was the last time you spoke to or messaged Brodie?'

'We spoke to him over video chat on Christmas day, it was nice, although I know Muriel had hoped he'd come home for Christmas and New Year, but it would have cost too much so we understood.'

'How was Brodie funding his travels?' I asked.

'When he came home from Scotland in 2020, he came to live with us, there was no point him trying to get his own place when we weren't sure what restrictions were going to be put in place or even how long he'd be home for. Then he managed to get a job on one of these webchat services that a lot of companies were using then, it was for Royal Bank of Canada. We didn't take any money off him for living here so he saved up, that coupled with the fact that he's been working whilst he's away has paid for everything. Is there anything else you need to know?' Muriel asked.

I shook my head, 'I think that's everything for now, thank you so much for talking to me today and I will do everything I can to find Brodie.' I didn't say alive and well, like you sometimes see on the telly, I never say that.

I'd considered asking Graham and Muriel if Brodie had ever had any issues with drugs, but that's the sort of question that immediately gets parents' backs up, and besides it was very possible that he could've had, but they wouldn't necessarily know. I thought about Alana for a moment, would I know, would she be able to hide something like that from me, not that I could believe for one second that she'd take drugs, but still no matter how close we are I was sure there were things she kept to herself.

Chapter 8

After I'd finished the video chat with Brodie's family I sent his sister Lilly a quick message, asking her if it would be possible for us to speak one on one explaining that I'd got the feeling she'd been holding something back earlier, that I understood there might be things she wasn't comfortable talking about in front of her parents.

She replied saying there were a couple of things Brodie had told her in confidence but if I thought they might be of some help in finding him she would be happy to talk to me, we agreed I'd video chat her in the afternoon, her parents were going to visit her uncle and she would be home alone.

Ellie popped to the local store to get a top up of the essentials, we told her there was plenty of stuff in the cottage, but with Sonya arriving tomorrow she wanted to make sure that we wouldn't run out of milk and bread.

When she returned she looked flustered, the cold had turned her nose bright red. 'The place is swarming with police down there, well perhaps that's a bit of an exaggeration, there's four extra uniformed officers and a few others who must be detectives, which is a lot of extra people for a small place.'

'You hear any gossip?' Alana asked.

'Mac, the guy that runs the shop said he was going to have nae juice and crisps by the end of the week but joking aside everyone is really worried about Brodie. I overheard a couple of the officers and it's clear they think they're looking for a body. No one thinks he could have survived out there by himself in this weather, especially injured.'

'Mum doesn't think he's dead, do you?' Alana said looking over at me as I helped Ellie put away the groceries.

'Well, not by natural causes anyway, I think they'd have found him by now if he'd simply stumbled off the road injured and disorientated, and if he was injured why didn't he call for help? I checked and I had signal where his car was.'

'Oh, that was the other thing they think he didn't call for help because his phone battery died, because it's not been on since around the time he left the Hogmanay celebrations.'

'That's not possible,' Alana chipped in before I had the chance to formulate a response. 'He showed me, he had one of those battery charging back up things, you know like I keep telling you that you should get,' she nodded her head towards me. 'He said sometimes he's been places that it's not so easy to charge up, so it was essential, he showed me it when we were talking about travel, said that he didn't go anywhere without it.'

'It could have run out of charge as well.'

'It's possible, but really unlikely,' I said.

Our conversation was interrupted by a sharp rap on the door, Ellie went to answer it and a couple of moments later she called for me. Stood in the doorway was a woman about the same age as me, short dark hair, jeans, hiking boots and a thick jacket, the furry edge matted by snow flakes. The rain from earlier had turned to snow which was now laying firmly on everything it touched, and with the size of the flakes falling it showed no sign of going away any time soon.

'Are you Rowan McFarlane?' She asked in a way that made me instantly realise who she was.

'I am, and you must be the DI in charge of the Brodie Cullen case.'

She frowned, 'how do you know who I am?'

'Well, you look like police, you sound like police, and you seem pissed off at me and we haven't even met yet, so you've got the trifecta,' I smiled.

She stared at me.

'Can I help you with something, would you like to come in?'

'This shouldn't take long,' she replied.

'Fine but how about we do it inside so we're not asking Ellie to try and heat the whole area.' I stepped back to allow her in.

She stomped her boots against the mat taking off mud and snow.

'Is it okay if I take DI...' I looked to the woman for her name

'Hampton.'

'...into the living room,' I continued.

'No problem,' Ellie replied.

I waited until I'd shut the door before I spoke, 'do you want to have a seat while you tell me what it is that's pissed you off and then warn me to stay out of your case or would you rather do it standing up?'

'I'll stand.'

'I thought you would.'

'I don't know who you think you are, but this is a missing persons case not a fun project for an amateur. If something happens to Brodie Cullen because his family has put too much faith in you then I will see to it that you are prosecuted for interfering in a police investigation.'

I perched on the arm of the sofa, the idea that sitting whilst someone stood gave them dominance had never really washed with me.

'I'm not an amateur, I'm a professional, this is my job. I'm sorry you're butthurt that Brodie's parents have secured my services to find their son. I don't take kindly to being threatened by anyone, let alone the police, so let me be clear with you, if you disregard Brodie's parent's wishes and don't keep me in the loop and that leads to something happening to him then you can be the one explaining to them why their son was the victim of your pride.'

'I have no intention of risking this investigation…'

'It's Brodie's life, not the investigation you should be concerned with risking. Now the way I see it is we can go about this one of two ways, first you can dig your heels in and refuse to include or involve me in any capacity and basically create a situation where we both waste time going over the same ground which ultimately only causes us both delays and puts Brodie at greater risk or you could wind your neck in, we could start this conversation again, agree to at least be civil, I mean you never know we could end up being friends, stranger things have happened, and work together. Also, I'd strongly, and I mean this with respect, strongly recommend that before you accuse someone of being incompetent that you at least do a quick Google search and talk to your local man, because I'm certain that PC Sinclair would have told you I've been brought in as a police consultant on more than one occasion.'

She uncrossed her arms placing her hands on her hips instead and looked me up and down, was she considering how she'd introduce me to the team, or if she could get away with locking me in a small cupboard, it was hard to tell.

'It's not like we'll be able to avoid each other, especially with Sonya staying here.'

'Sonya?'

'Dr Grother, police pathologist, I understand she's been brought in because she has some expert knowledge that might help the case.' I was careful not to give away the fact that Sonya had shared everything with me.

A momentary flash of rage flickered across her face before she let out a laugh, relaxing her arms, she held out her hand for me to shake, 'Hi I'm Chris Hampton, I'll be the DI on this case, I understand you've been employed by the family, let's work together.' She spoke in a slightly stilted mock acting way.

'Pleased to meet you I'm Rowan, a damn good private detective and generally a massive pain in the ass, who should definitely have met you before getting herself involved, I'd be delighted to work with you.' I matched her tone.

'I actually did Google you, you've got a pretty impressive track record, intimidating some might even say.' Chris sat on the armchair.

'Thanks, I want you to know I have no intention of undermining you, I mean I know I can be full on, and I generally think I'm right, but ultimately we have the same goal.'

'Right,' she paused for a moment. 'This is my first case like this, I mean I've dealt with missing persons and things like that before, but this is the first time I've been in charge, and I know there are people who'd like to see me fall on my face.'

'You need to put them out of your head, it's not about them, it's about finding Brodie.'

'Or his body.'

'You think he's dead?' I asked.

'No, and I don't think you do either. My boss thinks we'll turn up his body in some weird place in a few days and he'll have died from exposure…but you think there's more to this than a burst tyre, and so do I.'

Chapter 9

Chris and I chatted for another half an hour or so and agreed we'd catch up the next day after Sonya had arrived.

'Are you two going to play nice, or are you desperately missing George at this moment?' Alana asked when I came through to the kitchen after Chris left.

'George is, of course, great, but Chris seems nice too, she's driven to find Brodie and we're more or less on the same page.'

'I thought you might have come to blows, I was genuinely surprised to not hear raised voices when you went into the living room,' Ellie said.

'She's been learning to play nice with others,' Alana laughed.

'Less of the cheek please I'm still your mother, although there is an element of truth in that, I have learnt there's a lot to be gained to working alongside people occasionally, I just don't want to make too much of a habit of it.'

'What's her take on the case?' Ellie asked.

'She's under pressure from her boss to treat it as a missing, presumed dead case, but she also agrees with me that there's too much that doesn't add up. Anyway, I need to grab a quick sandwich then I've got a video chat with Lilly.'

'Didn't you speak to her this morning?' Alana asked.

'Yeah, but I could tell she knew something and that she wasn't likely to say whatever it was whilst her parents were in earshot, so we arranged a separate call.'

Lilly was in what I guessed was her bedroom when she appeared on my screen, she was sitting at her desk, behind her I could see a shelf of trophies and a few ribbons hanging down.

'What sport do you compete in?'

'Oh, fencing. Brodie did it first, I went along to watch and then ended up joining the class, he only went for a few months, but I loved it, still do.'

'Did he not like getting shown up by his wee sister?'

She laughed, 'it wasn't that, he got really into cars, started going to all these race meets and stuff, then dad got him a 1967 Mustang to restore and he just wanted to spend every evening working on that, so he stopped the fencing.'

'Were cars just a hobby or did he race?'

'He raced karts for a bit, but he was more interested in the mechanics of them, and the set up, he used to talk about it all the time.'

'Why did Brodie want to come to Scotland in the first place?'

'Flora looked after us a fair bit when we were little, she would tell us stories of her childhood and the place she grew up, showed us photos and it was beautiful, Brodie got the travel bug early on, he took every opportunity to go on school trips and when he was at uni he did a year abroad in Germany, he stayed with Emil's family for the year and when he came back I joked with him that he sounded more German than Canadian.'

'What happened when he was here last time?' I asked, it was the question I'd been working up to.

She looked down for a moment, 'no one knows this but me okay, so unless you really have to, please don't tell anyone.'

'Okay, I'll do my best.'

'He met a girl on a night out in Edinburgh, she was living in Glasgow, they went out a few times and he really liked her, I could tell because he had that soppy look on his face whenever he spoke about her.'

'Your parents didn't know about the relationship?'

'No, mum was always concerned that he'd meet someone overseas and then not want to come home to Canada, she didn't want to lose him she said, Brodie said that she was being melodramatic, that if he met a girl they might want to come live in Canada. Honestly, I'm not sure if Brodie ever really intends to settle down here anyway, but I'd never tell mum that.'

'Was it a serious relationship?'

'He moved through to Glasgow to be closer to her, then he moved in with her. I think he was in love with her.'

'Is that why he was upset when he came home in 2020, because he had to leave her behind?'

'No, she died a couple of weeks before he came back, he was really devastated. I'd never seen him so cut up, it was like the grief had crushed his soul. And then he didn't want to tell mum and dad because he'd lied about her in the first place, so for the first few weeks he basically stayed in his room, barely talking, hardly eating. But slowly he seemed to recover, and I thought that he was getting past his grief.'

'How did the girl die?'

'Overdose…'

'She killed herself?' I interrupted.

'Accidental, Brodie said that they were out for the night, and someone must've slipped something in her drink, she had some health conditions and took a bad reaction, she was dead before the paramedics arrived, she died in his arms and there was nothing he could do to save her.'

'Did Brodie tell you her name?'

'Lauren,' Lilly said.

'Lauren Davidson?'

'Maybe, I'm not sure of her last name, sorry. Do you know her?'

'I know of her. Her family are from Strathcarron. Do you think that's why he chose to come here specifically?'

'Maybe, I know that he left the trip with Emil and his friends early to go to Scotland, he said he had some unfinished business there, I thought that he meant he hadn't managed to complete his trip last time.'

'Has anyone gone through his room at home yet?'

'No, I'm not sure if the police have asked my parents to look for anything though, why?'

'Did Brodie keep a diary?'

'No, nothing like that, he liked everything electronic, so it was either on his phone or his laptop.'

'Hmm, could you do me a favour anyway and look through his room.'

'What am I looking for?'

'Anything that seems out of place, also anything about Scotland, Strathcarron, or what happened to Lauren.'

'Okay sure, what do you want me to do with it if I find anything?'

'Take lots of photographs and email them to me. There was one other thing I wanted to ask, I didn't ask your parents because I didn't want to offend them, but has Brodie ever been in any trouble, I don't mean a speeding fine, but anything to do with fighting or drugs?'

Lilly tried to hold back a laugh, 'Brodie is the last person who'd take drugs, he barely even drank, a beer at a barbeque that sort of thing or maybe a glass of wine over dinner, he said he didn't like how being drunk made you feel. Brodie is a bit of a control freak, not in a bad way, he just liked to have control over his environment, and his senses. He broke his arm when he was 15, the doctor gave him strong pain killers and he said he'd rather be in pain than take them because of the way they made him feel.'

'Thanks, did he ever get into fights when he was younger?'

'Nothing serious, he could take care of himself but preferred to walk away though, he didn't like the drama.'

Chapter 10

Lilly told me she would message me if she found anything in Brodie's room and then our call had been cut off by the return of her parents. I couldn't shake the feeling that the unfinished business he had mentioned to his sister wasn't actually completing a scenic tour of the Scottish Highlands. Something must've happened to change his plans, to make him decide to leave Emil and their friends and come here. But what?

I wondered how easy it would be to speak to the David-sons, Callum had indicated that they felt the police had failed them by not looking into their daughter's death more thoroughly, but they might respond more favourably to a private detective. Before I opened that particular can of worms though I wanted to do some more research on what happened in Glasgow, find out if any of the other bereaved family members thought there was more to their loss than an accidental overdose.

In just under an hour of research I discovered that of the 7 people that died, 2 further families had been unhappy with the cause of death being listed as accidental overdose from recreational drug use. One woman, Jackie had been out with her younger cousin for her hen do, Jackie had a small baby at home, this had been her first night out since becoming a mum and she'd almost cancelled. Her husband spoke to the press saying that he would never forgive himself for persuading her to go out that night, but he was adamant that Jackie would not have willingly taken drugs, she was still breastfeeding her daughter and wasn't even drinking. Jackie's cousin, Vicky, said that Jackie had been on Diet Coke all night and hadn't even had any of the bottle of prosecco they'd had at the start of the evening.

The family of 17 year old Emily Paterson said that there was no way that their daughter was a recreational drug user, she was hoping to be on team GB for the next Olympics and her running club regularly did spot tests on the athletes' urine. The police responded saying that the deaths of all involved were a tragic accident but cautioned that it was a very real risk with taking recreational drugs. When asked if they thought it was possible that some of the club patrons had their drinks spiked, they conceded that it was a possibility, but with the majority of people affected either admitting to purchasing it or having a history of recreational drug use it was unlikely.

Rod Harris said that no one person purchased enough of Blue42 to spike other people's drinks. The families asked for a review of the case which was carried out and the conclusion was that it was possible that some of the people affected had unknowingly consumed the drug but that there was nothing to suggest that they had been targeted or that there was the intention of killing anyone.

And yet a huge amount of harm had been caused. But how did this connect to Brodie. Lauren died in Glasgow, surely if he had come to look into what had happened to her that's where he would have gone, but he hadn't gone to the city, he'd flown into Aberdeen and come straight here. I wished I'd met him, I wished I knew what kind of man he was, then I'd be better placed to know if this visit had been a pilgrimage to the home of the love of his life or if it had been him following an investigation. And if it were the latter did that mean that the source of Blue42 and the cause of Lauren's death originated in this tiny village in the middle of the Highlands?

I wandered back through to the kitchen where Alana had just put the kettle on.

'Tea or coffee?' She asked.

I looked at my watch, 3.30pm. 'Coffee please.'

'Cake?' Alana said.

We'd celebrated Christmas with Maureen and Eddie, then the day before our departure north they'd turned up at the door laden with goodies including, a Christmas cake and boxes of shortbread and rum truffles.

'That would be lovely.'

'Next year I think I'll invite Maureen and Eddie instead of you pair,' Ellie laughed.

When we were all sitting with our drinks and cake I asked Ellie, 'how well did you know Brodie?'

Ellie thought for a moment, 'not that well, enough to say hello to, I helped a local school put on their Christmas play and Brodie came to help build some of the set. He was good at his job, he spoke to the children, and they liked him. We passed the time of day, he said he loved it here and would be sad to leave.'

'Did you ever see him in a social setting?'

'No, I mean other than at the shop from time to time.'

'Not in the hotel bar?'

Ellie laughed, 'I'm not there much myself, but other than the other night I never saw him there, which isn't that strange, Grant Fraser had him up before the sun and out working.'

'Would you say Grant is well liked?'

'Aye I would,' for a moment Ellie had the twang of a local accent. 'Everyone seems to respect him and his family.'

'Respect isn't the same as being liked though.' Alana said.

'That's true, I'm sure he'd had his fallings out, you can't live in a place all your life and not have them, but no one I know has had a bad word to say about him,' Ellie said.

'When you saw Brodie at the bar, when you said he seemed drunk, what was his order?' I asked Alana.

'Whisky, he wanted it to bring in the New Year, it was heading close to midnight, and he didn't want to have an empty glass he said.'

'But you had spoken to him earlier in the night though, had he been drinking then?'

'He was just drinking Irn Bru when I'd been talking to him before, that's why I was so surprised to see him in that state at the bar.'

'His sister said he didn't like to drink much, the idea of him having a drink to see in the New Year tallied with how she described his drinking habits, but getting fall over drunk did not.'

'Do you think he got some bad news and was drowning his sorrows?' Ellie asked.

'No,' I replied.

'What then, he knocked back a couple of whiskies and didn't realise how strong it was and because he wasn't used to drinking, he was more effected by it than he expected.'

'No, I think someone drugged him.'

'What?' Ellie almost shrieked.

'Sonya said that there were traces of the drug Blue42 in the blood found on his jacket, assuming that was his blood then I think it's safe to say that he didn't deliberately take it. Blue42 is a Rohypnol mix which could easily have made him seem drunk.'

'But why? Why would anyone want to drug him?' Ellie asked.

'When I find that out, I'll know where he is.'

'Didn't you say that a ton of people died after taking that a few years ago?' Alana asked.

'Seven people, one of whom Brodie was in love with.'

'That can't be a coincidence,' Alana said.

Chapter 11

The rest of the afternoon I toyed with the idea of reaching out to Jackie and Emily's families, but in the end decided now wasn't the time. I didn't want to ask them to rake over very painful information with nothing more than a vague hope that someone might be held accountable for what had happened to their loved ones.

If the investigation led me that way, then I would reach out then, when I had more to offer. Chris phoned a little after 6pm to say that a further search of the area had turned up no sign of Brodie, she asked if I'd like to drive the route Brodie took the night he disappeared. I said that I would, and we arranged that she would pick me up at 8am. Inwardly I had groaned, even after years now of trying to correct my body clock the idea of early mornings always filled me with dread.

I checked my messages and found a reply from Flora:

Thank you for getting in touch, I've spoken to Lilly Cullen today and I know you're trying to help find Brodie. Lilly mentioned that Muriel told you why I left Scotland and you must be wondering if my circumstances have anything to do with Brodie. I don't like explaining myself to strangers, but in this case I'll make an exception, but only because I don't want you chasing a red herring instead of finding Brodie safe and sound. When I left Scotland it was to avoid marrying a man I barely knew to appease my father and Canada was far enough away that I knew he wouldn't come after me.

I didn't imagine he would force Elsa, my sister, into that same marriage, sadly she died in a car accident the following year, killing her, my nine week old niece and her husband who was four times the legal limit at the time. The shock caused our father to have a heart attack and die.

I've never been back to Scotland because of the massive amount of guilt I felt over their deaths. As far as Brodie is concerned, the only connection between my story and his is that I told him and Lilly stories about the village when they were little.

Please find Brodie, I don't think I can cope with adding another tragedy to my conscience.

Regards Flora.

It was probably the only response I was going to get from Flora and for the most part it explained the situation. I still hated the coincidence but for now I would take her at her word and not follow that thread of investigation any further.

I was looking forward to Sonya arriving tomorrow afternoon, I had questions about Blue42 and I was sure she'd have more knowledge of what happened in Glasgow in February 2020 than I had been able to find online.

The next morning at 7am my fitness watch vibrated on my wrist, I turned it off and lay in the bed on my back for a moment, Alana's steady sleeping breaths a calming white noise. I pulled the covers back gently and crept out of the room and into the shower. I took my clothes and dressed in the living room so as not to disturb Alana. At 7.55am I pulled my coat on, grabbed my bag and went outside to wait for Chris so I didn't risk her knocking on the door and waking Ellie and Alana.

She was punctual at 8am, I was glad to be in the warmth of her car, even being outside for 5 minutes had let the chill seep in a little, there was no way Brodie could have survived if he was, as her boss believed, stuck out in the middle of nowhere.

'How's things going at HQ?' I asked as we drove off.

'I think half the team think it's a waste of resources spending this much manpower looking for a dead body, they think we're only throwing so much at it because he's a foreigner and it makes us look bad if we don't.'

'And the other half?'

'A bit more curious, but mostly going through the motions. I've got a couple of guys in the team that really want to get their teeth stuck into the investigation though which is at least something.'

'What are you hoping to find this morning?'

'I don't know, I've driven roads like this all over the highlands and yes they can be a bit on the narrow side, but by and large they're in good condition.'

'Are you looking for something that might've caused his

puncture or are you thinking someone might've tampered with his tyre at the hotel?'

She smiled, 'I'm leaning more towards the latter. We get it a bit with environmental activists messing with the car's valves, if you knew what you were doing it wouldn't be hard to sabotage the car in the carpark without anyone really knowing. It can make a bit of a noise, but out here in the winter the wind makes enough of a noise to disguise that.'

'And with Brodie drugged I doubt he would've noticed anyway.'

'That's what I was thinking, although it does feel a bit over the top to drug him and tamper with his car, why not just let all his tyres down and then he'd have been stranded,' Chris said.

'But if they'd left him stranded at the hotel then someone would've offered him a lift, even if he had decided to walk it − there are too many variables, I think they wanted him to get away from people so they could intercept him with more likelihood of being unnoticed.'

'It was a bit of a gamble though, only one road going this way, someone could've easily driven past and seen them.'

'True, although if they did it could have looked like a good Samaritan helping out a stranded motorist,' I said.

The stretch of road from the hotel to Brodie's turn off had been resurfaced at the end of last year, even the passing places were smooth tarmac.

'I've asked forensics to look at the valves when they're checking out the car, should know in the next day or so if they were tampered with,' Chris said.

We stood in the spot the car had been pulled off the road, I looked to see if I'd missed anything a couple of days ago when I was out here with Callum.

'The discarding of the jacket bothers me,' I said.

'I know what you mean, if he was injured then I understand he might take it off to treat his wound, but it would've been cold, so you'd think he'd have put it back on and if he wasn't alone then why leave evidence like that behind?'

'I've been wondering that as well – and all I can come up with is they didn't realise that it had been dropped. Hopefully Sonya will be able to tell us more this afternoon.'

'Do you know Dr Grother well then?' Chris asked.

'Yeah, I've known her for a long time, but we've become really good friends these last 5 or 6 years.'

'She good at her job?'

'One of the best.'

'My boss wasn't too keen on bringing an outside pathologist in, but his boss said that she was the expert in this Blue42 drug. She's asked if we could get any of Brodie's hairs from a comb or shaver in his room and send it to the lab for her. Do you think she's planning on doing a hair drugs test, to see if there's any sign of prolonged drug use in Brodie's hair?'

'That would be my guess,' I said as we wandered further up the road.

'We should head back, I think we're wasting our time, I mean not *our* time, but police time combing through the great outdoors looking for him, I don't think he wandered off.'

Back in the car we drove in silence for a few moments. 'What's Chris short for?' I asked, not out of any real interest more to break the quiet.

Her cheeks reddened slightly, 'I'll tell you on one condition, you have to promise not to take the piss, okay.'

Now I was intrigued, 'Okay, I promise.' I put 3 fingers up in an old fashioned scouts salute, 'Scouts honour.'

She sighed, 'It's short for Cristal, like Cristal Carrington from Dynasty. My mum was a huge fan and she thought Cristal Hampton sounded fancy, not in fact realising she had given me a very popular stripper's name. I have no idea why my dad went along with it, but I started going by Chris as soon as I could, even in primary school I hated it.'

I tried to stifle a laugh.

'Oh no you don't, you promised not to take the piss.'

'Okay,' I said biting my lips gently between my teeth. 'Does she admit now it might've been a bit of a mistake.'

'No, she bloody doesn't, she says it's just because we live somewhere rural and if we'd been from one of the big cities I would've fitted right in. She's the only one in the family that uses it, but honestly one of the worst things is when I meet new people, especially if I'm dating and they ask about my name.'

'It could be worse.'

'Yeah, thankfully Hashtag wasn't a popular option when I was born otherwise God knows what I'd have ended up with.'

We pulled up outside Ellie's cottage.

'Do you want to come in?' I asked.

'I'd better get back to the team and try and restore some order. I'll call round later though when Dr Grother is settled.

I hesitated before opening the door of the car.

'Everything okay?' Chris asked.

'I don't want you to think that I'm holding out on you so I wanted to check that you know there's a connection between Brodie and the deaths in Glasgow from Blue42.'

'What do you mean?'

I closed the door to keep the cold out. 'When Callum and I searched Brodie's room at the Fraser's we found some photographs, one of them was Brodie with a woman called Lauren Davidson.'

'Okay.'

'Lauren was one of the young women that died in Glasgow, she's from Strathcarron.'

'I thought this was his first trip to Scotland.'

'That's what he told everyone, but he was here before the pandemic, he was in love with Lauren.'

'You think there's some connection? I thought they were all ruled as accidental deaths though.'

'They were, but Lauren's and two other families asked for a review, they didn't believe their loved ones willingly took drugs.'

'Yeah, but that's what all families say, they never like to admit that maybe their daughter was into the recreational drug scene, people have a very rigid idea of what a drug user looks like and when they don't see that reflected in their family member, they don't believe it.'

'I know and ordinarily I'd agree, but Lauren had some pretty serious health conditions, Jackie had a baby she was breastfeeding, and Emily was training to be an Olympian – they don't fit the mould any which way you look at it.'

'I'm sure the investigation was carried out properly.'

'I'm not saying that it wasn't…'

'What *are* you saying?'

'I'm saying that you've got three very obvious anomalies that don't fit the theory that these were accidental overdoses of people who knowingly took a recreational drug. Then when you add in the fact that Brodie lied about knowing Lauren, despite his sister saying that he'd found the love of his life in her, I think it's worth considering that Brodie agreed with Lauren's parents and that he found out something that made him change his plans in Europe and head up here. It can't be a coincidence that Brodie was drugged with the same drug that killed his girlfriend.'

'Okay I'll take it into consideration and run it up the chain of command and see what my boss thinks.'

I opened the door again and this time climbed out into the nippy cold air. 'I'll see you later,' I said before closing the door and heading down the path back to the warmth of Ellie's cottage.

'How did it go?' Alana asked as I closed the door behind me.

'Good I think, Chris seems like a good detective…'

'But?' Alana asked.

'I guess I'm worried that because she doesn't have much experience that she'll be swayed by the opinions of her boss or the pressure they put on her to classify this as a missing, presumed dead case.'

'She's not a convert to all your theories yet then?'

'Not yet, but I've got time,' I smiled. 'Do you want a cup of tea?'

'Yes please.'

'Have you had breakfast yet?' I asked as I walked through to the kitchen.

'No I was waiting in case you hadn't had time to eat before you left.'

'I had one of Gran's shortbreads with my coffee but I'm starving now.' I looked at my watch, it was 10am. 'What time did you get up?'

'About half an hour ago, I was watching a documentary on my laptop before that.'

'Where's Ellie?' I asked, taking mugs out of the cupboard, trying to ascertain how many I would need.

'She went for a bath.'

'I'll put one out for her just in case.'

'Just in case what?' Ellie walked into the kitchen in a large fluffy pink dressing gown and matching slippers.

'In case you're out the bath by the time it's ready.' I made breakfast for us all, bacon sandwich and a cup of tea. 'Do you know the Davidsons?' I asked Ellie.

'A bit, she's nice but I don't think I've ever heard him say more than two words together.'

'Do you know her enough to introduce me?'

'If we saw her about definitely, but not in a let's go visit them at home way.'

'Is she out and about a lot?' I asked.

'Not really, but I think there's going to be a meeting in the hotel tonight, all the locals are going, Callum said something about getting everyone together to talk about Brodie, did DI Hampton not mention it?'

'No, she didn't, perhaps it slipped her mind.' I hoped the oversight hadn't been intentional because she must've known I'd find out anyway. 'Do you think the Davidsons might be there?'

'I'd imagine so.'

Chapter 12

It was a little after 3pm when Sonya arrived.

'Thank you so much for accommodating me,' Sonya said to Ellie.

'Honestly no trouble at all, any friend of Rowan's is welcome.'

Within a few minutes all the awkwardness of Ellie meeting Sonya had passed, and we were all drinking tea and eating Christmas cake.

'I've got a meeting with DI Hampton in an hour or so, have you met her yet?' Sonya asked.

'I met her yesterday and then we went out this morning to look over the route Brodie's car would've taken.'

Sonya smiled. 'Good, I'm glad you're getting along. What do you think of her?'

'Competent, but inexperienced, she has a good instinct for investigation I think, though.' I paused, 'what can you tell me about Blue42?' I asked.

'The first time I became aware of it was in November 2019.'

'Did someone die then?'

'No deaths, but three hospitalisations, that's what brought it to our attention, I've been working as part of a larger group on drug pathology, following drug trends and looking at new ways for us to help with rehabilitation and treat anyone who takes a bad reaction.'

'What is it?'

'It's a mixture of Rohypnol and a variety of other drugs which makes it very dangerous, there's been an increase in the number of synthetic drugs, like Spice which is a synthetic cannabinoid, that's much more dangerous than cannabis, and the results can be devastating. Blue42 is just another in what seems to be an ever-growing list. The difference here, though, is that unlike its predecessors it's not only addictive, it has a scarily high mortality rate, as demonstrated in Glasgow in February 2020.'

'Doesn't that sort of defeat the purpose of making a drug though,' Alana said. 'Surely you want your customers to be alive and addicted?'

'You're right, and I can't imagine that the supplier intended for people to die, like you say alive and addicted is what they're looking for, but also drawing that much attention to yourself is hardly good for business either. Apart from having the police looking for you it's not exactly a good sales pitch, take this drug, you might have a good time, or you might end up in the morgue.'

'It didn't stop people taking Ecstasy in the 1990s though, people were dying then and still every weekend people were going out and taking it,' I said.

'That's true, people between the age of 18-25 tend have a bit of a belief that they're immortal, that it won't happen to them,' she looked at Alana and smiled, 'no offence.'

'None taken, you're right anyway, I saw it all the time last term in halls.'

'People taking drugs?' I asked trying not to sound like an outraged parent.

'Drugs, drinking till they passed out, pills to help you focus and study for tests,' she looked at me, 'and no I've never been tempted, so don't worry.'

'I wasn't worried,' and it was true, Alana was young, and I was certain that she had done and would do things she wouldn't tell me about, but drugs and drinking to excess were not amongst my concerns.

'Do you think Brodie is connected to the deaths in Glasgow?' Alana asked Sonya.

'No way of knowing at the moment, but I doubt it.'

'Has a test been carried out on Brodie's hair?' I asked.

'Yes, and there was no sign of drug use, which makes me conclude that it was much more likely that he didn't take it voluntarily.'

'It was his blood on the jacket?' I asked.

'Yes, the jacket has gone for further forensic examination to see if they can find any traces of foreign DNA which might help us narrow down who we're looking for. Are you going to be joining me for the meeting with DI Hampton?' Sonya asked me.

'As long as she doesn't have any objections, which I can't see that she will.'

When Chris arrived she looked tired.

'You alright?' I asked.

'Been on the phone to my boss for the last 45 minutes and I think he used the expression "tragic accident" at least twenty times.' She gave a slight shake of her head. 'I'm beginning to get the impression that he only put me in charge because he thought there was nothing to investigate.'

'Where does he think Brodie is?' Sonya asked.

'Out in the wilderness. Sorry I shouldn't be bringing my internal problems to you Dr Grother, that's not what you're here for.'

Sonya shot me a look, 'trust me I spend plenty of time listening to Rowan complain, I'm sure I can manage to be a sounding board for you as well whilst I'm here. And stop calling me Dr Grother, it's Sonya.'

'Thanks Sonya, shall we crack on then?'

Ellie and Alana stayed in the kitchen while we went into the living room, I didn't like to tell Chris that I would likely share all the details of the case with Alana at least.

Chris asked Sonya to explain about Blue42 and she repeated what she had told me earlier on. 'That's all we need out here where hospitals can be far away and not easy to get to.'

'I think if you had a wider scale problem of Blue42 being used in the area you would already have seen an increase in hospitalisations, if not then certainly GPs reports due to the side effects.'

'If that's the case that means Brodie was deliberately targeted, which does fit with what Rowan and I both think happened, they used the drug to make Brodie less able to defend himself, put him in a position that his car would come off the road so they could...' she looked away and sighed, 'unfortunately I can't finish that sentence, we haven't been able to find a single reason as to why Brodie would be targeted.'

'How could they know he would try to drive himself and not ask for a lift or get a taxi?' Sonya said.

'I think Brodie would've realised that he'd been drugged, he probably knew he was in danger and was trying to get away. If he didn't ask for help, he either didn't realise how impacted he was by the drugs or he was afraid of getting someone else involved,' Chris replied.

'I still think this has something to do with Lauren Davidson,' I said.

'Why do I know that name,' Sonya frowned.

'She was one of the people who died from taking Blue42, her family are from the area, and they never believed that she willingly took the drug.'

'Didn't the police do a full review of that case though?' Sonya asked.

'They did, but I've been looking at the families who challenged the findings and I agree with them that it doesn't seem plausible that they were recreational drug users,' I said.

'We already spoke about this?' Chris said folding her arms giving me a hard stare.

'The truth is the police don't always get it right, pathologists don't always get it right, sometimes mistakes are made, but it seems to me that Rowan is right, it's the closest thing we have to link Brodie to Blue42,' Sonya said.

'I'm not implying that all police are incompetent, most aren't, but I do know from personal experience that sometimes, for whatever reason things are over looked and, as you haven't managed to find anything else, and because Brodie really needs our help, perhaps we should make sure we've at least fully investigated this angle,' I paused. 'I'll understand if you don't want to open that can of worms, I can speak to the Davidsons, I think they'll be at this community meeting this evening and perhaps even reach out to the other two families and if I find anything out I'll let you know, that way you can be seen to be doing exactly what your boss wants you to do and if I'm wrong none of this will come back on you. What do you think?' I asked Chris.

'Okay, you look into the Glasgow link, I'll continue looking into anything else that happened over the last few days here to see if it throws up any new leads,' Chris said.

'And I'll continue looking into Blue42 and seeing if any local doctors or hospitals have had any admissions that they might not have realised were related,' Sonya said.

'There is one other thing you could do for me,' I said to Sonya. 'Any chance you can see if a hair test was done on Lauren, Jackie and Emily?'

'No problem.'

'Right, I'd better go and get ready for the meeting this evening, I think a lot of residents are concerned that we're not doing enough to find Brodie and others just don't like us being around and asking questions.' Chris said as she left.

Chapter 13

I stood at the back of the room and watched Chris address the concerned locals, she answered questions without really committing to anything. I'd asked Ellie to point the David-sons out to me so I could approach them after Chris and her team had wrapped up.

Mrs Davidson was around ten years younger than her husband, they both had a weathered look that comes from spending most of your time outside no matter the season.

'Mrs Davidson?' I said approaching her as they headed for the door, she took a step back and looked me over without saying anything. 'I'm sorry I didn't mean to sneak up on you, I'm Rowan McFarlane, I'm a friend of Ellie's,' I pointed to Ellie, she saw and waved across. 'I'll get to the point, I'm a private detective and I've been asked by Brodie's family to help find him…'

'I'm not sure what you think that has to do with us,' Mr Davidson said.

'Brodie knew your daughter Lauren, they met in early

2020 and he travelled to Glasgow to be with her, from what his sister tells me he was in love with Lauren.'

'You must be mistaken, Lauren didn't have a boyfriend then, she'd have told me,' Mrs Davidson spoke this time.

I took out my phone and showed them a photo of the picture Callum had found in Brodie's room. They both stared at it for a couple of moments, tears welled in Mrs Davidson's eyes.

'She didn't say.' Mr Davidson put his arm around his wife and pulled her so close to him it was almost like she was absorbed into him, and they became one person.

'Brodie didn't tell his family either.'

'Was it his fault, the drugs?' Mr Davidson asked.

'No, he wasn't a drug user or a drinker…' I paused considering the best way to tell them everything I knew. 'From what I understand it was Brodie that first called for help, he realised that Lauren wasn't well and when she collapsed, he dialled 999 and took her outside for fresh air and he stayed with her until the paramedics came. He made sure she was outside so they could get to her right away…he was holding her when she passed.'

Mrs Davidson let out a broken gasp as she tried to control the sobbing that started.

'I don't want to do this here,' Mr Davidson said. I looked at him holding his wife and realised that if he let go, she would crumple to the ground.

'I'm sorry I didn't mean to upset you so much, do you want to go outside?'

Mr Davidson looked towards the doorway where a number of people stood milling around Chris trying to catch her attention and speak to her directly. 'No, let's go this way.'

I followed as he made his way through a door on the

other side of the room, it took us out into a corridor which looked like it led to the kitchens and the basement. A flight of stairs went somewhere, the guest bedrooms probably. He sat his wife down on the stairs and spoke quietly to her for a few moments until her breathing slowed and she regained her composure.

'I'm so sorry,' I said again, and I was, I should've suggested that we speak somewhere privately, I should've thought about the strength of the emotions I was about to rake up.

'It's okay,' Mrs Davidson's voice was quiet. 'All this time I thought she died alone and afraid, it might not look like it but it's a comfort to know that someone was with her,' she gave me a watery half smile and I felt the urge to cry.

I swallowed my emotions back down.

'I wish he'd introduced himself, all this time just pleasantries...' Mr Davidson said, 'but then it's not exactly an easy subject to broach is it. What I don't understand is why you think what's happened to Brodie has anything to do with Lauren, she's been gone years now.'

I took a deep breath, 'What I'm about to tell you isn't public knowledge and it needs to stay that way, so I have to ask you to keep what I'm about to say to yourselves.'

'We're neither of us much for gossip, we keep to ourselves and if you say this can't be passed on you can be assured that it won't be,' Mr Davidson said looking at his wife who nodded in agreement.

'You're aware that Brodie's jacket was found a little way away from his car and that it was blood stained. We know that was his blood and when it was examined, they discovered that there were traces of Blue42, the drug that killed Lauren, in his blood. I think that Brodie came here for two reasons, one I think he wanted to see where Lauren was from and I do, for what it's worth, think that he had every intention of introducing himself to you both…'

'and the other reason?' Mrs Davidson asked.

I bit my lip taking a moment to think about the best way to construct the information I was about to share. 'The other reason is I think that he agreed with you that Lauren didn't take that drug by choice, and I think he found out something that made him believe that he could prove that.'

'You think that what happened to Brodie is connected to Lauren's death?'

'I do, I think whoever was responsible for giving Lauren Blue42 is also responsible for taking Brodie and I think if I investigate what happened to Lauren, I have a good chance of finding Brodie.'

'How can we help?' Mr Davidson asked.

'I need to know everything you can tell me about Lauren, about what happened when she died, the information the police gave you and anything they told you after the review of the case.'

'Norrie will be pleased to know someone else is looking into this,' Mrs Davidson said.

'Norrie?'

'Norrie Smith, Jackie's husband, that man has been a powerhouse through all of this, caring for a wee baby and never keeping quiet about what happened that night, he's never stopped demanding someone re-examine the findings.'

'Do you think he'd speak to me as well?'

'In a heartbeat, I know you're looking for Brodie and the connection is Lauren, but the same person killed them both.'

'What about Emily's family, have you kept in touch with them?'

'No, I think they wanted to move on and put it behind them, they set up a sports scholarship in Emily's name to help underprivileged kids get into athletics.'

'Okay, can I give you my contact details and get you to ask Norrie to give me a call?' I handed my card to Mr Davidson. 'Tell me everything.'

'Lauren had been in Glasgow a wee while, she liked it there, it's not uncommon with the younger ones, they grow up somewhere everyone knows all your business, they see the same old faces day in day out, then they go off to uni and find themselves in a big city and they like the anonymity of it. After she graduated, she got a flat and a job, she seemed settled. I'm not going to lie I always hoped that ultimately, she'd come home and choose to raise a family here, but I didn't hold it against her that she'd chosen to leave.'

'Did she go out clubbing much?' I asked.

'Not really, I know people say you never really know what your kids do after they leave home, especially when they are so far away, but she tended to prefer to get a curry in and watch the telly.'

'Do you know why she went out that night?'

'It was someone's 25th birthday celebration, a lad she'd been to uni with, it was a whole bunch of her uni mates that went that night.'

'Do you have any names?'

'Not off the top of my head,' Mrs Davidson said, 'but we've got her graduation programme at home, I can find them from that.'

'That would be helpful. When was the first that you knew something was wrong?'

'The morning after she died,' Mr Davidson spoke now. 'We got a knock on the door, I could see the yellow jacket through the little window and when I opened it up and saw two police officers there I knew something was wrong, I mean it doesn't take a genius to work out it means some-one's died.'

He was right, I'd had that same god-awful gut-wrenching feeling when I'd answered the door the day I learnt that Jack had been murdered.

'I didn't think it would be Lauren though…' he wiped his eyes with the back of his hand, 'you don't expect to outlive your kids, it's not natural. We told them there was no way that Lauren would take drugs, I think they thought we were delusional at first. But we explained about her health condition, she would have known the risks and she wouldn't have taken them, she'd never even been drunk.'

'What did you think when the cause of death came back as accidental overdose of recreational drugs?'

'We were so angry we actually travelled down to Glasgow to speak to someone about it, they tried to fob us off and that was when we met Norrie, and once we knew that we weren't the only ones not buying their bullshit we pushed for the review, not that it did any bloody good though.'

'What did the review find?'

'They said there was no conclusive evidence to support either side, that all they could say was that they died from an overdose of Blue42, and we were the only three families kicking up about it, the others had accepted that their loved ones made a mistake and bought a dodgy drug and paid the price. We couldn't stay there long, everyone could predict a lockdown was on its way and we had the farm to run and anyway it felt like we were pissing in the wind, so we came home and offered our support to Norrie long distance.'

Chapter 14

Ellie and Alana were waiting with Sonya and Chris in the foyer of the hotel. 'How did you get on?' Chris asked.

'I opened back up a very raw wound, but they want to help in any way they can.'

'I'd better get back to the team and debrief them, but you'll let me know if you discover anything pertinent, won't you?' Chris asked.

'Of course.'

She left us and headed back inside the hotel. No one spoke much as I drove us all back to Ellie's cottage.

'I don't know about you lot, but I'm beat,' Ellie said. 'I'm off to bed.'

'I could do with a cuppa before I head up.'

'Me too,' Sonya said.

'No worries, I'll see you in the morning.' Ellie climbed up the stairs, I felt a momentary pang of guilt that she might feel relegated to her bedroom in her own home.

'You staying?' I asked Alana.

'No, I'll leave you to catch up, I've got some reading I was hoping to get through before I go back to uni.'

Sonya shut the kitchen door behind us, I was glad of the quiet, it had felt like a very busy, very noisy day. I was glad to be able to sit down with a cup of camomile tea and share my thoughts with Sonya.

I took a sip of tea and nibbled on a piece of shortbread.

'What is it?' Sonya asked.

I frowned.

'You've got that look you get when there's a thought rattling around in your brain that you want to share but you think is a bit out there.'

'You know me too well.'

'We did live together for six months.'

Sonya had moved in with me and Alana during the pandemic after her boiler gave up the ghost, she hadn't been able to get anyone to come and fix it and what had started off as a couple of weeks had turned into months, to the point that I'd missed her more than I cared to admit when she finally moved back home.

'I was thinking, what if we assume that Lauren, Emily and Jackie and probably some others did have their drinks spiked and what if it was indiscriminate, they weren't specific targets but someone wanted to make people sick, for people to die, they wanted to either attack the business or the people in it for some reason.'

'You mean the same way people use biological warfare.'

'Yeah.'

'You're talking about using something that's classed as a recreational drug for a what…a terrorist style attack?'

'Is that such a far-fetched idea? I'm not suggesting it was an actual terrorist attack, but that this was a deliberate act to cause maximum damage and harm.'

'But the bouncer admitted to selling it to make a bit of extra money on the side.'

'He also said he can't have been the only one dealing that night because he didn't have enough product for as many people to have taken it as did.'

'Someone else there could have been dealing.'

'How many high-level distributors of Blue42 do you think there were in 2020?'

'One, maybe two at a push, it was a new drug.'

'If you were pushing a new drug why would you have multiple dealers in one place, wouldn't it be easier to have supplied the bouncer with enough drugs that he wouldn't sell out?'

'I suppose,' Sonya conceded.

'Which means that if there was someone else in that club spiking drinks with Blue42 they weren't doing it for commercial reasons. Also, if you planned to cause carnage like that it would be ideal to set the bouncer up to be your patsy, with him being proved to be dealing, the police wouldn't be looking for anyone else to be involved in the distribution of the drug.'

'But why?' Sonya asked. 'What would anyone gain from that.'

'I don't know. Do you have any clue where Blue42 is being made?'

'The group I'm part of is an international group and in 2019 there were some reports of Blue42 in Germany, The Netherlands and Denmark, with the first ever death reported in Denmark the conclusion we've taken from that is that it's most likely being produced somewhere in mainland Europe.'

'Brodie was in Europe before he came to Scotland, maybe he found something out?'

'Why not take whatever he thought he knew to the police, why come to Scotland?'

'Because all he had was a vague theory that he couldn't prove, or because he had the idea that he could avenge his girlfriend's death himself,' I shrugged.

'That's a lot of maybes,' Sonya said.

'I've made a virtual visit request for Rod Harris.'

'I'm surprised he was willing to talk to you.'

'He might decline my request, we'll see, but from everything I read about him he was truly remorseful that people died because of him.'

'He was never willing or able to give the police enough information to help them find the person he was working for, by all accounts it was a fake name, driving a car with stolen plates on it. And from what I read the physical description was so vague it could've matched half of the male population of Glasgow and beyond.'

'I know, but perhaps after being inside for a few years he'll have had time to remember something, or I might ask him a question they didn't. It's got to be worth a try.'

'You really think he's still alive, don't you?'

'I do, you don't?'

'The levels of Blue42 found in his blood weren't high so shouldn't have been enough to kill him, just help incapacitate him. I think the more interesting question is, if he's being kept alive then what is it he has that they want?'

Sonya was right, that was what I needed to find out, but there was nothing more that could be done this evening so in the end we both went to bed.

When my phone began to buzz I'd mistaken it for my alarm and attempted to snooze it and it took a few moments for me to realise I was being phoned.

'Hello,' I croaked in a groggy half whisper, trying not to wake Alana as I got out of bed and crept down the stairs.

'Hi is this Rowan McFarlane,' the man's voice sounded unsure.

'Yes, who is this?' I asked, going into the kitchen and closing the door behind me. I took a quick glance at my watch, it was 7am.

'This is Norrie, Beth Davidson said you wanted to speak to me.'

I thought for a minute, none of the names making any sense to me, 'Jackie's husband,' I said in a moment of clarity.

'Yes, sorry did I wake you?'

'You did, but that's okay.' Normally I didn't like letting people know that they'd got me out of bed but on this occasion I'd rather him think I was sleeping than an incoherent idiot.

'When you have a little one you tend to forget what normal human times are.'

Jackie's baby had been three months old when she'd died I remembered, 'no problem, I appreciate you calling. I don't know how much Mrs Davidson told you.' It seemed wrong to call her Beth when she'd not given me her name.

'Not a lot and to be honest she wasn't making much sense last night, and if I'm honest I was only half paying attention because Isla was having one of those nights where she just wouldn't settle. All I really got was that you're a private detective, someone's gone missing and you're looking into Jackie and Lauren's deaths.'

I filled him in on who Brodie was and why I wanted to reach out to him.

'You think there's a connection between this lad going missing and what happened to Jackie?'

'I don't want to get your hopes up, but yes I think there's a good likelihood that the two things are connected.'

'And you're on our side?' He asked.

'What do you mean?'

'You believe us when we say they weren't druggies, not even recreational drug takers.'

I thought about Jackie going out that evening, not wanting to leave her baby girl, promising that she wouldn't be late and to call if she was needed, she'd most likely expressed some milk in the evening so that Norrie could feed their daughter before bed. Her almost not going and him persuading her to enjoy her cousin's hen night. I imagined her at the club, probably checking her watch thinking about how late she should stay out.

'Yes, I believe you.'

'Thank you, it's good to hear someone else say that. She was a good person and a wonderful mum, I still can't believe Isla won't get the opportunity to know her.'

'I'm so sorry.'

'Thank you, anyway I'm happy to help in any way I can.'

'Please don't take this the wrong way when I ask, but is it possible that any of the women she was out with might have bought some drugs?'

'There's no way one of them would've spiked her drink, they might've ended up killing Isla…'

'I'm not suggesting they spiked her drink I just wondered if any of them might've bought drugs for themselves?'

'I can't be one hundred percent sure obviously, but I don't think so.'

'Did any of them get sick that night?'

'Her cousin, Zoe, the one whose hen night it was, she

was taken to hospital and was in for four days but was ultimately alright and two of Zoe's friends were treated by paramedics in the church, that's where they took everyone whilst the place was locked down and the guys in hazmat suits came to check it wasn't anthrax or anything like that.'

'There would've been a post mortem on Jackie, do you remember if the pathologist mentioned if she discovered any underlying conditions that Jackie had that might've made her more susceptible to the drug?'

'She was asthmatic, I'm not sure if that could've been a factor.'

'What about Zoe?'

'No but she'd been on antibiotics up until a few days before the hen night, she'd had a chest infection.'

'When the police did a review of the case they told you that there was no evidence to suggest that anyone had intentionally hurt Jackie, is that right?'

'Yeah, their big concession was changing cause of death from "Death by Misadventure" to "Accidental Death" they said it was the only thing they could do in the circumstances to show recognition to the knowledge that Jackie didn't put herself at risk.'

Death by Misadventure would've implied that Jackie had died whilst voluntarily partaking in a risky activity such as recreational drug use.

'Why not an unlawful killing?' I asked.

'Because that implies someone acted in a way that might've led to her death without any intention of that happening, but what the police actually said was that they recognised that it was unlikely Jackie took the drugs knowingly but that it was possible that she accidentally ingested them by picking up the drink of one of her friends that had intended to consume them.'

'The implication being that someone in their group was a recreational user and put the drug in their own drink?'

'I think so, to me it just seemed like an excuse to close the case, they'd arrested Harris, the doorman and they weren't willing to look at any other possibilities.'

'What do you think happened?'

'Don't get me wrong I'm not naive, I know that there were probably dozens of folk in the club that night that bought the drug and were regular users of this type of thing. And I get that there's only so much investigating the police can do when it comes to these things, that it can be hard to get far enough up the food chain to make whoever's really responsible pay for what they've done.'

'But?'

'I think they could've done more. Rod Harris pled guilty so there wasn't a trial, but his lawyer reached out to the families of everyone that died to let them know how sorry he was. I wanted to go and visit him in jail, but with lock-down and a baby to look after I couldn't so the lawyer arranged a video chat. I asked him, Harris that is, why he did it.'

'What did he tell you?'

'That he was sorry, that it was his first time ever doing anything like this, that he had no idea how bad it was and that people were going to die. I almost felt sorry for him, he was crying more than me. I'd hoped it would give me closure, but it didn't. I wanted the police to be doing more to find the person that had got Harris to sell it and they told me they were, but here we are years later and nothing.'

'Do you think someone deliberately targeted Jackie that night?'

He was quiet for a few moments, 'I don't know. I suppose I don't think it was someone who knew her and wanted her specifically to die, but I think that someone spiked a lot of drinks that night in the hope that a lot of people *would* die.'

It was the same conclusion I had been drawing, the thing I struggled with is why, why would anyone do that. 'The club they went to had only recently reopened, hadn't it?'

'That was its grand opening night, I think that's why so many people went.'

'Why was it shut?' I asked, I'd read in the papers that it had failed some health and safety inspections, but I wanted to know if Norrie had any more local knowledge.

'Health and safety.'

'Do you know what exactly?'

'One of the barmaids went to go and get some stock from one of the storerooms, she wedged the door open because it was a self-locking security door. Someone shut it or it got knocked closed and she was trapped inside, the fire escape door had been chained shut by the owner who thought it was being used by the staff to nick stock without being seen. Someone turned the lights out, the switch was on the bar side, she went to go bang on the door to get let back in and she slipped on some rubbish that had been left on the stairs, fell and hit her head on the corner of a cupboard. No one noticed she was missing for a couple of hours and by the time they did and she was found, it was too late to do much to help her.'

'Would she have lived if she'd been found sooner?'

'That's what it said in the press.'

'And what happened to the owners?'

'Health and Safety inspection discovered three other fire escape doors chained shut and a whole pile of other breaches, they were fined but I don't think much else.'

'I'm surprised they were allowed to keep the club.'

'It was advertised as under new ownership when it reopened.'

'But it wasn't?'

'Technically it was, but all that had really happened was that it had been put in the name of another family member and that had been disguised by him having his entertainment company buy it. Same people different public face.'

Do you have any details on the girl that died?' I asked.

'Not to hand but I could look it up for you, I don't see what it would have to do with Jackie though.'

'Probably nothing, I just like to have all the background information I can.'

'I'll email you anything I can remember.'

'That would be great, thanks for calling me this morning Norrie, I know it must be difficult every time someone asks you to go back over it.'

'They don't ask as often as they used to,' he paused. 'I really hope you find this Brodie lad and that you find a way of proving that someone deliberately killed Jackie that night.'

'I can't make any promises, but I'll do my best.'

'All I want is for Isla to know her mum loved her and would never have done anything to risk not seeing her again.'

'I understand.' I said goodbye to Norrie with the promise to let him know if I found anything out.

Chapter 15

I'd been on the phone to Norrie for twenty minutes. He hadn't told me much I didn't already know about what happened that night in 2020, but what he had said about the reason the club had been closed was interesting.

I'd have preferred to be scrolling through the internet on my laptop, but I'd left that in the bedroom so instead I was drinking coffee and looking at the much smaller screen on my phone. Milly Stewart's death had been described as a tragic accident by some papers and the result of gross negligence by others.

The local community had been outraged, first by Milly's death and then by the realisation the club which a lot of the younger people went to every weekend was a death trap. Three of the five fire escapes were chained shut, which would've meant in the event of a fire approximately 500 people would have been trying to escape through the two remaining doorways. It would've been carnage and that was before you realised that the stock rooms were overflowing with junk or that the rubbish hadn't been being properly stored and disposed of. It was a minor miracle that Milly had been the only casualty of the club's mismanagement.

It was harder to find out more about the club's ownership. I checked Companies House and saw that it was now owned by Magic Entertainment, with a list of four directors, none of whom at first glance appeared to have anything to do with the original club owners. I hoped that Norrie would be able to provide me with some credible link between the two.

After Milly's death the club was closed and when Magic Entertainment took over, they fully refurbished and got a clean bill of health on every inspection. It looked like a lot of money had been sunk into making the place look new and inviting, to have been closed down on the opening night must've meant that Magic Entertainment had taken quite a financial hit. And there was no sign that it had reopened following the lifting of the restrictions or that it had any intention of doing so.

Just before 8am my phone buzzed again, this time it was Chris calling.

'Hey,' I said.

'You sound awfully bright eyed and bushy tailed.' I could hear the mock distain in her voice. 'I take it I haven't woken you then?'

'No, are you disappointed?' I laughed.

'Surprised.'

'Someone else beat you to it about an hour ago, anyway what can I do for you, I'm assuming you weren't calling to get an update on my sleeping schedule.'

'This early morning call of yours anything I need to know about?' Chris asked.

'Not at the moment, I'm still poking around in the Glasgow club deaths.'

'Okay, I was calling to let you know that the search team found Brodie's phone about ten minutes ago, totally smashed up, not sure we'll be able to retrieve much data from it.'

'Where was it found?'

'Approximately three miles away from where his coat was discovered.'

'How come no one saw it during one of the other searches?'

'It was probably concealed under the snow.'

'No sign of Brodie though?' I asked.

'No.'

'Odd, don't you think?'

'I've been told to concentrate our search teams on that area, if he wandered that way he must've been very disorientated, there's nowhere to take cover.'

'You don't honestly believe you're going to find him there, do you?' I asked hoping that I hadn't underestimated her.

'I'd be surprised, but I'd like to know how the phone got there though.'

'What's your plan of action for the day?'

'I have to go back to the station and update my boss on our progress, or lack thereof, this afternoon. What about yourself?'

'I'm waiting to see if Rod Harris agrees to have a virtual visitation with me, and if that falls through, I'm going to try to get in contact with Brodie's German friend Emil. Sonya said she thinks that Blue42 originated from somewhere in mainland Europe, so now I'm wondering if it was there that Brodie first found something out that made him cut his trip with his friends short.'

'Good luck, I'll catch up with you later,' Chris said before ending the call.

The kitchen door opened, and Alana came in. 'Everything okay?'

'Yeah, I got a phone call and didn't want to wake you, so I came downstairs.'

She put the kettle on, took two mugs out of the cupboard and put a camomile tea bag in one cup.

'How do you know I don't want coffee?' I teased.

'The coffee pot's empty which means you've had at least two cups already so I thought it was time for a tea,' she said without turning round.

I smiled, she was right. 'Are you sleeping alright bunking with me?'

'It's fine,' she paused.

'What's up?'

'Do you think you'll be finished on this case before we're due to go home?' She asked.

'Even if I'm not we can go home, get your stuff sorted, get you settled in the flat and then I can come back if that's what's worrying you. Are you looking forward to being out of halls?'

'It'll be nice to have a bit more privacy. I've got a video chat with my flat mates this afternoon, to help me to get to know them.'

'That's a good idea, are you nervous?' It was unlike Alana to worry about what people might think of her, but these were the people she was going to be living with, so I understood her trepidation.

'Not nervous, it's just that I don't know them and I'm only going to be there for a term and they're fourth years.'

'Look at it this way, you moving in for the term is helping them out loads, otherwise they'd be splitting the rent and bills 3 ways instead of 4 and they wouldn't have offered the room to you if they didn't think you were a good fit.'

Alana smiled and handed me the mug of tea. A few moments later Ellie and Sonya came in and the small kitchen felt full. Ellie began making breakfast for us all, I said I could get my own, but she insisted.

'Hello, Dr Grother speaking.' In the midst of the preparation, I heard Sonya answer her phone and then she stepped out of the busy kitchen into the hallway. A few moments later she reappeared.

'Sorry, I'll need to skip out on breakfast, I've got to go.' Sonya said.

'What's happened?' I asked.

'The police have found the body of a young man and they need my help.'

Chapter 16

I couldn't sit around doing nothing, waiting to find out if the body was Brodie, instead I decided to carry on working my case. Even if I was wrong and what happened to Brodie had nothing to do with Lauren's death, there was still something off about the events in Glasgow, and I'd made up my mind to dig into it a little further regardless.

I got an email from Lilly telling me that she hadn't found anything of any interest in her brother's bedroom. She included a photograph of Brodie and Emil and another few of Brodie, Emil and another two young men, this was the group he'd been working his way across Europe with. I emailed back and asked if anyone had tried contacting Emil to let him know what had happened or if she had a telephone number for him. Lilly said that she'd sent a text to Emil asking him to get in touch, but that she hadn't heard back from him, she gave me the mobile number she had for him. I replied saying that I would try to contact him, and I'd keep her updated of any developments. I didn't like to lie to her, but what good would it have done for Lilly and her parents to be half a world away worrying that Brodie's body might have been found, better to be ignorant now, and if it was the worst, know about it when it had been confirmed.

Rod Harris agreed to a virtual visitation and a time had been scheduled for 2.30pm today. I wasn't sure what speaking to him could really add but it would give me a more complete picture of what had happened in Nightlife, if nothing else.

My phone buzzed – it was a text from Sonya:

> It's not Brodie – that's all I know at the moment – keep it to yourself.

I breathed a sigh of relief and then felt immediately guilty, Brodie wasn't dead, but somebody else was, someone who had a family that would be looking for him and be devastated to learn that he was never coming home again.

I had so many questions for Sonya, they'd all have to wait until she was back here, and I could talk to her in private. I hated keeping the news from Alana and Ellie, especially as over lunch it was the main topic of conversation, in ordinary circumstances I would've told Alana, but it wasn't possible to tell her without telling Ellie and I was sure that it would be common knowledge before too long anyway.

I was glad to get away to prepare for my visit with Rod. I logged on to the prison visitor service and waited for him to appear on the screen. He looked tired, his years in prison had aged him compared to the photographs I'd managed to find online. I introduced myself.

'I'm not really sure what I can do for you.' He spoke with a strong Geordie accent that caught me off guard.

'I'm investigating a case that I think is related to the deaths in Nightlife in February 2020 and I was hoping you could tell me about what happened from your point of view.'

He rubbed his face with his right palm, 'God if I could go back and do it all again differently I would in a heartbeat. What do you want to know?'

'Start from the beginning,' I replied trying to be deliberately vague at this stage hoping that he'd start to tell me his story and include some details that might otherwise get missed with a more direct line of questioning.

'The November before, ma wee brother, Adam, came to see me, he'd taken a beating from someone, black eye, split lip, and I asked him what was going on. It wasn't unlike him to get himself into bother. More often than not it was because he woke up in the wrong persons bed or because he'd got a bit lairy at the pub. He told me he'd started playing poker and had got in over his head. He was in the hole for just over ten grand. I didn't understand how, but he'd put down his Rolex as collateral and omitted to tell them it was a fake.' Rod shook his head. 'I don't know how he thought he'd get away with it, but this time he'd messed with the wrong folk and they were threatening all sorts if they didn't get their money. Told me they'd already put a brick through my mam's window. I tried to get a loan from the bank, but I couldn't.'

'How did you find the loan shark?'

'He found me, I met him in the pub – I think the people Adam owed money to had figured out the best way for them to get what they were owed was through me.'

'What was he like?'

'The loan shark?'

I nodded.

'He seemed alright, obviously the interest rate was extortionate, but what else could I do?'

'How did you fall behind with the payments?'

'I only missed one payment – I had to get my car fixed.'

'Surely one payment wasn't enough for you to get so far behind that you needed to sell drugs.'

'You'd think, but it's not like he had a complaints department. Anyway I think they used it as an in to pressure me into selling the drugs for them.'

'Them?'

'The loan shark, Wesley, he introduced me to this German bloke named Andreas. He told me that he had a new party drug, said it was like ecstasy but better. Wesley said all I needed to do was sell the drugs – if I did that for six months he'd write the whole debt off, seemed like a good deal to me.'

'A little too good perhaps,' I said.

'In hindsight I should've known it wouldn't be simple.'

'What were you doing for work whilst Nightlife was shut down?' I asked.

'I'd been working for a security firm part time, and I was the doorman at another club, filling in whilst their regular man was away.'

'How did Wesley even know you were going back to Nightlife?'

'I'd told him that I'd be able to catch up my payments because I had the extra work coming,' Rod said.

'Did you tell the police about Wesley and Andreas?' I asked.

'Yeah, they arrested Wesley as well, two weeks after his sentence he had an "accident", hit his head and died.' Rod used his fingers to make air quotes around the word accident.

'You think it had something to do with Andreas?'

He shrugged, 'who knows, likelihood is that he threw

plenty of people under the bus to try and get a lighter sentence, I'm sure he wasn't short of enemies.'

'Did the police ever find Andreas?'

'I don't think so.'

'Take me back to that night in the club, what did you think when people started collapsing?'

Rod looked away and when he looked back his eyes were watery. 'My first thought was it was the drugs because I saw a couple of kids I knew I'd sold to. I called the police immediately.'

'Had you sold all the drugs you had with you?'

'That's the thing, I'd only sold about half of my consignment and as more and more people got ill I was confused, especially when I knew I hadn't given anything to some of them. I started to think it wasn't anything to do with the drugs, that it had to be something in the club, like the air conditioning. I swear I never meant for anyone to die.'

'Did you give the police the drugs when they turned up?'

'I gave them everything, I told them everything I knew, I tried to remember who I'd sold the drugs to. I said to them there was no way I'd sold enough for this many people to get sick.' The tears were falling now, his shoulders vibrating in silent sobs.

'Do you recognise this man?' I showed him a photograph of Brodie.

'His girlfriend died that night, Lauren Davidson. I know every one of my victims, I learnt their names and about their lives. I wrote to their families telling them how sorry I was and every morning I repeat their names to remind myself that no matter how awful it is for me in here that I'm alive, in twelve years I'll be free to carry on my life and they don't have that option,' Rod said.

'Did either of them buy any drugs from you that night?'

'No, I'm good with faces, it's my thing. But I do remember them, they came in with a group, another couple of girls and half a dozen lads.'

'Any of them buy from you?' I asked.

'No, but one of them worked for Andreas.'

'What made you think that?'

'He came up to me and said "Andreas says hi" – he was German too.'

'Was this him?' I asked holding up a picture of Emil.

'No.'

'What about either of these two?' I zoomed in on the faces of the other two young men Brodie had been traveling through Europe with and showed them to Rod.

'The one on the left, the blonde-haired lad. Right cocky little shit he was.'

'You're sure it was him?' I asked.

'Absolutely, like I said I've got a thing for faces.'

'And he was with Brodie and Lauren?'

'He was there, he was with a girl, she was draped all over him. I remember saying she was too out of it to let her in, and that's when he started talking about Andreas and I decided I didn't want to get into it with him.'

I would need to ask Lilly if she knew the lad's name, she was close with her brother and there was a good chance that he would've spoken to her about his friends.

'Did you see anyone else dealing that night?'

'The place was mobbed, it was hard to see much, people were stuffed in like sardines. There was meant to be someone keeping an eye on how many people we had in, so we didn't go over capacity, but something changed, because

I tried to contact the owners and tell them it looked like we were full, but they said it wasn't a problem,' he shook his head. 'I knew better, I should've stopped people going in, the police said it looked like I was keen to get more punters in so I could sell more drugs. The owners said that I didn't contact them to tell them, but I could show on my phone records that I did, but they both denied talking to me.'

'Anything else happen around that time that you think would be useful to know, perhaps something you didn't share with the police at the time?'

'I handed myself and the remaining drugs I had on me to police as soon as they arrived, I thought it might go in my favour if I fessed up right away, I pled guilty, which my lawyer said should help with a shorter sentence, but the judge didn't see it that way.'

I didn't say anything right away, he'd been put in a difficult position trying to bail out his brother, I understood taking the loan, and wanting to protect his mum, but at the end of the day he'd made a choice to sell drugs, it was hard to feel sorry for him.

In the end I simply said, 'thanks for speaking to me today.'

'You're welcome, I hope it helps you find the lad.'

His face disappeared and the screen went blank.

Chapter 17

I looked through my notes, running through some possibilities in my head. Was it possible that Brodie had been involved in Lauren's death, there was nothing to suggest that he took drugs, but that didn't necessarily mean he didn't sell drugs. But why would he deliberately spike Lauren's drink, if he knew about her health condition, he would've realised there was a huge risk of her becoming seriously ill. It didn't make sense, Lilly said Brodie was crushed when he came home, although you would be crushed if you accidentally killed the love of your life.

My brain felt foggy and confused, I stood up and shook my arms, then took a deep breath in, holding it for a second before letting it out with my mouth wide open and my tongue sticking out. I was sure I looked and sounded ridiculous, but I'd taken up yoga during lock down through a YouTube channel and this 'lion's breath' had become a way of me helping to re-centre my focus.

After a few rounds of breathing, I was sure Brodie did not have anything to do with the drugs, which left the option that one of his friends did and it was perhaps discovering this little gem of knowledge that had turned all his travel plans on their head. Was it possible that his friend had accidentally let slip information about what had happened to Lauren, enough to send Brodie back to Scotland to hold someone accountable.

My only issue with this theory was if there was some international drugs ring to uncover then surely the answers were more likely to be found in Glasgow than in the Highlands. My thoughts were interrupted by the sound of a car pulling up outside the cottage, I looked out of the window and saw Sonya.

I got up and opened the living room door so she'd see me as soon as she came through the front door.

Sonya stomped her boots against the mat trying to rid them of snow and mud, she looked over at me and held up two fingers, indicating she'd be with me in a moment. I hoped to have at least a quick chat with her alone before Alana and Ellie joined us. Sonya lined her boots up next to mine and padded through to join me in her socks.

'Are you okay?' I asked closing the door behind us.

'It's bloody freezing out there, but I'll be fine. They're moving the body to the morgue now, so I've come back to get some food and warm up, go through my notes before I do the post mortem tomorrow. Their usual pathologist won't be available for another few days, so I volunteered my services.'

'They're lucky you're here.'

'Perhaps someone should tell DI Hampton's boss that, he spoke to me like this would be my first post mortem, and reminded me that this was part of a police investigation.'

'Wow, just wow,' I replied.

'I strongly advise that the two of you never meet,' she smiled.

'Did you tell him how much experience you have, you literally lecture on this stuff.'

'No, I'm not going to argue my credentials with someone who would only know which end of a scalpel was which when he cut himself. He can have my help or wait, ironically the doctor that's his regular pathologist was one of my PhD students a couple of years ago.'

I shook my head, 'apart from the fact that Chris's DCI is a twat, what else can you tell me?'

'The answer should be nothing,' she chuckled and then pulled a tablet out of her bag and opened a file on it. 'Young man, mid-twenties, blonde hair, about five foot eleven, stabbed, hard to say how many times but at least five from first examination. He's been dead at least twenty-four hours, but it's cold out there and time of death will be hard to pinpoint with as much degree of accuracy as normal.'

'Murder then,' I commented.

'Looks that way, no one on the scene recognised him so Chris and her team are looking for missing persons from further afield to see if we can get a sense of who he was. I've suggested they do an international search, both his jacket and his jeans were German brands and he'd had them for a while. DCI Burke, and yes that really is his name, wasn't keen on this suggestion, he told me I was overstepping my position and it was much more likely that the deceased had been on holiday in Germany and bought some clothes whilst he was there.'

'And you disagree?'

'Neither item was new, and even with that I might've been more open to Burke's suggestion if he was only wearing one item, but to have two, plus the shoes were also a German brand, but one you can easily buy in the UK. I suspect he'll ignore me until he realises that I'm right and then I fully expect him to claim it as his own idea.'

'Once again, wow. Remind me to bring George a gift back won't you,' we both laughed. 'Can you show me any photos?'

She swiped through some pages until she came to a close up of his face, a face that despite the skin being an unnatural bluish white and the lips purple, was one I recognised immediately. 'I know who that is,' I said.

'What? How?' Sonya asked.

'Well, I mean I sort of know who it is. I don't have a name, but I've seen him before.' I scrambled through my phone to the picture of Brodie, Emil and their two friends and showed it to Sonya. She enlarged the photo looking from one screen to the other.

'You're right, they are the same person. Any chance you can find out *who* he actually is?'

'I'll ask Lilly,' I'd been intending to ask her more about her brother's friends anyway, I typed a quick email asking her for the names and if she had them, the contact details of the two men in the photo with Brodie and Emil.

'I should probably let DCI Burke know we have a possible lead on the dead man,' Sonya said.

'Wouldn't it be better if we found out more about him first, then we can give the information to Chris. Plus, wouldn't you enjoy knowing we'd proved you right before you fill him in?'

'He's coming to observe the PM tomorrow,' Sonya said.

'Not like you've not been observed hundreds of times before though.'

'It doesn't bother me him watching, it's the fact that I'm almost certain he'll feel the need to interject and I'm not sure my patience will stretch that far. Right, I need food,' Sonya said, getting to her feet and heading to the kitchen.

It was mid-afternoon before I heard back from Lilly, she said the other two men in the photo were brothers and she'd describe them as more friends of Emil's than Brodie and that her brother had been disappointed that they were going to be joining them on the trip through Europe. Ben and Karl Weber aged 24 and 26, although Lilly hadn't been sure which one was which, they had been easy for me to find on social media and identify that Ben Weber was the man Sonya would be carrying out a post mortem on tomorrow and the one Rod Harris had identified as knowing Andreas.

Chapter 18

DCI Burke had insisted that I come through with Sonya to meet with him, Chris told me he'd asked for a quiet word with me before the post mortem started because she'd had to tell him that information regarding Ben Weber had come from me.

It had meant another very unwelcome early morning for me and now I was sitting in Sonya's passenger seat looking at the beautiful scenery flashing past, irritated at being summonsed in this way.

'Don't let him get under your skin,' Sonya said. 'You're only here for a short time, so smile and nod and ignore him.'

'I'll do my best.'

'Hmm, well remember Chris has to work with him and you don't want her to suffer the brunt of something you do because you get to walk away after.'

I knew Sonya was right, she had over a decade of experience of dealing with the police, prosecution lawyers in court, students and probably more besides. It had taken years to build the relationship I have now with DCI George Johnston in Fife and until this point I'd never really grasped how accommodating of me he really was.

'Alright.' I said, noticing Sonya was clearly waiting for a response.

DCI Burke was not how I'd pictured him, instead he was tall and grey haired and looked very much like he'd have been at home in a Highland Estate, shot gun under one arm and a bunch of lifeless pheasants in the other.

'DCI Burke, a pleasure to meet you,' I said putting out my hand for him to shake. Out of the corner of my eye I caught Sonya stifling a laugh.

'Rowan McFarlane, I presume?'

'Indeed.' I wanted to ask who the bloody hell else he thought I'd be, seeing as there was only the three of us stood in the corridor.

'I thought we should take a moment to talk in private whilst Dr Grother readies herself for the post mortem,' he nodded towards a closed door and I followed him through.

The room was stark, a small table and two plastic chairs, grey walls which could have done with a repaint to cover over the multiple chips.

'Do take a seat,' DCI Burke said.

I sat, he stood behind the other chair resting both his hands on its back. I'd seen this move more times than I cared to remember, this idea of asserting dominance by being higher up and talking down to me. I sat relaxed, my hands resting in my lap.

'I understand from DI Hampton that you have developed an interest in this case.' DCI Burke continued.

I didn't say anything.

'I'm sure you can understand why that greatly concerns me.'

'Not really,' I replied.

'When a member of the public actively tries to insert themselves into an investigation, I need to ask myself why, what have they got to gain.'

'I'm not getting involved as a member of the public, I'm getting involved as a private detective and as such what there is to gain should be self-explanatory.'

He sneered, 'I'm quite sure we don't need the help of an amateur.'

'I beg to differ, because without me you wouldn't have a clue who the deceased is. And I'm not an amateur, I'm a fully accredited professional private detective.'

'Accredited or not I do not want you involved,' he said.

'What I do has nothing to do with you.'

He shifted slightly and I could see annoyance in his eyes. 'I don't know what they let you get up to in Fife but let me make myself clear, you will not be afforded any of those courtesies with my team.'

'What I "get up to" in Fife is helping the police in their investigations, which if you've taken the time to look you will see has led to the solving of multiple missing persons cases throughout Scotland,' I said.

'I hope you're not suggesting that the police were incapable of solving them without your assistance. Perhaps I am not making myself clear enough for you, you are to stay out of this investigation, you are not to ask people questions, you are not to have clandestine meetings with DI Hampton, you are not to ask Dr Grother anything.' A small purple vein in his temple pulsated.

'Let me be very clear with you,' I said standing up. 'I have been engaged by Brodie's family to investigate his disappearance and I intend to do that…'

'Now you listen here…' he interrupted.

'No, you listen – you might rule the roost in regard to the police, but you do not have any authority over me, I will continue my investigation, and if you insist on hampering me then I'm sure that Brodie's parents will convey to you their upmost disappointment themselves. As for your request for me to not ask Dr Grother anything that would be tricky seeing as we are living together at the moment. Furthermore, I have been nothing but respectful towards you and I don't think it's too much to ask for the same.' I walked past him to the door and walked out into the corridor.

'This conversation isn't over,' he called at me from the doorway.

I looked over my shoulder, 'it is for me, and if I'm not mistaken Dr Grother is ready to begin the post mortem.'

I could see Sonya through the glass panel, she shot me a look and I was reminded of our earlier conversation, still she couldn't have expected me to sit there and let DCI Burke berate me, nor would she have thought it reasonable for him to demand I stop investigating. I offered her a weak smile and a shrug of my shoulders. She gave a barely imperceptible shake of her head. Then Burke appeared next to me.

'I hope you don't think you're getting to stay for this.'

'You've not left me with a lot of options, Sonya brought me here at your request and I can't leave until she's finished so I might as well watch.'

'I don't want you to get sick on my shoes, these can be quite upsetting the first time.'

'It's not my first time,' I said without looking at him. It was my second and honestly, I'd rather not be watching, but I didn't want him knowing that.

'Fine, but you don't get to ask questions, just stand there and be quiet,' DCI Burke barked at me.

He tapped on the glass wall that separated Sonya from us several times throughout to ask inane questions, after the third time she had reminded him that she would answer his questions at the end and not to interrupt her further, after that she had taken to simply ignoring his raps. I could see he found this frustrating and that vein that I'd watched pulsate as he spoke to me, was becoming more and more pronounced.

By the time Sonya had changed and come through to the little office at the side DCI Burke was tapping this foot, glancing at his watch, and sighing loudly. I admired Sonya's reserve as she carried on as though he wasn't there at all.

'I know you're new to all this but how much longer is all this going to take,' he waved indiscriminately at the paper-work on the desk.

'It takes the time it takes to be done correctly.'

'Does someone else need to check it?' DCI Burke asked.

'For what?' Sonya asked without looking up.

'Mistakes,' DCI Burke said as though that was obvious.

'Does Dr Anstruther normally have his work double checked?' Sonya asked.

'Of course not.'

Sonya paused, put down her pen and turned to face him, 'then why do you think I would need my work checked?'

'Because as is painstakingly obvious you've never worked on a murder case before.' Burke looked pleased with himself.

'Is that so, and what makes you say that?'

'Well when I asked you about it yesterday you didn't say you had,' he had his arms crossed.

'You didn't ask me, you told me I wasn't as competent as Dr Anstruther and treated me like I was a grad student, which is ironic because Dr Anstruther *was* my PHD student once. Purely for the purposes of encouraging you to stay quiet enough to allow me to do my work properly I'm happy to share my credentials with you. I have carried out hundreds of post mortems related to unexplained deaths alone, several of those murders, I have given evidence in court and I've been a police pathologist for almost a decade, I lecture in Forensic Pathology at Edinburgh University. Does that meet your exacting standards?'

'Well…' Burke shuffled his feet slightly, 'you didn't make that clear…otherwise I wouldn't…' he trailed off.

'I shouldn't have to explain myself to you. Now please be quiet so I can complete my work and then I'll happily answer your questions.'

I watched his face, now a deep shade of crimson, his eyes lowered looking at what must've been a very interesting spot on the floor. I watched Sonya work, wondering if she was deliberately taking her time to punish him. Eventually she spoke and broke the silence.

'His body was out in the cold for some hours and there's been very little insect activity due to the time of year, making time of death much harder to approximate, he was out over night and I'd suggest that he's been dead less than 24 hours. His stomach contents showed that he'd eaten a couple of hours before he was murdered. I'll send it for full analysis but it looks like it was probably a pot noodle. He was stabbed 11 times, with what was most likely a chef's style knife, the sort with a slight curve in the blade designed for chopping herbs etc.'

'Quite a common thing then,' DCI Burke said.

'Yes, however we did have a bit of luck, the tip of the

knife broke off in one of the ribs, it might be enough to get a more detailed description of the knife, but certainly would help us accurately identify the murder weapon should your team find it,' Sonya said.

'Excellent. Anything else you can share with us at this stage?' DCI Burke asked.

'I think it's fairly apparent that he didn't die where his body was found, he would've suffered huge blood loss and forensically that's hard to clean up well enough to completely avoid any detection. I found some blue fibres on the body and in the wounds, this could be transfer from something the killer was wearing but more likely what he was wrapped in for transfer. We should know more about what they came from in a day of so. There were no defensive wounds on the hands and arms…'

'You think he knew his attacker then?' DCI Burke interrupted.

'It's impossible to tell…'

'I thought lack of defensive wounds was a good indicator that a victim knew their attacker?' DCI Burke interrupted again.

'Not necessarily, but you're correct in some circumstances, however you're unlikely not to put up a fight at all whilst being repetitively stabbed, even by someone you know.' Sonya continued quickly not allowing Burke time to interrupt a third time. 'In this case I believe that Ben Weber had been drugged, and was therefore incapable of defending himself.'

'Drugged, right I see, do you know what with?' DCI Burke said.

'I did a quick check for presence of Blue42 in his blood and it came back positive. I'll send a larger sample to my team so it can have a full analysis and toxicology run on it and that will allow us to see if it's the same batch of Blue42 that I found in Brodie's blood.'

'And that's important, is it?' Burke asked.

'I think it's worth knowing, whether or not that turns out to be important will be down to your investigations,' Sonya said looking at me.

'Right, well, I'll let you finish up your paperwork,' Burke said to Sonya. 'And you can let me know when you get the other test results back.'

Sonya agreed that she would and then we both watched him leave.

'Well isn't he a charismatic chap,' I said.

'There was only so long I could hold my tongue for, what did he say to you?'

'The usual, stay out of his investigation, I wasn't welcome here, that I didn't know what I was doing, he even had the audacity to suggest that I might be involved in the death in some way and that I was trying to insert myself into the investigation because I had something to hide.'

'I'm sure you told him your thoughts on that,' Sonya smiled.

'I was polite,' I paused for a moment tipping my head to one side and replaying the conversation in my head. 'Well, I wasn't rude, but I also told him he didn't get to tell me what to do.'

Chapter 19

I'd brought my laptop with me to the lab so I set myself up on a table in the corner of the room so I could work whilst Sonya was busy.

I decided to send a direct message to Karl Weber through social media. I wondered if he knew his brother was dead, or what his involvement in any of this was, but I was investigating Brodie's disappearance and there would be nothing unusual about a detective reaching out to his friends.

> Hi, my name is Rowan McFarlane, I'm a private detective and I've been hired by the family of Brodie Cullen to help find him. He went missing on the 31st December and has not been seen since. I understand from his sister, Lilly, that you and your brother were travelling through Europe with Brodie and Emil before Brodie decided to come to Scotland. I was hoping you would be free to talk to me as I'm trying to gather some background information on Brodie.

As usual I left my email and telephone number, then I sent the same message to Ben Weber, despite knowing he was lying dead only a few metres away from me in the morgue. I needed Karl not to know that I knew, it should be unthinkable for one brother to kill another, but I knew that it was a possibility I had to take into consideration. This way Karl wouldn't be suspicious if he had access to his brother's social media. I sent another similar message to Emil, adding that Lilly had passed on his telephone number and asking if it was okay to give him a call.

In my inbox was an email from Norrie, he'd been very thorough including any and all newspaper articles that even vaguely mentioned the club, the drugs, and the deaths. There was surprisingly little. But then most news at the end of February/start of March 2020 had been eclipsed by the pandemic. I imagined carrying out an investigation of this scale in those circumstances can't have been easy.

I zoomed in on the photographs from the newspaper, in two of them I noticed the same figure stood near the closed club, at first, he looked like he was a passer-by, caught accidentally in the camera lens, but to be captured twice in almost the same place was unlikely. It was hard to make out any features from the grainy black and white newspaper photograph. I sent a quick email to the publication asking if they could email me a copy of the original photograph, perhaps then I would be able to confirm my suspicions.

The first response to my direct messages came from the most unlikely of the recipients, Ben Weber. Considering I'd only this morning watched Sonya perform his post mortem the idea that he was now replying to me was intriguing. For a moment I wondered if we'd been wrong, and it was in fact Karl that had been murdered until Sonya reminded me that Karl was a good six inches taller than Ben.

Thank you for letting me know about Brodie. I was with Brodie before he came to Scotland. He said he was coming to visit his girlfriend, there had been some sort of emergency. I haven't heard from him since then. I'm not able to give you much background information, he was really Emil's friend, and this trip was my first time meeting him. If you want to talk about anything else regarding our trip until that point, I have provided my number below. I'm in the UK too now so this is my UK number. Ben

I looked at the number, it looked familiar. I opened the file for the case and went to the photographs I'd taken from Brodie's bedroom at the Frasers' – the number "Ben" had given me was the same as the one Brodie had scribbled on the back of his till receipt on the 27th December. The same day that he cut off all communication with his family back in Canada. Something had changed that day, and whoever was pretending to be Ben was right at the heart of it.

I stepped out into the corridor to call "Ben" – 'Hi this is Rowan McFarlane,' I said as soon as the phone was answered.

'The private detective that messaged me?'

'Yes, thanks for getting back in touch so quickly.'

'Not a problem, although I don't think I can be much help to you,' he said.

'Sometimes the most insignificant of things can help,' I replied. 'When was it Brodie left you to come to Scotland?'

'I don't remember the exact date but a few months ago at least.'

'What did he say was the reason for him coming?'

'Something to do with his girlfriend.'

'You don't happen to remember her name, do you?' I asked.

'Laura or Lauren, I think. I don't quite remember.'

'And you're in the UK now?'

'That's right.'

'How long have you been here?' I asked.

'I arrived just before Christmas, and I stay until end of January.'

'And whereabouts are you staying?' I asked hoping that my asking all these questions about him wouldn't make him suspicious.

'Glasgow, it is a very nice city.'

'You've been before of course,' I said.

There was a pause before he answered, 'why do you think that?'

It wasn't a denial, which was interesting. 'Brodie's sister told me that he met you and your brother Karl when he was in Scotland with Emil the first time.'

'Of course,' he said but there was a stress in his voice now. 'I had forgotten about that because our trip was cut so short by the pandemic.'

I was trying to decide if I should let him know that I knew that Ben and Karl were in the club with Brodie the night Lauren died, but I didn't know who I was talking to yet and it was too early to show my hand fully. 'Did you keep in touch with Brodie after that?'

'Not really, I think we sent each other the occasional message now and again, but we weren't close.'

Was this fake Ben hedging his bets, thinking that it was likely there had been at least some correspondence between the two in the intercepting months? 'Are you close to Emil?'

'He is more my brother's friend than mine, but we get along just fine.'

'Did you all come to Scotland together, you, Karl and Emil?' I asked.

'I came with Karl only, I do not know where Emil is at the moment, but Karl would likely have an idea.'

'I messaged Karl as well, but I've not heard from him yet, are you staying together?' I asked.

'We were,' his speech was hurried. 'But Karl found a job in Aberdeen for two months and I need to go home before end of January so I couldn't join him for this part of our trip.'

'Are you going home to anything special?'

'I have a job in Munich starting in February.'

I wanted to ask what he'd be doing, in ordinary circumstances I probably would have, but I was conscious that with every question I asked whoever I was talking to was forming an impression not only of me but of what I might already know. 'Well thanks for talking to me, could I ask that if you do hear from Brodie that you ask him to get in touch with me or his family, there are a lot of people very worried about him.'

'Of course,' he said.

I said goodbye and hung up. Who had I just been talking to, the accent had been German from the little I knew, but it could have been anyone. The real question was, why pretend to be Ben, what did they think they could gain from this charade?

Chapter 20

Sonya was packing up her things when I went back into the little office. 'You about ready to head back?' She asked.

'If you've done everything you need to.' I said before telling her about my call from the afterlife.

'Nothing more I can do here until the test results come in and that will likely be tomorrow at the earliest. Besides breakfast seems like a lifetime ago and I could do with some lunch. Are you going to tell Chris about the call?'

I looked at my watch, it was nearly mid-day. My stomach growled at the thought of lunch. A few moments later we were in Sonya's car driving back to Ellie's. I sent a text to Chris asking her to come to the cottage this afternoon. She had the resources to trace the telephone number.

Alana and Ellie were making lunch when we arrived, Ellie had taken Alana out for a bit of a drive so at least one of us was getting the opportunity to see the sights.

'Sausage sandwich okay for you both?' Ellie called from the kitchen.

We agreed that it was.

'You were very quiet on the drive back,' Sonya said.

'Getting a telephone call from a corpse will do that to you,' I joked.

'You're worried about something.' Sonya replied ignoring the flippant comment that she'd come to recognise as my way of deflecting from what I was really thinking about.

'I'm concerned you're going to end up with three more dead bodies and I'd really like to prevent that happening.'

We were just finishing up lunch when there was a knock at the door, I went to answer assuming that it would be Chris and was surprised to see Callum instead.

'Oh Callum, sorry I wasn't expecting you,' I said.

'DI Hampton sent me, she said to let you know DCI Burke is down at the investigation HQ and she can't get away whilst he's there, he has her under strict instructions not to talk to you or help you in anyway.'

'Well, isn't he quite the charmer.' I thought back to my conversation with him this morning, I wasn't shocked, I'd clearly pissed him off and this was his childish way of retaliating. Still, I didn't need his permission to investigate, I'd done plenty of that on my own, but unlike Burke I wasn't petty enough to let any more people potentially die for the sake of my pride.

Callum shifted uncomfortably not sure whether to agree with my assessment of his boss or not. 'She said if you have any information pertinent to the case you could give it to me and she'll try to catch up with you this evening.'

Alana had come through to the hall and was stood behind me, 'hey Callum, we weren't expecting you, are you hungry? We've got some sausages left from lunch, I can knock you up a sandwich if you want.'

Callum's cheeks flushed, I glanced at Alana, no sign of

embarrassment there, I wondered if the PC had taken a liking to Alana and if the feeling was mutual. 'If it's not too much trouble,' he said.

'No, it's fine,' Alana replied.

I stepped out of the way to let him come past me and into the kitchen, a few moments later he was tucking into his sandwich and enjoying a nice hot cup of coffee.

Sonya and I sat at the kitchen table with our laptops out giving the impression of working whilst watching Alana and Callum deep in conversation.

Sonya leant over towards me and said in a whisper, 'do we have a romance blossoming here do you think?'

I scowled, 'he's too old for her.'

She tried not to laugh, 'He's only about 23 or 24.'

Sonya was right, it wasn't much of a difference and Alana had been through enough in her life that she was probably more mature than most 24 year olds, but still I couldn't see her with Callum. I didn't know what my objection was, I hadn't felt this way when she'd dated Xavier at university, perhaps it was the idea of her being in a relationship with a police officer, one who at the moment at least felt like he was on the opposite side of the investigation to me.

'I'd better be off,' he said downing the last of his coffee. 'Thanks for lunch, it was great.' He was speaking directly to Alana.

'Can't have you out there fighting crime on an empty stomach,' she giggled.

And in that moment I realised what it was I didn't like, in every interaction they'd had Alana had been there as a domestic host, he liked her because she made him lunch and listened to him talk, but I hadn't seen him show any interest in her.

'I'll see Callum out,' I said standing up quickly, ignoring the glare from Sonya. 'I've got a couple of things I need him to share with Chris.'

He looked a little disappointed. I closed the kitchen door behind us and as I started to open the front door I said, 'do you like my daughter?'

He blushed, 'yeah, she's really nice…'

I interrupted him, 'she's a lot more than sausage sandwiches and cups of coffee you know, she's studying to become a forensic anthropologist. That's about another seven years of study.'

'I get it, she's super smart so I'm not surprised. I understand you being protective. I've got goals as well. I sat my sergeant's exam last year and passed, I'm just waiting for a position to open up somewhere. I want to get to at least DCI, I like that she's ambitious, that's one of the best things about her.'

I tried to remind myself that the limited times I'd seen them together were not the extent of their communication and I wondered why Alana hadn't shared this with me and how I could ask her without sounding like I was being too intrusive.

'That's okay then, it's not that I don't like you…'

'It's that you have high standards for Alana, I get it. I think you'd like my mum,' he smiled. 'Was there anything you actually needed to tell me for DI Hampton?'

It was my turn to blush slightly, 'there is actually, you remember that telephone number that we found written on the receipt in Brodie's room?'

He nodded.

'I got a telephone call from that number this morning from a man claiming to be Ben Weber.'

'But he's dead.'

'I know, that's why I think you should see what you can find out about that number – it would be good to know where they were calling from, the man said Glasgow, but…'

'What if it was closer.' Callum said.

'Exactly.'

'Do you think that means they don't know that we've discovered the body?'

'Possible, or that they don't think I know you have or that we haven't identified that body as Ben. The man had an accent, probably German. I sent messages out to Karl and Emil as well and I'll let you know if I hear back from either of them. And say to Chris to pop by if she can later on if DCI Burke has left her in peace.'

'Okay dokey. I'll let you know if I get anything from the telephone number.'

I watched him walk up the path to his car and drive off. I went back into the kitchen.

'You finished enquiring after his intentions towards me now?' Alana smiled and exchanged a look with Sonya.

'For now,' I said.

'Good. I'm off to watch an online lecture from Harvard School of Anthropology,' she replied and headed off up the stairs.

I went back to my laptop and found a response from Emil:

Hi, I'm sorry everyone is worried about Brodie, there is no need for you to keep looking for him, we are together and well. He asks that you let his family know he'll be in touch soon. We are travelling to Germany together and will catch up with everyone properly when we get there. Emil.

I spent a few moments considering how to respond. Was Emil also in danger, I thought it was very likely that he was, and if whoever was holding him and Brodie found out that I was on to them I'd be putting them even more at risk.

Thanks for letting me know, I'm glad to hear Brodie is fine. Can you have him call the number at the end of my message, it's for DI Hampton she is in charge of the police investigation looking for him. I'm sure once she speaks to Brodie and everything is cleared up then she'll be able to close her investigation and mark it up to a misunderstanding.

I'd considered not mentioning the police, but with whatever was going on with Brodie, whoever had pretended to be Ben earlier today must know that the police are involved. I hoped that my message was enough of a play dumb that the sender believed I didn't know anything.

I sent Chris a text telling her I really needed to speak to her and that I understood that she might not be able to get away, but could she call me. There was a chance that the message sender might call her, and I wanted her to at least have a heads up about it.

Ten minutes later my phone rang.

'This better be important,' Chris said in a hushed voice.

'It is,' I found myself almost whispering in response. I quickly told her what had happened so far today.

'You think this person might try and contact me impersonating Brodie?'

'I think they might. What would that mean for the investigation?' I asked.

'If it had happened before we found Ben Weber's body

then I think DCI Burke would have pulled me back, but it's a murder investigation now and there's no denying the connection between Weber and Brodie, only a fool would conclude that Brodie's disappearance and Ben's death aren't connected,' she paused. 'And I know you probably think DCI Burke is a fool, he can be, but even he thinks it's all intertwined. I'll probably be taken off lead though, putting me in charge of a missing persons case is one thing, but a murder changes that.'

'That sucks, who do you think he'll put in charge?' I asked.

'There's a couple of DI's that have had experience of suspicious deaths, but he might put himself in charge due to the international implications.'

'Urgh,' I said knowing that with DCI Burke in charge it would make my job so much harder.

Chris stifled a laugh. 'He's alright when you get used to him.'

'I don't think I'm going to be here long enough to get used to him. Did you get a chance to look into that telephone number I spoke to Callum about?'

'We did, it pinged off a tower not far from here, which at least is a good thing because it means they haven't gone far. DCI Burke is going to be speaking to the press later today about Ben, but we've agreed because of the contact you had this morning we're not going to identify him. His family understood why we wanted to keep it quiet for at least a few days.'

'That's good at least. I'm planning on paying a return visit to Grant Fraser's place in case we missed anything there the other day.'

'You'll let me know if you find anything?'

'Yeah of course.'

'Oh, and just so as you know when DCI Burke starts complaining about it I'm going to deny any knowledge of this conversation,' Chris said.

'I just don't understand why he's so resistant to help. So far I've given him an ID for a murder victim and a phone number to follow up.'

'He doesn't trust you, don't take it personally, it's a bit weird having outside help and I wasn't sure how I felt about it at first, and besides perhaps you two aren't that dissimilar, you don't strike me as the sort of person who accepts help happily either.'

I paused, I felt a little insulted by the comparison, but the real sting was the fact that there was some truth in her words. 'I get it I suppose, it irks me that's all.'

'You've got too used to that cushy number you've got with the DCI down your way. But he does appreciate the information, even if he's not very good at showing it,' Chris said.

'I'll take your word for it.'

'Listen I can get a PC to check on you occasionally, if you like, now that it appears you're in the cross hairs of someone who may well turn out to be a killer,' Chris said with some hesitation.

'No thank you, I'm more than capable…'

'I wasn't saying you weren't capable, I wouldn't be doing my job if I didn't show some concerns for your safety.'

'Your concern is noted, but honestly the last thing I want is to be followed around by some PC, that would likely be more hazardous to everyone's safety.'

Chris snorted a laugh. 'Okay then.'

'I'll let you know if I get any more communications from beyond the grave,' I said before ringing off.

Chapter 21

I listened to DCI Burke on the radio and found myself feeling slightly impressed at the way he handled the barrage of questions coming his way. He gave a good description of Ben and appealed for anyone who might be able to identify him to call the hot line. When he was asked if he thought that the body had anything to do with the missing man, he replied saying there was nothing to suggest that the two were connected and that they were being investigated as completely separate cases.

Not being able to see him I couldn't know if his body language had given off any cues that might contradict his words. I felt a slight moment of remorse for the way I dealt with him the first time, had I heard this before meeting him I might have taken a different approach, but then I remembered the patronising way he spoke to Sonya and how quickly he'd dismissed my input as worthless, and the feeling passed.

I drove round to the Frasers' unannounced accepting

the risk that they might not let me in. Grant Fraser looked particularly displeased to see me. He opened the door and looked me up and down, a dark expression forming on his face.

'Hi Mr Fraser, sorry to drop in unannounced like this, I'm Rowan McFarlane, we met the other day with PC Sinclair.'

'I know who you are, what do you want?' He responded.

'Behind him I heard the clink of cutlery on plates and said, 'I hope I'm not disturbing your dinner.'

'We've just finished.'

'I was hoping that I could take another look at Brodie's room,' I said.

'I'm sorry I'm not comfortable letting you do that.'

'His parents have asked me to check on a few of his possessions,' I replied.

'You should come back with the police, and I might think about it,' Grant Fraser said.

'That's a shame,' I said pursing my lips and sighing, 'I was hoping to be able to go back to his mum this evening and let her know whether the keepsake she gave her son to travel with is here or if he might have had it on him.' It was a lie, a story that I fabricated in the moment, but I hoped it sounded realistic enough to pull on Grant's heartstrings. 'I'll let her know you won't give me access to his possessions,' I continued before turning away from the door.

'Wait,' he said.

I turned trying to hide the look of satisfaction from my face.

'You'd best come in, the woman has been through enough.' He stood back and opened the door wide enough to let me pass.

'That's good of you,' I said. 'I won't be long.' I climbed

the stairs and went into Brodie's room, Callum and I had a good look through it the day after Brodie disappeared, but I had a nagging feeling that I was missing something. I closed the bedroom door and stood for a few moments looking around, it looked exactly the same as it had when Callum and I had been here, except now it was dark outside. I pulled on a pair of neoprene gloves and got to work.

I decided to start with his bed and work out. I carefully peeled back his duvet, gently patting it down as I went, then I did the same with the sheet and the pillows, finally I lifted the mattress, under the mattress had been a favourite hiding place for teenagers throughout time and I hoped that Brodie might've chosen it too. No such luck.

I put it all back together before moving on to the wardrobe. I took every garment out, checked all the pockets, still nothing. Next the chest of drawers, Brodie had kept his things neat. I took a pile of socks from the first drawer and laid them on the bed as I thought about the message allegidly from Emil suggesting that Brodie wasn't missing, but instead was on his way to Germany. Had the writer really believed that it didn't look suspicious for Brodie to disappear in the middle of the night leaving all his belongings behind.

As I replaced the socks I heard a crinkling sound coming from one of the pairs, I ran my hand over the sock, something was definitely inside. I undid the pair and pulled out a piece of folded up paper. It was a printout of a page from the internet, advertising a shepherd's hut as an Airbnb. I scanned the details, it wasn't far from here, but the most interesting thing was the telephone number to call if you wanted to book. It was the same number that I'd received a phone call from this morning and the same one that Brodie had scribbled on the back of his receipt.

I needed to find this shepherd's hut. I put the page into an evidence bag and put it inside my shoulder bag so Grant would be none the wiser that I'd discovered anything. I continued my search through the clothing. In the bottom drawer I found a pair of jeans and inside that tiny pocket that you get on the front of your jeans I found a memory card, the type that's typically used in a digital camera.

Forty-five minutes later I was finished my search, I went back down the stairs. Grant sprang up from his seat as my foot touched on the bottom step.

'Is that you then?' He asked.

'Yes thanks.'

'Did you find what you were looking for?'

My mind was blank for a nano second before I remembered the sob story I'd given him to gain access. 'Unfortunately not, I'm assuming he had it on when he went missing.'

'What was it?'

'A Saint Christopher,' I said thinking on my feet. 'Patron saint of travellers, it was his grandfathers, his mum gave it to him to keep him safe on his travels.'

'Oh right, I remember him wearing something like that, I told him he needed to be careful that he didn't get it caught in any of the machinery. I suggested he take it off, but he said he never did.'

I couldn't believe I'd actually hit on a lie that hit home so well. 'I'm hoping that it will bring his mum a bit of comfort knowing that he has it with him then.'

'I'm sure it will, is that you away now?'

'Yes, that's me,' I said.

'Maybe give me a call first if you need to come back,' Grant said.

'I can't imagine I'll need to bother you again, but I'll

certainly let you know if I need to come again. Thanks for letting me look around, sorry for disrupting your evening.'

He walked me to the front door and watched as I walked back to my car, the door was still open as I began to drive away.

Chapter 22

Back at Ellie's cottage Alana and Ellie were in the living room discussing the merits of rural versus city life, I listened as Ellie spoke about how much joy she'd got from teaching at the nearby community centre. Alana looked up and gave me a little wave, I waved back and headed into the kitchen where Sonya was sitting at the table working.

Sonya and I sat at opposite ends of the table with our laptops out. I typed "s shepherd's hut" into the Airbnb search, but nothing came up. Then I did a wider search, "shepherd's hut holiday rental Scottish Highlands" this time a list of results appeared. On my seventh try I found the page that Brodie had hidden in his sock. It was on a website that advertised unusual or traditional properties for holiday rental in the UK and Europe, "Traditional Experiences" - booking was by telephone only.

I flicked through the pictures, it didn't look out of the ordinary, in fact I realised as I looked through the photos that I'd seen these images before. I went back to a previous search, a company named 'Highland Shepherds' I moved the pages so I could see them side by side. The exterior hut was different but there was no doubt the internal photographs were identical.

I needed to find the hut. The ones on Highland Shepherds website were mostly in the Fort William and Ben Nevis area, miles away from where I was. I looked though the other properties from Traditional Experiences' website. There were several in Germany, two in the Netherlands and one in France. Other than the shepherd's hut there was a place just outside Glasgow, it was an old-fashioned gypsy caravan, the contact number for it was the same as the shepherd's hut.

I looked back to the sheet of paper that Brodie had printed out. As I picked it up the large kitchen light caught behind it revealing a faint mark on the back of the page. I turned it over and squinted at the pencil marks, hoping this wasn't a sign I was starting to need glasses. I stared at the writing trying to work out what it meant before it hit me, these were OS Map co-ordinates.

I went through to the living room where the topic of conversation had changed to why so few women's clothes actually had pockets, a topic I had ranted about more times than I could remember, I smiled.

'Sorry to interrupt, you don't happen to have an OS Map of this area, do you?' I asked Ellie.

'I think there's some on the bookshelf in the upstairs hall, not sure if any of them are for here though.'

I thanked her and left them to it again. Upstairs after a couple of minutes rummaging through a large stack of maps I found one of the area and took it back downstairs to lay out on the kitchen table.

I spread it out and looked for the co-ordinates that

Brodie had written down and marked the place with a pencil 'X' it was hard to be certain but it looked like it was on the edge of Grant Fraser's land. It was too late now to go and look, it would need to wait until morning.

I took the memory card out of the evidence bag and turned it over in my hand before sliding it into the slot on my laptop. I waited impatiently as the photographs uploaded.

'I'm going to leave you to it and head to bed,' Sonya said as she began packing up her things. 'I should have the hair follicle drug test results back tomorrow for the Glasgow victims and Ben Weber by the end of the day.'

'That's good, although I'm pretty sure you'll find no trace of prior drug use in at least three of the Glasgow victims.'

'I'm just relieved that the senior pathologist at the time thought to take follicle samples, otherwise we'd never be able to check.' She paused, 'don't stay up too late, it's no good burning the candle at both ends.'

'I'll head up soon I just want to take a look at what's on this memory card first.'

Sonya left the kitchen, I heard her pop her head into the living room to say goodnight to Alana and Ellie before heading up the stairs.

With all the photos now available I began to click on them. There were several of the outside of the shepherd's hut, the windows had been boarded over from the inside, on the door there was a combination style lock. I clicked on the next image, it was taken from inside the hut, but it wasn't the cosy warm interior that had been displayed on the website, instead there were some wooden shelves, each holding plastic tubs, the sort that you would ordinarily see used for food storage, Maureen had several like this for bringing people homemade cakes and biscuits in.

Each shelf was photographed, there must've been at least a dozen boxes, they'd been split into four sections and each box in the section had something written on the top. They were numbered, the first three boxes had '1' scribbled on the top then a series of letters that could mean anything. I'd ask Sonya tomorrow if she knew what they might mean. The sections followed a numerical pattern of 1-4.

The kitchen door creaked as it was pushed open, I jumped.

'Sorry,' Alana said. 'We were just coming to tell you we are heading up to bed and see if you were going to come up as well.'

I considered staying in the kitchen to finish looking at the images, but instead decided to take my laptop upstairs and finish looking at them in bed. I didn't want to wake anybody up by staying down here into the early hours of the morning.

When we were both in bed I said, 'it won't disturb you if I keep working for a bit will it?'

'No, it's fine, have you found something useful?'

'I think so. I think Brodie found a stash of drugs.'

'Here?' Alana said shocked.

'It looks like it, I'll know more tomorrow when I walk out to the co-ordinates I found in Brodie's room.'

'But why here?'

'I've been wondering about that as well, but it does make sense. The drugs are either made here or they're made in mainland Europe and brought across on a fishing boat or something like that, stored here and then when 'tourists' pass through they pick up the drugs they've been tasked with selling and off they head. No one would bat an eyelid at people from all over the world coming here but only staying a day or two.'

'But that would mean that someone from round here was involved. Why would they get involved in drugs?'

'Money, that's usually the reason.'

'Can I come with you tomorrow?' Alana asked.

I wanted to say no, the motherly instinct always wanted to keep her at arm's length from every investigation I did, but she wasn't a little girl anymore. The company and a second pair of eyes would be nice. 'Sure, as long as you do what I tell you.'

'Thanks.' She lay down. 'I'm going to get some sleep.'

I went back to the images, Brodie had taken the time to open every container and inside each were dozens of little bags containing a small number of tablets. The following few images were blurry and looked like they might've been taken by accident. Then two pictures of the hut from a distance then six each showing a man I now knew to be Ben Weber entering the hut and then, according to the time stamp on the photos, leaving five minutes later.

The time and date on the next pictures were from later the same day, the 26th of December and it showed another man entering the hut and leaving a few minutes later. I zoomed in on the image and confirmed my suspicion that it was Karl Weber.

How must Brodie have felt to discover that two people he had considered friends, who'd been with him as Lauren lay dying, were quite possibly the ones responsible for spiking her drink and causing her death.

On the morning of the 27th of December Brodie had taken a string of photos documenting Grant Fraser arriving at the hut, opening the door and then seconds later coming out and then being on the phone to someone and he did not look happy. That was the same day that Brodie wrote down that phone number on his receipt and the last time he contacted his family.

Chapter 23

I had lain awake for ages last night wondering how I would've acted if I found myself in Brodie's shoes. He had last spoken to his family on Boxing Day, I guessed that later he'd begun to formulate a plan and either wanted to keep his family away from what he was doing or he needed a clear head and no distractions whilst he took action. Most likely it was a bit of both, I decided in the end.

After breakfast and wrapped up warm, Alana and I headed out to find the shepherd's hut. It was freezing and even with thick socks and leather walking boots my toes still felt cold.

'Who do you think it is then, that's involved from round here?' Alana asked.

'It looks like it's Grant Fraser.'

'Really, why do you say that?'

'He was in the photographs that I was looking at last night.'

'Are you going to tell Chris?'

'Not yet, if I tell her now and give her all the evidence, she'll need to arrest Grant and if he tells the police anything about the organisation that he's working for and they find out, they might just cut their losses and kill Brodie and Emil and leave.'

'You think they're alive then?'

'For now.'

'Why do you think Ben Weber was murdered?'

'It's hard to know for sure,' I said, 'my guess would be that he was considered the biggest liability.'

Our walk took us along a path adjacent to the Frasers' small holding. I was relieved that there was no sign of anyone out and about, although being with Alana would have allowed me to easily write off the sighting as us just taking a walk to clear away the cobwebs. It took us almost another hour before we saw the shepherd's hut. No one had searched this far in the hunt for Brodie, in part because it was so far from where his car had been abandoned, but mainly because he'd have had to walk past the farmhouse to get here.

I stopped as we got a bit closer to it, noticing that the door had been forced open, I signalled to Alana to wait whilst I double checked there was no one there. I tentatively moved towards the hut, pushing the door open a little further with my foot, it was empty. Alana joined me and we stepped inside, I wasn't sure what I'd expected to find, the plastic containers were strewn across the space, all of them empty. I took some photographs.

'What's that?' Alana asked pointing to a corner of the room.

I crouched down and shone my torch into the space. I pulled on a pair of gloves and took out a small evidence bag scooping up two blue-white tablets and a small pile of what I presumed were tablets that had started to dissolve into the wooden floor.

'I think this is what's left of the drugs stash that used to be here,' I said. 'Come on let's get out of this hut and take a look around.'

I pushed the door back to the semi-closed position we'd found it in and started to look around the area outside the hut. The ground was hard and frosty, there was no way of knowing if the footprints in the mud had been made recently.

'I think I've found something,' Alana called from behind the shed.

I walked quickly round to join her, she was looking down at a dead fox, I frowned.

'I wondered if maybe it had managed to ingest some of the drugs, it looks like it just dropped dead and that's pretty weird. Have you got a spare pair of gloves?'

I reached into my bag and handed her a pair, she slipped them on before kneeling down next to the animal, she turned its solid body over and ran her hand through its fur. 'No sign of any wound or gun shot, probably died about a few days ago, given how it looks, it's cold out here though and with no shelter and being so small it's not easy to narrow it down. You should probably tell Sonya at least. This fox is going to become another animal's dinner and I don't know if the drugs in its system would kill that as well.'

She was probably right, Sonya would have no choice but to tell Chris, I wondered if the hut stood on Grant's land and if there was anything that would associate him with it. I took some photos of the dead animal and agreed that we would tell her when we got back.

When we arrived back at the cottage Chris was sitting in the kitchen drinking coffee and talking to Ellie and Sonya.

'I wasn't expecting to see you today,' I said as we joined them, glad to be back in the warmth. 'Are you here to see Sonya?'

'No, you actually. I've had a complaint,' Chris said.

'A complaint?'

'From Grant Fraser, he said you turned up at his house last night at an inappropriate time and demanded to be let into Brodie's room, he said you practically forced your way past him into the house and only agreed to leave when he threatened to call the police. I said I'd come and have a chat with you, I think I've talked him out of pressing any charges.'

'That's not what happened,' I said.

'Why don't you tell me what did happen then,' Chris said.

'I did go over yesterday evening, but it wasn't that late and I asked if I could see Brodie's room, his mum had asked me to see if his Saint Christopher was in with his stuff and I said I would look.' I hated lying to Chris and would much rather have told her the truth, but for now the lie was necessary. 'I explained that to Mr Fraser and he said I could look around, I thanked him and I was in Brodie's room for about half an hour, I didn't find the necklace and I left, he asked me to call first if I needed to visit and I said I would. I did not barge into his home, nor was I forcibly removed from it.'

Grant Fraser was trying to discredit me, make the police look at me as a suspect or at the very least as someone who shouldn't be trusted. On one hand I was annoyed but on the other this meant that he was concerned that I had discovered something.

'Why would he make up a story like that?' Chris asked.

I shrugged, 'why would I push my way into someone's home, I've been doing this job long enough to know that's not the way to go about things. What would I have to gain from that behaviour?'

Alana and Sonya had been quietly chatting on the other side of the kitchen and I could see Sonya glancing in our direction. Then Sonya's phone rang and she went to stand in the hall to take the call.

'It's weird though, why would Grant Fraser want to make us think you did that, it feels like deflection,' Chris said.

Sonya came back in, 'sorry to interrupt but one of the forensic techs just called to tell me that a walker stumbled across a shepherd's hut that looked like it had been broken into, they went to check it out and think it might've been used as a storage location for Blue42.' Sonya shot me a sly smile.

'Right, we'd better get over there and check it out,' Chris said to Sonya and then turning to me, 'perhaps it would be a good idea to stay away from Grant Fraser for the time being.'

'Noted,' I replied.

Sonya and Chris were gone for a couple of hours and when they returned, they brought a strong smell of wood smoke in with them.

'You two been walking through a bonfire?' Ellie asked.

'Something like that, by the time we got to the shepherd's hut it was on fire,' Sonya said.

'How did it start?' I asked.

'Petrol would be my guess,' Sonya said.

'I'm guessing that whoever it belonged to realised that they'd been discovered and were trying to cover their tracks,' Chris said.

'Hmm, suspicious,' I replied.

'About as suspicious as the fact that when we got there neither the forensic tech or the walker were anywhere to be found,' Chris looked at me.

'That is odd.'

'Anyway, it wasn't all lost, I found a dead fox near the fire that I think might've ingested the drugs, I've sent it up to the mortuary, so I'll be heading up this afternoon to take some samples to send away for testing,' Sonya said.

'That was lucky,' I said.

'Right well I'm going to see if I can figure out who this hut belonged to and find out why they might've wanted to torch it,' Chris said. Then before she left she turned to me, 'I have a strong feeling that you know more than you're telling me, I'm not entirely sure why you're holding out on me, but I'm trusting that you have your reasons. I'll be finished for the day, all being well, around six tonight, then I thought we should sit down and have a catch up, off the record if needs be.'

'Sounds good to me.'

'Also you should know that DCI Burke will be announcing Ben Weber's identity to the press today, I did hope he would hold off more than 24 hours, but he's in charge of the investigation now so it's his call.'

'Let's hope that doesn't put Brodie in any danger then,' I replied.

Back inside Sonya said, 'do you two want to tell me what's going on?'

'Don't look at her, she was just chumming me along,' I said talking about Alana. 'When I was in Brodie's room last night, I found a page he'd printed off from the internet about a shepherd's hut for rent – but then there were also photographs of it being used by Ben and Karl Weber as well as Grant Fraser and pictures of containers of drugs inside. Brodie must've discovered that it was where the drugs were being stored. We went to check it out this morning, it was Alana that thought the dead fox might be useful though.'

'And did anyone see you there?'

'I didn't think so,' I looked at Alana.

'Me either,' she said.

'Could it be coincidence that someone set it alight only a couple of hours after you'd been there?' Sonya asked.

'I hate coincidence but if Grant Fraser is involved then maybe it was because I rattled him last night by going back to Brodie's room. Perhaps he decided he'd report me to the police and then burn the evidence so there was nothing connecting him to the drugs or Brodie's disappearance.'

'Show me the photos, the ones you got from Brodie's room,' Sonya said.

I opened my laptop and waited while she scrolled through. 'Any idea what the markings on the top of the containers mean?' I asked.

'Probably a code for what they've added in to bulk it up, looks like they're still trying to come up with the right mix, or it could be a code for which dealers take what and where they sell it,' Sonya replied. 'That's a terrifying amount of Blue42 though, I should really pass this on to the police liaison I'm working with on this,' she looked up at me, 'if there's that quantity in the UK then it needs to be more widely known as this amount will lead to some serious issues and likely more deaths as well.'

'I understand.' Ideally, I would have preferred to be able to keep this discovery quiet, but it was already over a week since Brodie had discovered it and god knows where it might've travelled to by now. I'd no intention of being the cause of more deaths. 'Can you give me till tomorrow?' I asked.

'I have to make a report today that says I believe a large quantity of Blue42 was being held here, I can't take the risk of not reporting it, but I'll give you one more day before I do the full report with those photos you just showed me,' Sonya replied.

Chapter 24

I was sitting in the kitchen staring at the photograph Brodie had taken of Grant Fraser standing outside the shepherd's hut looking pissed off, I'd tried zooming in but there was no way of being able to see inside the hut. A thought had struck me when I'd originally looked at the pictures, because if I were Brodie and I discovered a stash of drugs like this, knowing that they were probably part of the same chain that had been used to kill my girlfriend I might just be inclined to steal the drugs. And, if that's what Brodie had done, then right now he was worth keeping alive, at least for as long as he didn't give up their location.

Alana cleared her throat, I looked up. 'You deep in thought there mum, are you alright?'

'Yeah sorry, I didn't notice you come in.'

'I gathered, are you going to share what's got you not paying attention to who's coming and going, I could've been anyone.'

'I'd have noticed if it was someone that wasn't meant to

be here,' I smiled. 'I was just thinking that if I were Brodie, I would've taken those drugs and hidden them somewhere.'

'That would be a pretty reckless thing to do, and you wonder why I'm always worrying about you.'

She was right, of course, it was reckless, drug dealers were not renowned for being reasonable. 'I know, I just meant if I was in his shoes, he probably feels like he's nothing to lose.'

'I wonder where he hid them. Do you think that's what he was talking about when I overheard him on the phone on Hogmanay?'

'It's possible, especially if he just took the drugs without thinking a plan of action through, I'd not be surprised if he was speaking to Ben or Karl, I can imagine they were keen to get the drugs back before they had to admit that they were gone.'

'What about Grant, where does he fit into all of this?'

'I don't know, we know from the photographs that he knew about the shepherd's hut, so it would make sense that he was involved in the whole process.'

'Are you going to tell Chris everything?' Alana asked.

I thought about it for a few moments, if I were back home and working with George would I have told him straight away? These days the answer was yes, we had enough trust and understanding between us that we would've worked out the best way forward together, with him periodically reminding me that this was a police investigation, of course. Still, I liked and respected Chris, and if it was only her, I doubted I'd have as much hesitation, but DCI Burke gave me less confidence.

'I haven't decided yet.'

The kitchen door opened, and Ellie walked through, 'you two look serious, is everything okay?' She asked.

'Just talking about Brodie,' I replied.

'It's awful that he's not turned up yet, his family must be out of their minds with worry. When I went down to the shop this morning everyone was talking about it, especially with the police finding that other lad dead.'

'What are people saying?'

'That Brodie must be dead too,' Ellie replied.

'Was Brodie friendly with anyone in the village or surrounding area?' I asked.

'Hmm, I know he went over to Mr McLeod's house a few times to help him out with repairs, he's in his 80s now so can't really do the big jobs himself anymore.'

'I don't think I've met him.'

'No, he tends to keep himself to himself, doesn't like coming out to the hotel, pops into the village sometimes, I'd been here months before I met him.'

'Do you know how he and Brodie met?'

'No idea, but he's Lauren Davidson's grandfather so maybe Brodie decided to find a way to meet him?'

'Do you know where he lives?' I asked.

'Not far from here, he's got a croft, not that he has any animals any more,' Ellie said.

'Can you give me directions?'

'I think so, are you going to visit him?'

'I've nothing else to work on and it's worth following up I think, do you want to come?' I asked Ellie, not because I really wanted her to, more because I was feeling guilty that I was living in her house and then leaving her out of everything.

'No, I was intending to get some planning done for the classes I'm doing with the local high school next term, I'm trying to decide if doing a musical is a bit beyond their collective talents or whether I should go for something traditional like Shakespeare, but that can sometimes turn the kids off drama.'

'I'm sure you'll find the perfect compromise,' I said to Ellie, then turned to Alana, 'what about you, would you like to come?'

'Why not.'

I was glad Alana had agreed to come with me, not because I didn't want to do it alone, but because I'd noticed how older people responded to Alana, they warmed to her almost immediately and that had been a useful secret weapon to get people talking in the past, I was hoping it would work just as well this afternoon.

I got lost once on the way to Mr McLeod's croft, taking a wrong turning which ended up in a twenty minute detour whilst I found somewhere I could turn around. Eventually though, I drove up the road to his house, it was little more than a dirt track, and his was the only house on it. The white paint on the outside of the croft looked like it had been refreshed relatively recently, I wondered if that was Brodie's handiwork. I knocked on the door and we waited. After a few moments I began to think he was out, or had simply looked out a window, seen a stranger's car and thought he didn't want to speak to us so had decided to ignore my knock, but after a couple of minutes waiting we heard noise from the other side of the door and finally it was opened.

Mr McLeod was a tall man, over six foot I would guess, which meant that he likely had to bend down to get through the doorway into his own home. He lent on a wooden walking stick which had the head of an eagle as a handle. He looked at us for a few moments.

'Hi Mr McLeod, sorry to drop in unannounced like this, my name is…'

'I know who you are, you'd better come in.'

We went through the wooden doorway and followed him into the living area, a coal fire burned in the hearth making the room feel toasty warm. We took off our coats and sat down on two of the four armchairs.

'How do you know who I am?' I asked.

'It's a small village, word gets about.'

'Do you know why I've come to visit?'

'Well now, you're a private detective and I understand you're happily pissing off that moron Burke by investigating Brodie's disappearance and you've likely heard that he helped me with a few jobs, so now you've finally caught up with me, you've probably got some questions. But first, if you don't mind, I think we should have some tea and some clootie dumpling.'

'Isn't that a pudding?' I asked.

'I'm old, I eat what I like when I like.'

'Instead of tea do you have…'

I opened my mouth to speak and he put his hand up to silence me. 'Please don't ask for coffee I don't have it, don't like it and I don't entertain enough to make it worth my while keeping it in. Now you wait here I'll be back directly.'

Alana smiled at me and as Mr McLeod left the room, she leaned across to me and whispered, 'I think you've finally met your match.'

We waited quietly whilst he was out of the room. There was an old rug in front of the hearth, I imagined it had once been vibrant reds and blues, but it was faded and threadbare now. Besides the four chairs the only other pieces of furniture were a small coffee table and a large, ornately carved mahogany sideboard. On the top, sitting on stands, were a couple of decorative plates with pictures of birds on them, and a few family photographs. I stood up to take a closer look, there was one of the old man, looking about twenty years younger, sat on the wall outside the croft with a woman of a similar age; one I recognised of Mr and Mrs Davidson, on their wedding day, Mrs Davidson in a big meringue of a dress, they looked happy. Then there were several of a girl with long dark hair at various ages including on her graduation day. I heard the rattle of china and sat back down, not wanting him to catch me snooping.

The tea was in a large brown pot and the mugs looked like they'd been purchased in the 70s, beige with a speckle of brown spots and images of garden vegetables on the sides. There was milk in a jug and a small bowl of sugar. He put the tray down on the table and went back out of the room without saying a word, a few seconds later he returned with a second tray carrying three plates of clootie dumpling and some forks.

The clootie dumpling smelled amazing, it was one of Alana's firm favourites and we'd made a point of having it at least once a year on Burn's night. The fruit and spices of the steamed pudding quickly filled the room.

'It's warm,' he said. 'I only made it a wee while before you arrived.'

We both thanked him and took a couple of mouthfuls before I asked him any questions. 'It's delicious, thank you.'

'You're welcome, I don't often have visitors to share it with, so it's nice to see you.' He looked at Alana, 'now I know your mother's name, but I don't think you're the subject of as much gossip so perhaps you could help me out.'

'I'm Alana,' she smiled at him.

'Very good, are you at university Alana?'

I waited whilst Alana told Mr McLeod, who insisted

half way through that we call him Archie, all about her course, answering all of his questions.

'That's a very smart girl you've raised there, you must be proud,' Archie said to me.

'I am, very.'

'As much as I'm sure you're enjoying eating my dumpling and drinking my tea I'd hazard a guess this isn't a social call.'

'You're right, I wanted to ask you about Brodie, I heard he came up here and helped you with a few bits of maintenance.'

'Aye that's right, such a nice young man, nothing was too much trouble for him.'

'How did you two meet?' I asked.

'I think the question you really want to ask is did I know that he was Lauren's young man, and the answer is yes. He told me, but of course I recognised him from the photographs Lauren had sent me on my smart phone.'

I tried to hide my shock that he was so up to date with technology.

'Lauren got me it, she said it would help us keep in touch. I don't use it so much anymore, but I keep it because it has all her photos and voice messages on it.'

'Did you tell him you knew who he was?'

'No, but he told me when he was painting the house, I told him I knew, and I think it was a great relief to him to be able to talk about Lauren with someone else who knew and loved her.'

'What sort of things did he talk about?' I asked.

'How much he loved her, all the plans they'd made together, they were planning on travelling, maybe even moving to Canada, getting married, having a family of their own. When Maggie, my wife, died I found it hard to get out of bed in the mornings, Lauren wasn't much age then, but she would call in on me several times a week and we would sit and read together, or play chess. I told him I understood how much it hurt, but that he was young, and Lauren wouldn't have wanted him to spend the rest of his life alone.'

'What did he think about that advice?'

'He wasn't ready to hear it, he needs to get past this idea that he let her down, that in some way he was responsible for her death, or that he could've prevented it.'

'Do you know why he hadn't been to see Lauren's parents yet?' I asked.

'He was afraid they'd be angry at him, I was planning on doing the introductions myself, they were strict with Lauren, not out of a desire to control her or curtail her life, but because they loved her and they nearly lost her, they were afraid that any little thing she did might cause her harm, they wanted to keep her close and they mollycoddled her. Of course, that had the opposite effect, she felt suffocated, couldn't wait to get away to uni and then when she was away I knew she'd never leave the big city and come back here to be under their watchful eye.'

I glanced at Alana and thought about how hard it had been to let her have her freedom after all that had happened, at one time I thought I was going to lose her, I understood that desire, an almost physical need to keep her close so that I could be sure that nothing bad happened to her ever again. I'd realised that was irrational and unfair, but it hadn't been easy.

'Her mother, my daughter Beth, didn't want to have any more children after Lauren, didn't want to go through that again, she wanted to focus all her energy into Lauren and now Lauren is gone.'

'Is that why she only told you about Brodie but not them, do you think?'

He nodded his head slowly. 'I think so.'

'What do you know about Brodie's friends Karl and Ben Weber?' I asked hoping that the change of direction wouldn't make Archie clam up.

'Friends?' He raised his eyebrows and looked at me.

'What would you call them?'

'I'd say that sometimes it's a case of keeping your friends close and your enemies closer.'

'What do you think about Ben's body being found not far from where Brodie went missing?' The information hadn't been officially released yet, but I couldn't imagine that Archie had any part in what had happened to Ben Weber, or that he was likely to use our conversation as the basis of any village gossip.

'I don't think Brodie had any hand in that if that's what you're suggesting.'

'I'm just asking your thoughts,' I smiled.

'I think karma might've caught up with him.'

'Why do you say that?'

We looked at each other, both considering how much the other might already know and wondering how much to give away. It was a standoff.

'Sometimes bad people meet bad ends,' Archie said eventually.

'And you think Ben Weber was a bad person?' I asked.

'You don't?'

'I think he was a drug dealer.'

'And drug dealers are as a whole bad people, in my experience.'

'What's your experience?' I asked.

'I was in the police all my career, it's not a new thing

drugs passing through villages like this one, especially if you're near the coast. Drug addicts, now them I sympathise with, that's an illness and they need help. But the filth that bring that stuff into this country and sell it to people knowing full well the crap it's full of, they don't deserve my sympathy, they deserve what they get.'

'What did Brodie tell you about the drugs?'

'The ones that killed Lauren?' he looked up at me. 'He told me everything.'

Chapter 25

I leaned forward in my chair, 'what does "everything" mean?'

'He told me about how Emil introduced him to two brothers he'd met travelling, he said they were alright, Ben got on his nerves though, and he thought even then he might've been involved in something illegal, too flashy is how he described him.'

'When did he find out that he was involved in drugs?'

'You're getting ahead of yourself, if you want to know what everything means, you're going to have to relax and let me tell it.' Archie said.

'Sorry, please continue.'

'When Brodie decided to go to Glasgow to spend more time with Lauren, he thought he might see Emil a few more times but he thought it would be the last he'd need to put up with the other two, but they all followed him through to Glasgow. Originally Brodie and the others were staying in a hostel and then Lauren asked him to stay with her, I think it was in the hopes that they could spend some more time together.'

Archie took a sip of his tea and pulled a face, 'cold, you sit tight and I'll make some more.' He collected the mugs on to the tray and carried them out of the room.

I would've happily told him I couldn't give two hoots about tea, but he'd made it clear that he would tell this story in his own way and if I wanted to hear it then I would need to be patient.

After the second round of tea was brewed and poured Archie lifted the mug to his lips and took a sip, 'much better, now where was I?'

'Lauren invited Brodie to stay with her,' Alana said.

'And that seemed to do the trick for a while, but it ended up that the Weber brothers had made friends with some of Lauren's friends and that's how they all ended up going out together that night. Brodie told me that he had to tell Ben multiple times to leave Lauren alone because he was making her feel uncomfortable.'

'Do you think that's why he drugged her?' I asked.

'What did I say about being patient,' he scolded me in a friendly tone.

'It's possible, but that answer may also lie closer to home.'

'In what way?' I wanted to ask him if he knew what involvement Grant Fraser had in it all.

'My granddaughter was a bonnie lass and she turned heads, even heads that shouldn't have been turned. I wonder have you chatted to Anna Greenhouse?'

I shook my head.

'She's a nice girl, her and Lauren were best friends, Anna stayed here in the village and works for her dad. I think you'd find a conversation with her particularly illuminating,' Archie said.

I smiled, there were clearly things he didn't want to tell me, but he was pointing me in the right direction, all I had to do was follow the clues.

'I'll find time to have a chat with her. Can I ask did Brodie come and visit you on the 27th of December?'

'Might've done, I don't always remember the dates of things, one of the joys of getting old.'

I felt like Archie was more than capable of remembering dates, he was as sharp as a tack.

'Why do you ask?' Archie continued.

'I was wondering if he asked you to look after anything for him.'

'Why would he do that?'

'Perhaps he wanted to keep something safe?'

'Not sure this would be where I would try and hide something, if you were looking for a hiding place there would be ample opportunities elsewhere that are much better choices than my wee croft.'

'Like where?' I was hoping for him to drop me another breadcrumb.

'Do you read the newspapers?' Archie asked.

'I do, mostly online though, why?'

'A few years back when I was still working, they were installing new lockers at the train station in the Kyle and inside one of them was over £100,000 in cash. I suppose that whoever left it thought that it was a good hiding place, but the reason those lockers were getting replaced was because they kept getting broken into. Of course, you see it on the telly don't you, people using these sorts of things for years, but it's not realistic.'

'I've heard of people using lockers in airports as well,' I said, 'but you don't think they're good hiding places?'

'They're alright, but the smart place to put something so that it's kept safe, that's lost and found. That stuff gets locked up and you can't get it back without actually speaking to someone.'

'Not so useful if you were trying to hide £100,000 though, might be a bit trickier to prove it's yours.'

'Did I tell you my nephew's son Adam, works in lost and found.' His eyes twinkled as he spoke.

'No, you hadn't mentioned it,'

'Lovely lad, he's working tomorrow, you should pop through and see him, you could go to see Anna in the morning, her father's office is in the Kyle, then after pop in and say hello to Adam, you tell him I sent you and tell him, all is well when you have goodness in your heart.'

'Thank you Archie.'

'You're welcome, now time for me to take a nap and you to head of back to your friend's cottage.'

'It was lovely meeting you,' Alana said.

'You too, keep up the good work with your studies,' Archie replied.

'He was nice,' Alana said as we drove back to Ellie's. 'Why do you think that he wants you to talk to Anna?'

'I don't know, but I trust him, he cares about Brodie.'

'Then why not just tell us what he knows rather than sending us on all these quests?'

'Maybe he thinks that whatever the information is would be better coming from Anna,' I replied.

'What are you going to tell Chris?'

'Bugger, I completely forgot she was coming over, I need more time.'

We pulled into the driveway outside the cottage, Ellie was making dinner when we went inside.

'Hope you're hungry, I've made sweet and sour,' she said.

'It smells amazing,' Alana replied.

'Sonya said she'd be back by five, so I told her I'd have dinner ready for us all by then.'

'Good that means I'll have time to eat before Chris arrives.'

Dinner was delicious, Sonya had spent the morning doing a post mortem on a dead fox and the afternoon going through test results and she and Alana had been excitingly discussing the process as we ate.

'You were right,' Sonya said to me, 'Lauren, Jackie and Emily's hair showed no signs of drug use.'

'And what about the fox?' Alana asked.

'Toxicology report came back and there was a huge amount of Blue42 in its system, I would be surprised if it didn't die within minutes of ingesting it. I think it's fair to say that there were some tablets discarded on the hut floor and the fox licked at them. From the results I would estimate that it ingested around 4 tablets.'

'Have the forensics team been able to salvage anything useful from what remains of the hut?' I asked.

'Not a thing. Whoever set fire to it used petrol as an accelerant, and it wouldn't take long to burn something that small.'

'How much petrol do you think was used?' I asked.

'It wouldn't have needed much, one petrol can I suspect, it's all wood after all.'

Chris arrived as I was helping Ellie with the dishes.

'I'll take over for you,' Alana said taking the tea towel from me.

I took Chris through to the living room and we both sat down.

'You care to fill me in?' She said, 'because I know that Sonya made that story up this morning.'

I looked at her, she looked tired and no wonder, she'd been working all hours since she took on this case. I liked her and I wanted to help her, this would be the moment I discovered if I could also trust her.

'You're right, I do know more than I've told you, but if I tell you, you have to promise not to go to DCI Burke yet, I need you to at least give me to the end of tomorrow.'

She rubbed the palm of her right hand across her face, 'I don't know if I can do that.'

'Then I can't tell you.'

'This isn't a bloody game, Rowan.'

'I know that, I'm not playing one, I'm doing my job and I want to do everything I can to find Brodie alive.'

'And you still think that might happen?'

'I do, I need you to trust me. I promise you that as soon as I have more information I will bring it to you.'

'Alright, okay, we'll do it your way.'

'Thank you.'

'Start talking then,' Chris said as she sat back in the chair.

'When I was searching Brodie's room I found a couple of things that I thought might be interesting, the first was weird and it seemed important more because of where it was stored than what it was.'

She listened as I told her about the items I'd found in Brodie's room, then I showed her the photographs from the memory card. The website that had advertised the shepherd's Hut for rent had been taken down, but I had taken dozens of screenshots.

'Bloody hell,' she sighed as I finished.

'I know, it's a lot.'

'Why didn't Brodie just report the drugs to the police?'

'I think he was probably concerned that they would be gone before they got there, or maybe he was driven by impulsive emotion.'

'If Burke found out that we withheld this information…'

'How would he find out?'

'How much does Ellie know, is she likely to share anything she's heard?' Chris said.

'She doesn't know anything, and even if she did, she knows how important confidentiality is in my investigations.'

'What's your plan of action now?'

'Archie McLeod gave me a couple of cryptic clues, I'm going to be chasing those up tomorrow, I'll call you when I get back.'

'Do you think Grant Fraser is involved?'

'It looks that way to me.'

'The shepherd's hut was right on the border between his small holding and the main farm that belongs to his brother. They both deny knowing anything about it, Grant says he thought it was Henry's and Henry said that he assumed it was Grant's and he was taking a bit of a liberty with the land.'

'That's a bit odd isn't it, I've not met Henry Fraser, what's he like?'

'A farmer,' Chris laughed. 'I know they're not all the same, he doesn't come down into the village much, he was in the hotel on Hogmanay though, so you'd probably recognise him if you saw him.'

'Do the brothers get on?'

'Passably, they don't appear to be the type of family that

have each other around for Sunday lunch every week, but they don't seem to be at odds with each other either.'

'It has to belong to one of them though, I don't believe that some random person put a shepherd's hut on the Frasers' land and just hoped that neither brother would notice.'

'Unless it was someone who knew them and the land boundaries well enough to know that if they placed it right in that spot each brother would be likely to think it belonged to the other.'

'I suppose it's possible, it feels too convoluted though, and there's too much risk involved.'

'I've put a uniformed officer watching both brothers for now.'

'Has no one ever had any suspicions about them before now?'

'Nope, no criminal records at all, Grant Fraser got a speeding ticket a couple of years ago, but that's not unusual around here though. I'd better be getting back to the hotel, I don't want anyone wondering where I am.'

'Couldn't you say you popped home to see your family?'

'That would probably piss off Burke even more than if I told him the truth, he's big on the idea that you should only focus on the case and nothing else matters.'

I walked Chris to the door and watched her drive away, closing the door I looked at my watch, it was only 8pm, but I felt exhausted. I stood at the bottom of the stairs, trying to decide if it was still too early to go to bed.

The kitchen door opened. 'What are you doing mum?'

'Thinking,' I smiled.

'Ellie's making hot chocolate, do you want some?'

I paused.

'She's got marshmallows and whipped cream,' Alana continued.

'Go on then, you've twisted my arm.

Chapter 26

The next morning I left to go and speak to Anna Greenhouse, Alana stayed behind with Ellie, they had plans to visit Plockton, there was a craft market being held there. It had been a cold night and there were nasty patches of ice on the road and I was thankful that there were only a half dozen other cars on the road.

Anna worked at her father's accountancy firm, I'd called yesterday afternoon to make sure she'd be available to see me.

'You must be Rowan,' she said as I walked up to the reception desk.

Anna was short, maybe 5'2" and heavily pregnant, 'yes, thanks for seeing me at such short notice.'

'No problem, I've been moving my clients over to the other accountants for the last couple of months, I'm basically down to reception duties now, we can talk in one of the meeting rooms,' she paused. 'Do you want a coffee?'

'It's okay, don't put yourself out for me,' I replied, despite the fact I would've loved a coffee.

'It's no bother, Greg, my husband, owns the coffee shop down the street, I'll text him to bring a couple along, although I only get decaf these days.'

Greg arrived with impressive efficiency, gave us our coffees and me a slightly suspicious look before kissing his wife on the forehead. 'You feeling okay,' he said, one hand on her bump.

'I'm fine.'

'Okay, but go home if you're not – let me know and I can get Bobbie to cover so I can drive you.'

'I'm fine, go away I'm busy,' she laughed and then turned to me, 'he's very over protective at the moment.'

'I'm not surprised, you can't have long to go.'

'Four weeks,' they said in unison.

'Don't worry Greg, I won't keep her long.'

'Okay, well I'd better leave you to get on.' Greg left closing the door behind him.

'I was surprised you wanted to speak to me,' Anna said.

'You were Lauren Davidson's best friend I believe?

'Since nursery,' she looked sad.

'And you kept in touch after she went to Glasgow?'

'Yeah, we spoke all the time, it's easy these days.'

'Were you not tempted to go to university?' I asked.

'No, I met Greg when we were both sixteen, he always wanted to run his own business, his dad and him got the coffee shop when he was seventeen and now he runs it by himself. And honestly, I was happy here, I have a wee craft business selling stuff online and at craft fairs and I knew dad would give me a job. I know that sounds terrible, but I work here part time and I did my qualifications whilst I worked. Greg and I have a nice life, absolutely no regrets.'

'Did Lauren always want to leave?'

'Not always, but by the time we were in our mid-teens

she knew she wanted something different, her parents are lovely, but they were always in her business, she wanted her own space.'

'Archie suggested that you might be able to help me understand *all* the reasons Lauren wanted to leave.' I hadn't been sure what to ask, Archie had been keen for me to talk to Anna, but at the moment I was getting another version of the story that everyone had told of Lauren.

She took a sip of her coffee, 'A village is a small place, same faces all the time, it's not like growing up in a big town or city, sometimes relationships happen that definitely shouldn't.'

'Did Lauren have that sort of relationship?'

Anna scratched her head, 'I wouldn't even call it a relationship, she had a thing with a married man, it only lasted a couple of weeks, one of the few times her parents were away and she was on her own.'

'Who was the man?'

'I don't think I should say, Lauren's gone and it's not like he had anything to do with her death, that was just a terrible accident.'

'Was it Grant Fraser?'

Anna's coffee cup was halfway between the table and her mouth, she held it there, frozen for a moment, 'what makes you say that?'

'I'm right, aren't I?'

'Yes.'

'Why don't you tell me what happened.'

'We'd both worked up on his small holding and on Henry's farm in the summertime, a little bit extra pocket money and Grant could be a bit...handsy, always patting you on the bum, coming up behind you and putting his hands on your shoulders and rubbing them. It always made me feel super uncomfortable, but I think Lauren was flattered by the attention.'

'How old was she?'

'Seventeen, it was the summer before she went to Glasgow. Because her parents were away he offered to drive her home, normally my dad would do it, but I was going out with Greg that night so she said yes. I don't know the intimate details, all I know is the next day she tells me she's not a virgin anymore and then I hardly see her for the next two weeks.'

'How did it end?'

'Lauren was getting fed up, a boy in the village, Douglas, asked her on a date and she said yes, Grant went mental and she told him what they had was a bit of fun and anyways he was married.'

'How did he take that?'

'Badly, he slapped her across the face. I had to make up a story that she wasn't very well to get my mum to come and take us home early. After that he would message her dozens of times a day, she blocked his number but he got a new phone. She was relieved when the end of summer came so she could get away from him. She said that for the first couple of months he messaged her non-stop, telling her he loved her and that he would leave his wife and they could be together and then it just stopped. She never knew why and frankly she didn't care, we both assumed he'd moved on to some other poor sod.'

'Did he ever give her any trouble when she went home for the holidays?' I asked.

'He was hostile towards her, but nothing outright, snide remarks that sort of thing, but they got less the longer she was away.'

'Did you know Lauren was in a relationship with Brodie before she died?'

'Yeah I did, I met him, well Greg and I both met him, we went down to Glasgow for the weekend a couple of weeks before she died, he was nice. I thought he was good for her.'

'Did he know about her history with Grant do you think?'

'I certainly didn't tell him and I'm not sure whether she would've or not, we never ever spoke about him. I did think it was a weird coincidence when I bumped into Brodie when I was visiting Archie and he told me he was working on Grant's small holding.'

'What do you think Brodie would've done if he'd known?'

'Leave probably, he never struck me as the sort who liked conflict, but I don't know him well enough to know for sure.'

'Did Lauren tell her granddad about Grant?'

'Yeah, she was really close with him, that's one of the reasons I still visit him all the time, when Lauren left for Uni she made me promise to keep an eye on him and I did and then when she died I made a silent promise that I would continue to do that for as long as he lived,' Her eyes became watery as she spoke, and then a large tear trickled down her cheek.

'I'm sorry, I didn't mean to upset you.'

She reached into her pocket and pulled out a paper tissue and dried her eyes, 'it's okay, it's the hormones, my emotions are all over the place right now.'

'Do you think Archie would have confronted Grant about leaving Lauren alone?'

Anna thought for a couple of moments, 'Maybe, he was

very protective of her and he wasn't the type to be shy about it, that plus he was in the police for long enough, he wouldn't have thought anything about dealing with a sleezy creep like Grant.'

'Thanks for seeing me this morning, I really appreciate it,' I handed her my business card. 'Give me a call or send me a message if anything else pops into your head.'

'Sure, but why do you want to know about this stuff, I thought you said you were trying to find Brodie, do you think Grant Fraser has something to do with his disappearance?'

'I'm exploring all avenues, I've no idea what's happened to him, so I want to make sure I don't miss any lines of investigation.'

She seemed to accept my explanation, but as I left I saw her picking up her phone, I wondered if she was calling Archie to ask why he sent me to her or her husband to tell him about our conversation. Either way it couldn't be long before the locals started asking questions about Grant Fraser's involvement in all of this.

Chapter 27

The train station was much smaller than I expected so it didn't take me long to locate the Lost and Found office. I pressed the buzzer outside the door and took a step back looking up at the building.

A voice spoke through the intercom, 'Hi how can I help you?' The man said.

'Can I speak to Adam please,' I replied hoping that there was only one.

A few moments later the door opened and a man in uniform and an orange viz vest stood in the doorway. He was probably in his mid-thirties, mousey brown hair, he looked tired.

'Adam?' I asked.

'Yes,' he frowned.

'Is there somewhere we can talk?'

He ushered me inside, where there was a small metal desk and two chairs in the corner of the room.

'How can I help, have we spoken before?'

'No, actually it was Archie McLeod that suggested that I

come and speak to you. My name's Rowan McFarlane and I'm a private detective and I've been hired by the Cullen family to look for their son Brodie – you'll have probably heard about him going missing.'

'I have, what's this got to do with Archie and me?' He sat back in the chair and folded his arms.

'Archie thought you might be able to help me.'

He shook his head slowly, 'I don't see how I could be of help.'

'That's a shame, one other thing, all is well when you have goodness in your heart.' I'd made sure to memorise the phrase exactly and didn't want to have to refer to my notes when I was talking to Adam.

Adam smiled, 'why didn't you say that in the beginning, hold on a second.' He stood up and went to a locked metal door, unlocked it and disappeared inside. A few minutes later her re-emerged carrying a large dark blue holdall. 'I think this is what you're after,' he dropped it on the ground next to me.

'Have you looked inside?'

'No, Archie asked me to store it for him on a no questions asked basis, so I did.'

'Weren't you worried about what might be inside?'

'No, Archie told me he was doing it to help Brodie out so I agreed.'

'You knew Brodie?'

'Not well, but I kept in good contact with Lauren, and she introduced him to me, they were happy. I liked him, thought they seemed like a good couple.'

'Have you seen much of Brodie since he came back to Scotland?'

'We went out a couple of times for coffee and a catch up.'

'Did he tell you why he'd chosen to come here?' I asked.

'He wanted to meet Lauren's family.'

'Was that the only reason?'

'What else could it have been?' Adam asked.

'What did you think when Lauren died from a drugs overdose?' I said changing my tack a little.

'I thought her drink was spiked.'

'Did you think it was an accident?'

'I *did*,' he looked away from me, his eyes landing on the holdall.

'Did something happen to make you think it wasn't an accident?'

'When Brodie went back to Canada we kept in touch, he was insistent that there was something more going on the night Lauren died. At first, I thought it was grief talking and over time he mentioned it less and less. I was made up when he told me he was going traveling with his mate Emil through Europe. I hoped that it would allow him to move on, I admired how much he loved Lauren and that he maybe wasn't ready for another partner, but I didn't want to see him letting life pass him by.'

'He wasn't originally planning to come to Scotland though, was he?'

'I don't know, he did tell me I suspect, but I didn't write it down or anything.'

'What did you think when he told you he was going to be working for Grant Fraser and living at his house?'

'I was surprised, I assumed it was the only work he could get in the area.'

'Did Lauren know Grant Fraser well?'

'It's a village, it's hard not to know people well. And she worked on his small holding a couple of times in the summer, lots of kids did,' Adam said.

'I've heard that he could be a bit handsy with some of the teenage girls, do you know anything about that?'

He took a few moments before replying, 'I'd heard that he could be a bit much, there may have been a couple of fathers who helped him see the error of his ways.'

'Any chance Lauren's dad was one of them?'

'It was a long time ago, it's hard to remember,' he smiled.

'That must've been hard to explain away, probably a bit embarrassing for Grant.'

'That was sort of the point, and I haven't heard of there being anymore issues, was there anything else, only I really need to get back to work.'

'No this is great, thanks.' I picked up the holdall and headed towards the train station car park.

I put the bag in the boot, resisting the urge to look inside. I'd do that back at Ellie's. As I drove out on to the main road I became aware of a green Land Rover Defender following me just a little too close for comfort. I couldn't make out the number plate, it was too muddy and with the winter sun it was hard to see who was in the driver's seat. I took a deliberate wrong turn that took me in a loop through a small square of houses, the Land Rover followed. It was about a forty-five minute journey back to Ellie's, I considered pulling into a parking spot and seeing if it passed me, but that came with risks. Moving I had options, stopped I was more of a target.

I used my hands free to call Chris.

'Everything okay?' She asked.

'I was following a couple of leads in the Kyle of Lochalsh today, I'm heading home now, and I'm being followed.'

'Are you sure?'

'Yes, there's a green Land Rover Defender and it's been behind me since I pulled out of the car park.'

'Can you give me the registration?'

'No, it's splattered with mud, and I can't make it out.'

'Are you sure you're not being paranoid, Defenders are a bit ten a penny round these parts, it'll likely be someone going the same way as you, try not to over think it.'

'I'm not, I took a couple of obvious wrong turns and it followed.'

'Okay how far from here are you?' Chris asked.

'I'm about halfway back, I've pinged you my location for you to follow. Do you think you could meet me at Ellie's I have something I think you'll want.'

'Sure. Listen just keep driving normally, but if they try and run you off the road or anything then let me know.'

I ended the call and looked in my rear-view mirror, and then at my sat nav. I took a moment to be thankful that Alana wasn't with me today, we'd been chased once before, and it wasn't something I wanted her to experience again.

Out on the quiet roads that connected the highland villages there were very few other cars around, very few potential witnesses should the person following me decide to take action. My only saving grace was that Land Rover Defenders are not known for their speed and nimbleness, at least that gave me an edge as I made my way to Ellie's cottage. If I hadn't arranged to meet Chris there I would have been inclined to drive by leading this threat away from my friends and family.

Finally, the turning for Ellie's cottage came into view, I could see Chris standing next to her car waiting for me. I pulled into the drive and the Land Rover sped up and drove on.

Chapter 28

'Did you get the registration number?' I asked getting out of the car.

'Yeah, I'll get someone to run it.'

'Thanks for coming over,' I said whilst I opened my boot and lifted out the holdall.

'What the hell is in there?' Chris asked.

'I honestly don't one hundred percent know, but I think it might be the drugs from the shepherd's hut.'

'Do I want to know how you came to be in possession of them?'

'We don't know that I am yet, let's go inside and find out.'

The front door was opened by a worried looking Alana, 'are you okay?' She asked.

'Yeah, I'm fine, calling Chris was just a precaution.' I carried the bag into the kitchen and put it on the table. 'Sonya, you might want to see this as well,' I said.

She got up and came to stand next to me. I pulled open the zipper to reveal several plastic tubs containing what looked like Blue42. The markings on the lids looked identical to the photographs Brodie had taken.

Sonya went to her bag and pulled out a screw top test tube with some liquid in the bottom, 'if you give me one of the tablets I can run a quick test on it,' she said to Chris who was already pulling on gloves.

Chris handed her a tablet and we all stood and waited as Sonya dropped it in the liquid and gave it a shake. The clear fluid changed to Magenta. 'Positive for Blue42,' Sonya confirmed.

'How the hell did you get hold of this?' Chris asked me.

I should of course tell her the truth, but I wanted to keep Archie and Adam out of it for now. 'The official version is that I got a tip off that Brodie went to the train station in the Kyle of Lochalsh on the 27th of December and he was seen going in with a big bag and when he came back, he didn't have it – I went to check that out and discovered it in the lost and found.'

'And the truth?'

'Archie McLeod suggested that I speak to his nephew Adam who works there. Archie and Brodie had been getting to know each other pretty well and Brodie trusted Archie to help him, Adam was also friends with Brodie. I'm not sure if Adam knew what he was storing, but I'm certain that Archie knew what was in the bag. Did you know that Grant Fraser had a sexual relationship with Lauren Davidson when she was seventeen, he became quite obsessed with her from what I've heard.'

'I'll deal with Grant Fraser, but I'd appreciate it if you stayed away from him, for now at least,' Chris said. 'I'm going to have to let DCI Burke know about the drugs, this is just too big for me to keep him out of the loop.'

'Yeah, I know, that's okay.'

'I'm not sure if he's going to be pleased or pissed off to be honest.'

'I'm thinking the latter,' I smiled.

'I'm just going to go outside and call him.'

'You can use the living room if you want privacy,' Ellie said. 'I promise I'll keep everyone in here.'

'Okay.' Chris walked out of the kitchen closing the door behind her.

'What will happen to the drugs now?' Alana asked Sonya.

'I'll arrange for someone to come up and collect them, then they'll be tested and analysed so that we can get a better understanding of what drugs and filler material is being used, then that information will be used to allow law enforcement to be more aware of people who might be making it, but equally as important it allows scientists to understand how to treat an overdose from it and hopefully that will help save some lives.'

Chris came back in, she looked solemn.

'How did it go?' I asked.

'Not great, and you're not going to be happy either.'

'Why?'

'DCI Burke wants to send a forensic team over to look at your car and go through your possessions.'

'On what grounds?'

'The giant bag of drugs.'

'Which I brought straight to you, without even opening.'

'I told you you weren't going to be happy.'

'Tell him I don't consent to my property being searched, so unless he can provide reasonable grounds or a search warrant, he can go to hell.'

'I thought you might feel like that, he says to tell you that being in possession of the drugs is reasonable grounds.'

'I'm not in possession of them. I picked them up, I told you about them and I handed them directly to you. You go back to him and tell him to try harder.'

'Technically it's not your property so it would be Ellie that would need to consent to the search.'

'Absolutely not,' Ellie said. 'Rowan is my guest and there is no way I'm going to let her be subjected to this by some jumped up bully.'

I could've hugged her right then and there, for now a grateful smile would have to do.

'Do you know what this woman put herself through to find my best friend and protect her? She isn't a criminal and this Burke bloke is going to have to do a lot better than that.' Ellie continued.

'I agree with Ellie and Rowan,' Sonya said, 'there isn't the required circumstances to force a search without a warrant and I suspect that DCI Burke knows that and he knows he wouldn't get one either.'

Chris shook her head, 'don't shoot the messenger, I'll phone him back.' This time she didn't leave the room, instead she dialled his number and put the phone on speaker.

'I'm just getting a team ready to come round now,' Burke said as soon as he answered not giving Chris the opportunity to speak.

'I suggest they stand down…'

'Absolutely not, this woman is a suspect in a murder case.' Burke interrupted.

'No, she's not, there isn't a shred of evidence that links her to Ben Weber or Brodie Cullen. She doesn't consent to a search, and we don't have reasonable grounds.'

'She has the drugs, there's your reasonable grounds.' Burke replied.

'I seriously doubt that any judge would agree that drugs that were immediately handed over to the police constituted reasonable grounds for a search.'

'Make it happen DI Hampton or I'll make your career prospects go away, I want Rowan McFarlane in one of the cells in the Kyle by the end of the day and that property searched, do I make myself clear.'

'What you're suggesting is illegal and I won't be any part of it.'

'Then consider yourself formally removed from this case, I will come down there and arrest the bloody woman myself.'

I'd been holding my tongue too long and wasn't about to be bullied by this odious man, and I was ready to tear him a new one. I opened my mouth to speak but Sonya held up her hand, her face giving away that she was almost as enraged as I was.

'DCI Burke, this is Dr Sonya Grother speaking, DI Hampton had you on speaker phone because she was calling to discuss the drugs and the arrangements I've made to have them transported to Glasgow. I understand that you're very keen to get this case wrapped up, however you seem to have overstepped the boundaries of your role.'

There was a moments silence. 'Not announcing yourself at the start of this call was very unprofessional,' Burke huffed.

'I hardly think you're in a position to be lecturing me about being professional when I've just listened to you bully DI Hampton and tell her to break the law by carrying out an unlawful search and an unlawful arrest.'

'You must've misunderstood me, I suggest you leave the police work to the police and stay in your lane.' Burke replied.

'I'm in my lane, and I did not misunderstand anything. Let me be clear your conduct this evening will be formally reported by myself, I suggest that you apologise to DI Hampton now and do not go ahead with your planned course of action against Rowan McFarlane.'

'I will not be threatened by a pathologist,' Burke said angrily, and I imagined his round face going from red to purple with indignation.

'I am not threatening you I am making you aware that as a police pathologist I will report your behaviour to the correct authorities within Police Scotland, and I'm giving you an opportunity to not make this situation any worse for yourself.'

'Fine, but the drugs come back here to our case head-quarters.'

'That was always going to be the plan, they'll be picked up tomorrow morning at 10am by Dr Begum and DCI Trevor Anderson. I'll email you across the relevant paper-work. To make you aware I have taken samples from each of the containers under the supervision of DI Hampton and these have been documented and signed for.'

Burke said nothing and the line went dead.

'Bloody hell that was intense,' Chris said. 'Thanks for stepping in, what happens now?'

'I'll make my report of his behaviour and it's likely he'll be removed from the case, other than that I don't know, that's out of my hands.'

Chapter 29

Callum arrived about twenty minutes later to collect the drugs, Chris signed them over to him. 'I thought there would have been two of you?'

'DCI Burke said we didn't have the manpower for it.' Callum replied.

'The people who followed Rowan are still out there, I'm not sure I like the idea of sending you off with a bag of drugs by yourself.'

Callum frowned, 'no offence but I think these people would be less likely to follow a police officer than Rowan. Rightly or wrongly, I don't think they see her as much of a challenge.' He tried not to make eye contact with me. 'Anyway I better get going, otherwise I'll have to account for every minute I'm away.'

'How is everything back at base camp?' She asked.

'I don't know what happened between you and Burke the jerk, but that dude is fuming, when he came out of the room, he was the colour of a beetroot.'

'Yeah, we had some disagreements on how the case should move forward. What's he doing now?'

'He left, he said he was going home to sleep in his own bed and that he would be back some time tomorrow. The rest of the team are pretty confused, he had them all ready to come storm somewhere, said we were closing in on the killer, and the next thing he's shouting at everyone to stand down and return to their hotel rooms.'

'He wanted to arrest my mum,' Alana said.

Callum's jaw dropped, 'wow, that would've been a bit embarrassing.'

'For your lot,' Alana replied.

'How did you persuade him to back down boss?' Callum asked Chris.

'I used my secret weapon.'

'What's that then?'

'If I told you, it wouldn't be a secret, right you'd better get going otherwise they'll be thinking you've done a runner,' Chris laughed.

We closed the door behind him, and Chris let out a loud sigh, 'it's been one of those days.'

'You want a cup of tea and a piece of millionaire's shortbread? I made it this afternoon,' Ellie said.

She looked at her watch, 'I can't I've got to go to drive through to the garage that's got Brodie's car and speak to the forensic techs that have been working on it, the boss wants to know if it's worth running any fibre analysis tests.'

'Alright, let us know if we can do anything to help,' I said.

She half smiled, 'perhaps don't do anything for the next couple of hours, I'm still getting my head round what's happened so far.'

I waved her off and then went back to join the others in the kitchen where Ellie had already made a start on making the tea.

'Thanks for this evening, your support means so much.' Sometimes I forgot how lucky I was to have this amazing bunch of close friends.

'You're welcome, although you know I wouldn't tolerate that sort of behaviour to anyone, right,' Sonya said before taking a sip from the mug of tea Ellie had put in front of her.

'I do, and I'm thankful for it.'

We spent the rest of the evening talking about the case and what was likely to happen to DCI Burke now. The ironic thing was that I had tried to warm to him, to see things from his perspective, after all I hadn't been a big fan of George when we first met and that had turned out pretty well for both of us. But there was no coming back from his behaviour, I knew that in different circumstances I would be spending the evening in a police cell worrying about whether I was going to be framed for a murder I did not commit.

I was just about to head to up to bed when my phone buzzed. 'Hey Chris, is everything okay?'

'Have you seen Callum at all?'

'Not since he came here to pick up the holdall, why?'

'He never made it back.'

'What?'

'He's gone,' Chris said.

'He can't be gone, can't you track his car?'

'We're trying that but so far we're getting nothing, I've got officers out searching the route our systems say he went…'

'What are you not telling me?' I asked.

'About five minutes after he left the cottage his vehicle slows down, stops for minute and then speeds off, we've got a notification that he tried to radio in then, but the signal was bad, and no one could make out what he was saying. He activated the panic button on his radio, next thing we lose contact with him and the vehicle altogether.'

'I'm sure he'll turn up,' I said only half believing it myself.

'I knew I shouldn't have let him take the drugs by himself, I should've insisted that someone else escorted him. If they've got the drugs then why would they bother keeping Callum alive,' her voice broke as she finished the sentence.

'Don't think like that,' I replied, although I was also thinking if they'd got the drugs then what was keeping Brodie and Emil alive. I felt a pang of guilt, this was my fault and then I stopped myself, none of this self-pitying was helping anyone and it wasn't the truth.

'I hope you're right.'

'Did you manage to get a trace of the Land Rover that followed me earlier?'

'Bugger. It completely slipped my mind to do it after everything with DCI Burke earlier.'

'Do you think someone was watching the cottage waiting for the drugs to be collected and when they saw Callum was by himself they took their chance?'

'Where would they have been able to watch from that we wouldn't have seen them and Callum would have mentioned it if he thought he'd seen something suspicious,' Chris said.

She was right, Ellie's cottage was in a wide open valley between the mountains, there wasn't anywhere that you could sit and watch from, without being easily seen by the occupants.

'Can we do anything?' I asked.

'Let me know if you hear or see anything suspicious, I've got to go.' Chris hung up before I had the chance to say anything else.

I was conscious that everyone in the kitchen had gone silent, all eyes on me.

'What's happened?' Alana asked, her quiet voice breaking the silence.

'Callum has gone missing, he didn't make it back to the hotel with the drugs,' there was no way to dress the situation up as anything better than that.

Alana covered her mouth with her hand, 'Is he going to be okay?'

'I honestly don't know.'

Sonya had gone pale too, not merely concerned for Callum's safe return but also thinking of all the lives at risk if that quantity of Blue42 fell into the wrong hands as it had almost certainly done now.

'I can't believe this is happening here, I didn't think anything like this would ever…' Ellie trailed off.

Sonya excused herself to go into the living room to make a few phone calls, I looked at Ellie and Alana, pale faced with shock. 'Why don't you two get off to bed, staying up all night worrying about him isn't going to bring him home any sooner.'

Alana protested, but was eventually persuaded, I waited in the kitchen until Sonya came back through.

'This isn't good,' she said sitting down opposite me.

'No.'

'I wouldn't be shocked if I ended up doing more post mortems before we go home.'

'No reason to keep any of them alive now,' I agreed. 'I should've taken the drugs straight to the police at the hotel. I could've prevented this.'

'I hate it when you do that, it's not noble to blame yourself you know.'

'I know, but it's true.'

'No, it's not. There's nothing to say that someone might not have come after the drugs there or on the transport tomorrow. These people have already killed one of their own, they're hardly a reasonable bunch.'

'I know, I really hope they find him.'

Eventually we both gave up and went to bed, Alana stirred as I climbed in next to her, but I managed not to wake her. I stared up at the ceiling, not thinking about Callum, instead thinking about what I had found out so far. Brodie had been travelling through Europe quite happily for weeks before he had a sudden change of plan, that must've been the moment he discovered that Ben and possibly Karl had something to do with the drugs that killed Lauren. What had they let slip that had sent Brodie here, it must've been something to do with Grant Fraser, that was the only thing that made any sense.

I must've dozed off because the clattering of gravel against the bedroom window jolted me awake, my heart racing. I checked my phone, it was ten past five. I got out of bed and pulled the edge of the curtain back to see who was trying to get my attention at this ungodly hour. It was hard to be 100% sure, but it looked like Grant Fraser was standing in the garden looking up at me.

I contemplated ignoring him, but my curiosity got the better of me. I grabbed the large hoodie and my jeans from the chair next to the bed and pulled them on. I picked up my boots and snuck out of the room closing the door quietly behind me. At the bottom of the stairs I put on my boots, and slipped my phone into my pocket.

I took a look back up the staircase, the cottage was still, I paused for a moment before opening the door, perhaps Grant had no intention of doing anything to me, but I've learnt it always pays to be prepared, I looked around for something that might work as a weapon. Ellie's home was annoyingly tidy, my foot knocked against an empty whisky bottle causing it to topple and roll to a stop next to my feet. I picked it up, it wasn't much but it would do, I lifted the latch for the door, turned the key and crept out into the garden looking across the gravel driveway, 'What the hell are you doing here?' I asked.

'I need to speak to you, in private.'

'It couldn't wait till daytime?' I asked wrapping my arms around my body trying to stop the cold sneaking inside my clothes.

'This is daytime, at least to me it is.'

'You knew what I meant. Why are you here?'

'Like I said I need to talk to you, and I need to be sure that no one else knows about our conversation. You look cold, do you want to come sit in the car out of this wind?'

I glanced over to where he'd parked in the road next to the cottage, his green Land Rover Defender looking uncomfortably similar to the one that had followed me less than twenty-four hours ago. 'No, you're alright, I'd rather not.'

'Suit yourself.'

I walked across the garden to a round wooden table, it's two chairs were lying on the ground to prevent them being blown over. I picked them back up and sat down indicating for Grant to do the same.

'I'm listening,' I said.

'I know what you think of me…'

'Do you, what's that then?' I interrupted.

'You think I'm a scumbag and…' he looked away from me down the dark empty road that went past the cottage, 'and a drug dealer.'

'Which part did I get wrong?'

'Both, I'm a decent bloke, I'd never get involved in drugs, I'm not like that.'

'If you say so, but I have to say I'm finding that increasingly hard to believe.'

'Please, just let me explain. I tried to explain to Brodie, but he wouldn't listen and perhaps if I'd pushed it, insisted he sit down and hear me out he would be here now and none of this would ever have happened.'

I was cold and tired and desperately in need of coffee, but that would have to wait. I weighed up the risks of sitting here talking to him, Alana would not be amused when she found out, but I was close enough to the cottage to scream and run back indoors if this went sideways.

'Okay.'

'I have a sort of permanent advert on the work away site, I need extra help all throughout the year and if I can get that for the cost of board and a bit of food then I'm happy with that, obviously it's been much harder over the last couple of years, so when I got the message about Brodie coming, I was delighted. And things seemed normal enough to begin with, I mean he wasn't chatty or anything and I figured he was the sort that liked to keep to himself. But then I noticed that when he wasn't working he was off walking with his camera, not like proper exploring walking, mostly across my land and I thought that was a bit odd.'

'Why?'

'Because it wasn't anything special, if you've had the chance to look around here you'll see that it's stunning.'

He was right this area had multiple opportunities for exploring and if I were staying for a little while I wouldn't have wasted time strolling around a few sheep fields.

'Then one night over dinner he brought up that he'd known Lauren Davidson in Glasgow,' Grant continued. 'Talking about what a travesty it was and how he hated the people who brought the drugs into the country and that they were murderers and he'd like to make every one of them pay.'

'Is that when you realised he was on to you?'

'Not quite, it's when I realised that he thought I was part of the problem.'

'It was your shepherd's hut that was being used to store the drugs in though, and that makes it hard for me to believe that you're not.'

'I knew nothing about that place until a few days ago...'

'Brodie took photographs of you going inside, how do you explain that?'

'Like I said I suspected that he thought that someone in the village had something to do with it, I figured that was why he went walking in strange places, so I decided to start following him, I didn't want him getting himself into bother.'

'Or you wanted to make sure he didn't catch on to you,' I said.

'You can think whatever the hell you like, but I promise you I had absolutely nothing to do with those drugs.'

'Let's say I believe you,' which I really wasn't sure was true at this point, 'how did you manage to get inside a shepherd's hut that was nothing to do with you?'

'I waited for Brodie to look round the place and leave and then I stayed until I saw it get opened. I used my binoculars to see the code.'

'How did you know someone would turn up that day?'

'I didn't, it was luck, although I waited almost six hours so I'm not sure how lucky that is.'

'Who came to open the place up?'

'Two blonde haired lads, I'd never seen them before. Of course, as soon as I saw the photograph of the dead man I knew he was one of them.'

'Why didn't you come forward then?'

'And say what?'

He had a point, with Brodie missing all suspicion would've fallen on him, but then if he was guilty, he would also have had good reason.

'Okay so you saw them going into the shed and then what?'

'They weren't in there very long, they came out, locked the door and off they went in the opposite direction. I waited about twenty minutes, and I went over to have a nose around, that's when I discovered the drugs – I mean I wasn't completely sure that's what they were, but what else could they be. I decided I would go back to empty the place out and drive it in to the police station, but when I got there the next day they were gone.'

'What did you think had happened?'

'Brodie was a smart lad, he would've done exactly what I did, wait to see someone going in, get the code, I figured he'd taken them. I tried to find a way to bring it up with him, if he'd told me I could've protected him.'

'He would never have told you, he believed you were involved, he even suspected that you had deliberately asked Ben and Karl Weber to target Lauren that night and cause her death as retribution for her shunning your advances.'

The colour drained out of him, 'Jesus, it was me – he

was calling *me* a murderer that night at dinner, I would never have done anything to hurt Lauren.'

'Why, because you loved her?'

He looked at the ground, 'our relationship was consensual, I'll admit I've been known to pat the odd bottom, but there was never anything in it, not till Lauren, and before you ask it wasn't all about the physical, although she was stunning. We would talk for hours, she liked to read the same things as me, we had shared interests and I'm not ashamed to say I was flattered by her attention. She made the first move, she was the one that kissed me, invited me to her house while her parents were away and asked me to get into bed with her.'

'Did you not think that you should've been the one to say no and set some boundaries?'

'It's easy to have 20/20 hindsight, I got caught up in the moment. This beautiful young woman wanted me, and I hadn't felt that virile for years.'

'Is that why you didn't want to let her go?'

'She made me feel alive and then it was over, it was like she flipped a switch and wanted nothing more to do with me, I struggled to believe it, I thought someone had got inside her head and influenced her. I'd got to know her, we'd shared something special, and I couldn't accept that she didn't feel that way, so yes, I made a right arse of myself and I embarrassed my wife, god knows why she stuck by me, I don't think I would've been so forgiving if I were in her position. And no doubt you'll have heard I went a bit too far and I got a bit of a kicking for my efforts, nothing that wasn't deserved, I lost myself for a bit.'

'And how did you feel when Lauren died?'

'Heartbroken, not that I could admit that to anyone round here, I went out into the field and screamed and bawled my eyes out. I never did stop loving her, I just pretended that way and got on with my life. I felt broken inside, I'd accepted that she didn't want to be with me but that hadn't changed how I felt.'

'How did it make you feel when you found out Brodie and Lauren had been a couple, where you jealous?'

'Of course, it stung like hell, but she was gone by the time I met Brodie and in some ways I pitied him, I knew what it was to lose her, there was some comfort in being around someone else who had loved her so deeply, someone whose grief I understood completely.'

'Earlier you said you'd tried to explain to Brodie, what did you mean?'

'I tried to tell him that I loved her too, I wanted him to know that I hurt almost as much as he did. But I didn't get very far, he told me Lauren had told him about me and it made him sick to have to sit at the same table and eat as me.'

I considered everything he'd said, now sitting before me he no longer seemed an imposing strong man, now he seemed small and vulnerable, and I found myself inclined to believe that he had nothing to do with the drugs or hurting Brodie, but if not him, then who?

'If I accept your version of events then how is that the shepherd's hut came to be sitting on your land?'

'It's a really remote part of the small holding, if you know where the old paths are you'd be fine, but it's not like I have any need to go out that way regularly, it could have been there months and I'd never had been any the wiser.'

It seemed hard to believe, but I had to admit that it had taken me some time to find it and the location was, by anyone's standards, remote. 'Why did you tell DI Hampton that I forced my way into your home, and do you know who burnt the hut down?' I asked.

'I was scared for you, I thought if I made a complaint you'd get warned off looking for Brodie and that it would stop anything bad happening to you, I can't feel responsible for another person getting hurt.'

'What made you think I was at risk and that I would need protection from you, I can take care of myself.'

'I'm sure you can, you'd been in Brodie's room twice I thought you must've found something I hadn't and with that lad turning up dead I knew whatever you had found was likely the same information that led to something terrible happening to Brodie and I didn't want to get up the next day and find that you were missing too.'

'Okay, but what about the hut?'

'It's not really on my land, it's more on Henry's.'

'Your brother? Are you suggesting that he has something to do with it?'

'Everyone thinks I just gave up the farm because I wasn't interested in having the responsibility, that I chose the small holding and the life I have. That's not how it was, when my dad got sick, it was me that did all the work, sure Henry gave the impression that he was the hard working one, but the only thing he did was make our parents life miserable, he was cruel to mum and mocked dad for being too weak to work. The day after dad's funeral he pinned me to one of the barns with a hay-lifter and told me the farm was going to be his, I was to take the small holding that was meant for him and tell everyone it was my choice. I agreed on the condition that I stayed at the farm while mum was alive…she died seven days later, the doctor said of a broken heart, official cause was a heart attack brought on by grief.'

'You suspected something else?'

'Henry is incredibly intelligent, I'm sure he could've found a way to make it happen. I didn't want to rock the boat. Eileen was pregnant at the time, and I was afraid for her, so I told her I picked the small holding so we could spend more time together as a family. Tragedy was that the baby was still born, Eileen lost a lot of blood and ended up having to have a hysterectomy to save her life, so there never was a family for us.'

Chapter 30

Now back in the kitchen I was hugging a mug of coffee with my hands and considering if I'd ever be able to feel my feet again. I'd been sat in the front garden for almost an hour with Grant Fraser and after he left, I found myself questioning everything I'd thought up to this point. It would be an easy way out to blame everything on his younger brother, most of his anecdotes couldn't be corroborated. He had sworn that he wasn't the one following me yesterday and like Chris he'd said that most people had a green Land Rover Defender, and surely if Chris had run the plates yesterday evening and they'd belonged to Grant then she would have had him picked up for questioning.

The door to the kitchen opened revealing a very tired looking Alana in joggers and a hoodie, 'what are you doing up?' She asked, half yawning at the same time.

'Grant Fraser came by to see me, I was chatting to him outside and now I'm trying to defrost.'

'What the hell? Why was he here, do you think that was sensible talking to him without anyone else around?'

'I don't think he's dangerous,' I replied.

'That's not what you thought yesterday, what changed?'

'He told me some things, and my gut says he was telling the truth.'

'I hope you're right,' Alana said.

'Me too.'

'Any news on Callum?'

'Not yet, I think Chris said something about having a rescue helicopter out looking for him.'

'Do you think he's alive?'

I considered my answer for a few moments, I'd always tried to not lie to her. 'I don't know,' I said honestly.

'I keep thinking why would they leave him alive once they've taken the drugs.'

'He's a police officer, killing him would be seen very differently to killing a drug dealer like Ben.'

'So we have to rely on the morals of drug dealers for his safety,' Alana replied turning away from me as she poured us both a coffee.

I walked over to her and put my arm around her shoulders pulling her into a hug. I felt my top getting damp from the tears she was so desperately trying to conceal. After a few minutes she pulled back and looked at me, her eyes red and puffy.

'I'm not in love with him or anything,' she said. 'I just liked him and he's not that much older than me, he had plans and dreams. There were things he wanted to achieve in his career, it's not fair.'

'It never is, but you can't give up hope yet.'

As I spoke my phone rang, it was Chris.

'Any news?' I asked.

'He's alive, pretty banged up, but alive,' she replied.

'Oh my God that's amazing, when did you find him?'

'The helicopter went out as soon as there was enough light, they saw his car in a ravine, we were able to get a rescue team out to him and he's been airlifted to hospital.'

'What the hell happened?'

'Hard to say but looking at the images I've seen so far I'd say he was bumped off the road and the car tumbled.'

'And the drugs?' I asked.

'In the car, I'm guessing they punted him further than was intended, it's not an easy place to get to, we had to have mountain rescue go in with our trained officers, it's going to be a bugger getting the forensic guys in and out.'

'Will Callum be alright?'

'I think so, he had hypothermia setting in and several broken bones and was slipping in and out of consciousness, but the paramedics say we got to him just in time.'

'That's great news on both counts, any chance you could swing by here today there's a couple of things I'd like to run by you.'

'Doubtful, I've got the guys coming to collect the drugs and they're now going to be travelling in a convoy to make sure they don't have any issues heading down the road and then I'm going to be dealing with processing this scene. DCI Burke isn't answering his phone and I'm not sure what's happening with him or if I should go over his head, so for now I'm up to my eyeballs. Is it urgent?'

'No, it can wait, hope your day goes well.'

Alana had been staring at me throughout my conversation, desperate for information.

'He's alive,' I said giving her another big hug. I told her what Chris had told me.

'Thank God,' she said.

'Thank God for what?' Ellie said as she came into the room.

'You'll never believe it,' Sonya said a moment later as she joined us.

'The drugs have been found and Callum is alive,' Alana said.

She looked up at us. 'How did you know that already?' Sonya asked.

'Literally just got off the phone with Chris,' I said.

'Bloody brilliant,' Ellie said. 'I think this calls for pancakes for breakfast.'

As Alana helped Ellie prepare the breakfast Sonya sat down at the table next to me. 'Who were you sneaking out to see in the middle of the night?'

'Grant Fraser, how did you know?'

'I'm a light sleeper, I heard the stairs creak and saw you go out the door, but I couldn't see who you were talking to because my room is round the back. What did he want?'

'He wanted to give me a bit of his family's history and point the finger of blame at his little brother Henry.'

'You believe him, don't you,' she said narrowing her eyes as she looked at me.

'I do. I'm not saying he's a good person, his behaviour with Lauren is still gross, but a drug dealer and murderer, I don't think so.'

'What now then?'

'Henry has access to dozens of barns and acres and acres of land where it would be easy to keep people concealed and quiet without running the risk of anyone ever coming across them.'

'Please tell me you're going to be careful, if he's the person holding Brodie then you've no idea what he's capable of.'

'I know that, I don't intend confronting him by myself, but I thought I could go for a walk and get a sense of his land, where would the harm be in that, at the moment he has no idea that anyone suspects him.'

Chapter 31

Alana offered to come on my walk with me, but Sonya said she could do with some help in the lab and I was grateful for that. The grass crunched under my boots as my steps broke through the layer of frost, it was a cold day, my breath could be seen billowing in front of me as I walked, the chances of being covert and unseen were slim in this weather so instead I would need to be careful.

I walked past Grant Fraser's small holding out into the empty field beyond until I could see the charred grass and the remnants of the shepherd's hut, the field was on a hill and from here there was a clear view of the smallholding and the road bellow. If the arsonist had come this way, they could've been sure that there was no one about to see what they were up to.

I'd scanned Google Maps before coming out and knew that if I followed the bottom line of the field I would come to a large barn, in the online image it looked run down and roofless, but I thought it was as good a place to start looking as any. A twenty-minute walk took me to it.

Still run down and roofless, the barn looked like it had been decades since it had last been used for keeping anything dry inside. After a quick investigation I scored it off the list of potentially interesting out buildings and carried on.

The next building I came across was nothing more than two rotting wooden walls, I perched on a nearby rock and took a drink of water from my bottle and consulted the map again. The remainder of the farm buildings were considerably closer to the main house and the closer I got to that the more danger I'd be putting myself in.

I'd hardly walked for ten more minutes when I heard the faint rumble of a quad bike engine, I looked around but saw nothing, on a still day like today it could be some distance away I told myself, my heartbeat quickened just a little. I carried on walking, the sound getting closer, when it was too loud to ignore, I turned to see where it was approaching from.

Two bikes were heading in my direction, it was difficult to identify either rider from this distance, I lifted my arm and gave a friendly wave. Moments later they were pulling to a stop next to me.

'You're that private detective woman, aren't you?' The younger of the two men said. He had dark hair, mud on his face and blue overalls on.

I smiled my best customer service smile, 'yeah that's right I'm Rowan, sorry I don't think we've met,' I reached out my hand for him to shake.

'I'm Michael Fraser and this is my dad, Henry.'

I shook both their hands, 'nice day isn't it, glad it's not raining.'

'What are you doing out here?' Henry asked.

'Just out for a walk.'

Henry looked at me almost daring me to break his gaze, 'walking for business or pleasure?'

'A bit of both, I guess, walking helps me think. Is this your land?' I asked.

'It is,' Henry replied.

'You're not investigating us I hope,' Michael laughed.

'Just walking and thinking,' I smiled. 'Your farm is huge,' I continued. 'I didn't realise it was spread across such a large acreage.'

'Aye,' Henry responded.

'Must be a lot of work,'

'It is, makes it easier when you have a son to help out though.'

'And your brother's close as well, isn't he.'

'Aye but he doesn't have anything to do with the farm, he's happy pottering around with his small holding, that does for him.'

'Fair enough, I'd better not keep you back,' I said hoping that it would encourage them to move on.

'Not at all,' Michael said. 'We were just heading back up to the house, you'd be welcome to join us for a cuppa and mum usually has some cake waiting.'

I glanced at the quads.

'There's room for two on mine,' Michael said.

'I wouldn't want to be any trouble, besides I feel like the walk back from your house would be more than I'd bargained for.'

'I'm going into the village after, I'll give you a lift back to the main road if you want,' Michael said.

I had run out of polite excuses and providing I wasn't kidnapped, some tea and a slice of cake would be nice. 'Okay then, sounds lovely, thank you.' I climbed onto the quad and found that I had the choice of holding on to

Michael or a very muddy handle in order to stay secured. I chose Michael.

'Hope that wasn't too bad,' Michael said as he slowed to a stop not far from the main farmhouse. 'I tried not to go too fast so as not to get you all mucky.'

'Thanks.' I followed the two men towards the front door and into the large kitchen where Mrs Fraser had been baking and a pot of tea was waiting.

'Who's this then,' she said as soon as she saw me.

'This is Rowan, you know the private detective lady that's staying with the drama woman,' Michael said.

'Well, it's nice to finally meet you, I don't go down into the village an awful lot these days, busy you see. I used to go down to drop my baking off to the croft box, but Henry's been taking it for me lately. What brings you up to us then?'

'I wasn't intending on coming up this far, I was out for a walk to clear my head and then I got chatting to Henry and Michael and now here I am.'

'Excellent, there's plenty of food, so you help yourself, I can pack up a bit extra for you to take back if you want.'

In the space of a few moments I understood where Michael's friendly, chatty personality had come from.

'With two strapping men in the house I'm not sure I'd be thanked for taking cake away,' I smiled.

'Nonsense, I'll knock up another one. These two could never claim that they've been deprived, that's for sure.'

I accepted the offer of takeaway cake and sat down at the kitchen table grateful for the warmth and the food.

'I understand you're looking for the lad that was staying with Grant, is that right?' Mrs Fraser said sitting down and taking a fork full of cake.

'That's right,' I replied, I wanted to be polite, but I didn't want to give anything away.

'Are you having any luck with that?' Henry spoke for the first time since we'd entered the house.

'There are some indications that he left with the intention of heading home, no one's heard from him, but he had a few contacts in Germany so that's what I'm looking into now.' I smiled making sure to make eye contact with Henry.

'Do the police not think that dead lad is connected then?' Michael asked.

'I'm not sure what the police are thinking, I like to follow my own leads.'

'I heard the mountain rescue helicopter out this morning in the early hours,' Mrs Fraser said. 'I thought they might've found him, but then it's probably just some numpty that thought going hill walking at this time of the year was a good idea and ended up lost and cold.'

'We get that all year round,' Michael said, 'they come and they think they know what they're doing but they don't dress or plan for the weather, and then all of a sudden they're caught out and they need dial a rescue.'

'Don't mind him, he volunteers most summers with mountain rescue, and he can get on his high horse about it sometimes.' Mrs Fraser said swatting her son's arm.

It was good to know that news of Callum's *accident* hadn't travelled this far yet at least. When the tea was finished I thanked Mrs Fraser and then turned to Michael, 'any chance of that lift back now, I've been out for a while, my daughter will be wondering where I am.'

'No problem, we'll go out the other door, it's closer to the car.'

I followed him through a corridor and into a boot room. 'This is nice,' I said having a look around.

'Yeah, mum had it done a couple of years ago to stop muddy boots being traipsed through the house but honestly dad rarely uses it and mum has just accepted it, the labourers use it though for their bags and stuff.'

I glanced around and caught sight of a green and burgundy Glacier Nomad rucksack with a Tintin keyring hanging from one of the zips. I'd seen it before in one of the photographs Lilly had sent to me, sitting at the feet of Brodie's friend Emil.

'You okay?' Michael asked.

'Yeah sorry, just having room envy that's all, not sure these ideas would translate to a modern house like mine, but would you mind me taking a couple of pictures on my phone, my friend Mel is an interior designer and she's always looking for inspiration.'

'Sure, whatever floats your boat.'

I took some general photos making sure not to focus in on the backpack too much and draw his attention. 'Thanks, I'll send them to her later.'

'No problem.' He opened the door to where a green Land Rover Defender was parked. I walked round the front noting the mud smeared number plate making it almost unreadable then tentatively got into the passenger seat.

'It's not much more comfortable than the quad I'm afraid but it has got sides and a roof so you should stay clean and dry.'

'It feels like everyone has one of these here,' I replied.

'Yeah, they're a good work horse.'

'Do you like farming?'

'It's all I've ever known.'

'Will you take over the farm when your dad retires?'

'I'd like to but dad's not keen on the whole retirement thing, I took a look over the books and we've been doing better than ever recently. We took a pretty big hit through the pandemic but now we're more or less back to pre 2020 levels, I said to dad that maybe he should step back and him and mum could relax, do a bit of travelling or something, I know she's always wanted to.'

'Wasn't he up for it?'

'No, he got a bit narky at me for looking, saying he'll retire when he's good and ready but between you and me I think he'll drop dead ploughing a field one day. Do you like your job?' Michael asked.

'Love it.'

'Is it dangerous?'

'It can be, I've had my fair share of black eyes and bust lips.'

'Hope you left your opponent equally as bruised.'

I smiled, 'most times I do.'

'Do you think you'll find Brodie?'

'I hope so, did you know him at all?'

'A bit, we met in the village and had a few drinks together, but I'm usually kept busy with the farm so it's not like I have a lot of time to socialise, but I liked him, he seemed sound.'

'Were you at the hotel for Hogmanay?'

'Yeah, I got dad to drop me off and pick me up so I could have a drink.'

'Didn't he fancy coming along?'

'Not his scene, he prefers a quiet night in.'

'I don't think we were introduced that night.'

'No, there were a fair few folk I'd not seen in a while so I ended up catching up all night.'

'You didn't see Brodie then?'

'In passing but not to talk to. Is this me being investigated now?' He asked smiling at me.

'No, I'm just interested in what happened that evening. Do you get a lot of temporary labourers at the farm?'

'In the summertime we do, not so much at this time of year, not such a big demand for them.'

'Where do they stay when they come for work?'

'There's a bothy bunk house type building, it's got a dormitory, bathroom, basic kitchen, that type of thing, they get to stay there as part of their terms, most of them couldn't afford to do the work if they were paying to stay in the hotel as well.'

We had almost reached the main road. 'You can drop me here, it's not much of a walk back to Ellie's,' I said.

'Are you sure, I can take you if you like.'

'No, it's fine I know you have things to be getting done, thanks though.'

Michael pulled over and I jumped out the car and watched him pull away, surer now than I'd ever been that it was the car that had followed me home yesterday. If Michael was involved though he was a bloody good actor. I walked down the hill towards Ellie's cottage when I heard her calling my name.

'Ellie?' I said as she drew closer.

Ellie threw her arms around me in an exaggerated embrace. 'Thank God you're alright.'

I peeled her off me and frowned, 'why wouldn't I be?'

'Sonya rang and said that your location tag thing you sent her from your phone had shown you moved very suddenly from a field to the farmhouse and then you were there ages and then on the move again. She sent me out to look for you with strict orders to call Chris if I couldn't find you.'

I'd sent Sonya a location share this morning when I'd headed out, it was something I'd started doing since Alana went to university, with no one home to know if I didn't return Sonya could check and see where I was and raise the alarm if I was uncontactable.

'Why didn't someone phone me?'

'We did but you didn't answer.'

I looked at my phone, it had dropped to "E" with no phone signal. 'Sorry to have caused so much drama, you'd better let Sonya know I'm okay.'

Ellie made a quick call promising that she'd have me call and explain myself as soon as we were back at the cottage. After allowing Sonya to lecture me for a few minutes on the phone she finally calmed down enough to let me know that the drugs had been handed over to her colleagues from Glasgow and were currently on their way now.

I opened up Google Maps and looked at a satellite image of the area around Henry Fraser's farm. The bunk house that Michael mentioned seemed the most likely place to be keeping Brodie and Emil, it was self-contained, it wasn't meant to be occupied at the moment so there was little chance that Mrs Fraser or Michael, assuming that he wasn't involved, would have any need to go in. And when I located it I noticed that there was a back road that led directly to it meaning that people could come and go without anyone on the farm being any the wiser.

I brought up the photos I'd taken of the boot room and zoomed in on the one of the backpack, then I brought up the pictures Lilly had sent me and put them side by side on my computer screen. There was no getting away from it, this was the same bag, but what was it doing in Henry Fraser's boot room?

Chapter 32

I sent a quick email to Lilly asking if she had any contact details for Emil's family, I didn't have to wait long for a response, his younger brother, Frank, had become sort of like a modern-day pen pal for her, she gave me his mobile number and said that she would text him and tell him to expect my call.

A few moments later we were chatting.

'When was the last time you heard from Emil?' I asked.

'I've had texts but no phone calls for just over a week,' Frank replied.

'was there anything off about the texts?'

'Off?'

'I mean did they seem like the sort of texts Emil would usually send, was there anything about them that didn't feel quite right?'

'They were very short and the first few were in English, but I thought that maybe with him being in the UK it was a slip up.'

'Wasn't the plan for Emil and his friends to be working in mainland Europe?'

'Yes, but Emil told me before he went to Scotland that Brodie had got himself into some trouble, Emil felt responsible for it, he wouldn't explain why, he said that he had to go and help him and that he would be back soon.'

'How well do you know Ben and Karl Weber?' I asked.

'Not well, they were Emil's friends, they had travelled together before the pandemic, but I only ever met them in passing.'

'What did you think of them?'

'I don't know, Ben, the younger brother, was arrogant... full of himself, you know,' he paused. 'But Emil, he always saw the best in people, and thought it was because Ben was young. Karl was okay, quiet but in a way that made you feel a bit awkward.'

'What did you think when Lilly told you that Brodie was missing?'

'I was worried, obviously, I am very fond of Lilly, and I have known Brodie for a long time now, he's like a second brother to me, I hoped that he would be found quickly.'

'Has Emil mentioned anything about coming back home in his texts or travelling from the Highlands to Glasgow?' I asked thinking about the message I'd received that allegedly was from him.

'No, all his messages have been about how nice it is, the occasional picture of a mountain or some scenery, that type of thing, when I asked when he was coming home, he said not for a while.'

'Did you ask about Brodie?'

'Yes, he said he didn't know where he was and that he'd been out with the search party looking for him. I tried to call him several times, but the phone is never answered.'

'Could you forward me the photos and messages he's sent you since he came to Scotland and let me know if he messages again?'

'No problem…there was one thing that was odd, when I hadn't spoken to him for a while I began to worry, especially with Brodie going missing and I sent him a message, something in German, it's part of a nursery rhyme and when either of us are worried about the other we send the first line and the other sends back the second line, but this time when I sent it he responded with a laughing face emoji.'

'When was this?'

'Two days ago.'

'Thanks Frank, I'll let you know as soon as I find out anything.'

'Do you think my brother is in danger?'

'I think it's too soon to know, I don't like that he didn't respond in your agreed way to the text you sent, but I don't want to get ahead of myself and assume that he's in any trouble. You can trust me to find out what's happened.' I said.

'You'll call me as soon as you know?' Frank asked.

'I promise.'

I said goodbye and ended the call.

Emil was in trouble, the question was, was it because he was involved in the drugs, or because he had gone looking for Brodie?

I wanted to go back up to Henry Fraser's farm and have a poke about, find the barn and hopefully Brodie and Emil alive, but I couldn't do that today. It was one thing to be caught on his land once, that can be chalked up to a coincidence and Henry doesn't ask any more questions, but twice and he's going to get suspicious and the last thing I need is him getting twitchy.

I scrolled though my list of calls to the number that had called me a couple of days ago pretending to be Ben Weber and hit dial.

'Hello,' the male voice on the other end said.

'Hi, who am I speaking to?' I asked.

'I might ask you the same thing.' The German accent was still detectable but not as strong as when it had been claiming to be Ben.

'I asked first.'

'Do you always get what you want?'

'Mostly.'

'Why don't you guess.'

'Well, you're not Ben Weber.'

'Admit it, I had you fooled at first.'

'Not for a minute, especially when I was looking at his dead body while we spoke.'

'Oh, you see now I'm disappointed in you Rowan, that wasn't playing fair at all.'

'What's the end game then Andreas?' It was a guess that this was the same man Rod Harris had described, but this case had always been about the drugs, and he'd been there from the beginning. I metaphorically had everything crossed that my assumption would prove correct.

'Give the girl a cookie, she knows who I am. I want my drugs back and if I don't get them within the next 24 hours then your friend DI Hampton is going to be finding three more bodies.'

'Your drugs are gone.'

'What do you mean, gone?'

'Didn't you hear they're on their way to Glasgow, they were collected first thing this morning. Was it you that ran Callum Sinclair off the road last night or did you send someone to do that for you?'

'I don't know what you're talking about.' Andreas laughed.

'Well, if you don't know then it sounds like you haven't got your organisation under control at all, tell me, why did Ben have to die?' I took deep breaths, he was getting under my skin and I was struggling to not let it come across in my tone.

'Because all of this is his fault, I should've known better than to trust him, he never could keep his mouth shut.' He spat, even after killing the boy the anger remained.

'He let slip to Brodie that it was him that spiked Lauren's drink.'

'Ten out of ten,' Andreas said. 'Another cookie for the clever little detective.' He paused. 'Ben got careless, started being too flash with his cash and Brodie began to suspect he was into something illegal and when Brodie confronted him, Ben admitted that he was dealing drugs. Of course, he wasn't so quick to tell me that he'd been sharing so much of my business information. Charmingly it was his brother Karl that shared it, because he thought it might save poor Ben, but it was too late for that.

'Is Karl on your payroll as well?' I asked.

'You ask too many questions.'

'Well, that *is* my job. What are you planning to do with Brodie and Emil?'

'I think you've had enough from me for one day and don't bother trying this number again, this will be the last call it ever takes. And a friendly piece of advice, go away, go home, run in fact, run back to your quiet life, and stay safe.'

'I've never had a quiet life and I'll go home when I've found Brodie safe and well.'

'It would be a real shame if something bad happened to you or that pretty daughter of yours.'

'I don't recommend threatening me and mine, the last time that happened it didn't end well for the person making the threats.' I said and then I hung up, anger coursing through my whole body.

Chapter 33

I emailed the prison hoping to arrange another meeting with Rod but received a reply saying that he was in the prison infirmary and wasn't in a fit state to have any kind of visitor. I asked what had happened and was informed that he'd got into an altercation with a couple of the other inmates the day after my conversation with him. I asked that someone let me know when he was well enough to talk, but I suspected that he would have no desire to speak to me again.

It could be a coincidence, but far more likely was that someone in the prison also worked for Andreas and let him know that Rod had been speaking to me. I felt momentarily guilty, he had been willing to help me, to share his side of the story and from everything he told me he was truly remorseful for his actions.

My phone pinged a text:

That Land Rover that followed you yesterday – it's registered to Eileen Fraser, Grant's wife, we're going to pick him up now. New DCI says we might even have enough to charge him. Speak later. Chris

I wanted to text back that she/we'd got it wrong, that Grant Fraser wasn't the brother we should be worried about and to find out who had taken over from Burke, but I doubted she'd be in any position to talk right now. I'd have to wait and hope that she came by later to fill me in. It wasn't surprising that a new DCI had been sent in to take over running the case, with one lad missing, one dead and one of their own being run off the road and left for dead this case would be starting to attract some serious attention within Police Scotland. In fact I was surprised that it hadn't attracted more media attention.

I decided to phone George and see if news had trickled its way down to Fife.

'This can't be good,' he said when he answered the phone. 'You calling from your holidays.'

'Charming, how's things there?'

'Quiet. I haven't got you making trouble for me, so for once it's peaceful.'

'Ha ha,' I retorted.

'I hear the same can't be said for you though.'

'Do you, who's been keeping you up to date on my escapades then?'

'Do you want a list?' George chuckled. 'First Hargraves had a call from some relative of his up there checking you were who you said you were, and then a very angry DCI Burke called to give me his thoughts on involving civilians in police work and just this morning I got a call from a DCI Don Thacker asking me for the low down on you, and of course Sonya was whisked away to join you so I've spoken to her a few times.'

'Never thought I'd say this, but I wish you were here,' I said, and it was true I hadn't realised how easy working with George had become, despite our very different approaches we made a good team.

'Hold on, I had to pick myself up off the floor. You'll be pleased to know I sung your praises to everyone, which seemed to really piss off DCI Burke.'

'Thanks, do you know much about what's going on here?' I asked.

'I know the basics, I'm guessing you have a theory though.'

'I do, and I think this DCI Thacker is about to arrest the wrong person.' I gave George a quick breakdown of what had been happening over the last couple of days and my early morning visit from Grant Fraser.

'Have you shared your thoughts with Chris?' George asked.

'Haven't had the chance, obviously finding Callum and getting the drugs on their way to Glasgow has taken precedence.'

'With a bit of luck, it'll become apparent to them that Grant isn't the brother they need to be looking at, but you've got to admit that it's a bit odd that the car that followed you is registered to his wife.'

'I can't explain that either.'

'Any chance you're wrong, and this Grant Fraser has played you, made you think it's not him by pointing the finger of blame at his brother?'

'I suppose anything is possible, but I don't think so, plus like I said, Emil's backpack was in Henry Fraser's boot room.'

'Could they be in it together do you think?'

I thought for a couple of moments, 'unlikely, they don't seem to have anything to do with each other. I suppose that could be an act though.' I paused mulling over the thought. 'Could you do me a favour?'

'Depends what it is,' George replied.

'Thanks, could you run the plates for me and text me what you find out?'

'I thought you said the team there had already done that...'

'They have, but I'd rather it was done again, there's a lot of inexperienced PCs on this job and it doesn't hurt to be thorough, right?'

'Okay I'll do it and text you later, what are you going to do?'

'I'm not sure.'

'My advice would be, find someone who's been there a long time, that would be willing to talk to you, and find out how much truth there is to the inheritance of the farm story. If that's true, then there's a high likelihood you're right and the wrong man has been arrested.'

I thought about Archie McLeod, he didn't have much good to say about Grant Fraser, had even pointed me in the direction of someone who would tell me that he was a low life pervert. But he had also told me where Brodie had hidden the drugs, and I was sure he'd be far more invested in finding out who was responsible for killing Lauren than he would anything else.

'Thanks, I think I know someone who fits that description.'

'Let me know how you get on, won't you.'

'I will, listen before you go, what do you know about this DCI Thacker?'

'He's from Glasgow, he's young and ambitious, Amadeus has worked with him before, says he's all about getting the right results, and when I spoke to him, he didn't seem averse to having you on board, most DCIs are wary of a private detective working alongside the police, but he had done his research into you and knew that you have a good track record.'

'Does Amadeus like him?' I asked.

'I think it would be more accurate to say he respects him.'

'Good enough,' I replied. 'Well, I'd better let you get back to your mince pies, I've got a case to crack.' I laughed and we said our goodbyes.

I popped into the kitchen to let Alana know that I was heading out to speak to Archie McLeod.

'Do you want me to come,' she asked. 'Only I was going to watch an online lecture from the John Moores University in Liverpool, one of their professors there is one of the best in the world at forensic facial recon-struction.'

'You stay, I'll be fine, enjoy your lecture.' I smiled, Alana had wanted to go into forensics since she was in first year of high school, but I couldn't help thinking whether what happened with Jack and what I do for a living had strength-ened that desire considerably.

I stopped by the shop and picked up a bag of fudge doughnuts to take with me.

'I didn't expect to see you again so soon lass,' Archie said as he opened the door and let me in.

'I hope I'm not intruding.'

'Not at all, I'll get the kettle on.'

'I've brought some doughnuts.'

'That's very kind of you, but I made shortbread this

morning, so perhaps you can take those home with you or share them with your police friends.'

'No problem, homemade short bread sounds lovely,' I replied realising that he had very politely told me that he doesn't eat shop bought cakes.

I waited in the living room until he came back with a tray of tea and biscuits. 'Adam tells me you popped by and picked up some lost luggage,' he said handing me a plate of shortbread.

'Yes, thank you. It's on its way to Glasgow now,' I said taking a triangle and having a bite. 'This is amazing,' I said as the biscuit melted in my mouth. I would never admit it, but Archie's shortbread was even better than Maureen's.

'That's good, I'm pleased. Now what brings you back to my doorstep, not that I don't like your company, you under-stand, it's just that I thought you might be too busy for social calls so I can only assume that this isn't one.'

'You're right, I was looking for some information on the Frasers' farm.'

'Why's that then?'

'I'm trying to verify a version of events that was shared with me, and I thought you've lived here a long time and you'd likely know what was what. Grant Fraser is the oldest son and I thought that it was the general rule that the farm would pass to him.'

'That's how it should go.'

'Originally I was told that Grant Fraser didn't want the farm and now I'm considering how true that is.'

'Dougie Fraser was a good farmer, and I know he always talked about Grant taking over from him, so it was a surprise that he didn't,' Archie paused. 'But this is old history, and I can't see how it has anything to do with what's happening now.'

'It doesn't really, except that I'm testing a theory of whether if one part of what someone tells you is the truth then maybe the rest is as well.'

'Henry taking the farm put Grant in a bad way and of course not long after that he and his wife lost their baby, heart breaking, poor woman nearly died. I'd say Grant never really recovered from that. There was a time when he was never far from the pub and then after that there was a lot of chat of him playing away, but I think he finally came to his senses.'

'What sort of a man is Henry Fraser?' I asked.

'Standoffish, proud, course he's had his own tragedies, his first wife died in a car accident, they'd only been married a month or two when it happened. Her sister took to looking after him and then a couple of years later they married. No doubt that sounds a bit unusual for your generation, but here, certainly in the past it wasn't that uncommon. Martha Fraser, she's the salt of the earth kind, wouldn't hurt a fly and would stop to help a random stranger without a second thought, it's really her that keeps that place going, organising seasonal labour is about the only thing Henry is good for.'

I drank my tea and listened to Archie. 'Why do you think Grant gave up his birth right?'

'The way I remember it, there was a falling out between them when Dougie got sick, give him his due Grant did the lion's share of the work, but it was obvious that Henry was a bully to his older brother. I can't be sure but at the time I suspected that maybe some threats had been made. Grant's wife came to me in confidence and told me that they were being forced out of the farmhouse, but when I talked to Grant, he told a different story and there was precious little I could do.'

'No love lost between the brothers then, they didn't mend their bridges after that?'

'Not a chance, that pair would cross the street to avoid one another.'

'What about Michael Fraser, Henry's son?'

'Nice lad, takes after his mother luckily for him, not that he gets much time for coming into the village, Henry keeps him occupied up there.'

We finished our tea, and I ate a second piece of shortbread before I thanked Archie again for helping me with the investigation and headed home.

I had barely stepped foot back inside Ellie's cottage when I got another text from Chris:

Are you available – I need a favour. We've picked up Grant Fraser but he says the only person he's prepared to talk to is you. Chris

Chapter 34

Chris and DCI Don Thacker were waiting for me in the hotel reception area when I arrived.

'Thanks for coming,' Chris said. 'This is DCI Thacker,' she continued, indicating to the tall man stood next to her. I would have estimated that he was in his late thirties, dark hair, blue suit, shirt, no tie.

'I spoke to DCI George Johnston about you,' He said by way of a greeting. 'He speaks very highly of your abilities,' he paused to look at me. Was he waiting for me to display my gratitude for such a positive reference.

'Well, I *am* good at my job,' I replied.

'Yes, so I've heard, but I do want to lay down some ground rules before we begin.' He looked around the reception. 'Let's walk and talk.'

I followed him through some double doors to the section of the building that had been commandeered to run the investigation.

'Grant Fraser is our main suspect in a kidnapping, murder, attempted murder and drugs case so I can't afford to have you fuck it up, is that clear?' Don asked, stopping to get my response.

'No problem,' I replied, trying to decide when I would tell him that he'd arrested the wrong person. 'But what if it's not him?'

Don snorted a half laugh. 'The evidence against him is pretty convincing.' We had entered a small room that he had taken as his office. 'I know my predecessor wasn't quite as open to your involvement and there's been some suggestion that he might have behaved inappropriately, but please rest assured you won't have the same problem with me. I intend to solve this case and if that means working with a civilian I will, but I'd like you to remember this is my investigation, not yours – mine, and you're here at my request.'

I was desperate to reply that surely I was there at Grant Fraser's request, but I remembered what George said, Amadeus respected DCI Thacker and that did stand for something.

'I understand, and I think it's good that we're getting our cards on the table here. I was employed by Brodie Cullen's family to find their son, that's my case and I'm happy to work with you because you come highly regarded by people that I respect and trust. I am not your employee, our relationship will only work if it is based on mutual respect and trust, so why don't we start there.'

He narrowed his eyes and looked at me, 'they said you were a tough nut to crack,' he smiled and his whole face changed, suddenly warm. 'Okay, but there are rules. I want Chris in the interview with you, it will be recorded, you can't share what's said outside of the investigation and no matter how much he tries to wind you up you can't bite.'

'Deal,' I held out my hand and he shook it.

Don led me across the corridor to another equally small

room, this one looked like it was normally used for storing laundry. Grant Fraser looked dejected sitting on a plastic chair, staring down at his hands clasped in his lap, I cleared my throat. He looked up.

'Thank God, thank you for coming,' he said.

I sat down opposite him, a small melamine topped table between us. 'That's okay, Chris…DI Hampton said you wanted to talk to me.'

'They think I'm the murderer.'

'What makes you think I don't agree?' I asked curiously.

'Because you went up to the farm, that means you at least believed me enough to investigate.'

Chris shot me a confused look which I tried to ignore.

'I did, I met your sister-in-law and your nephew.'

A tired smile flitted across his face, 'he's a good lad, Michael.'

'DI Hampton says that it was your car that followed me back from the Kyle yesterday, or your wife's car anyway.'

'That's the thing, I only have the one Land Rover, I don't know where they're getting their information, but Eileen drives an old Ford Fiesta, there aren't any other secret cars and I wasn't even in the Kyle yesterday, I spent most of the morning on the phone to a supplier because they'd sent me the wrong feed for the sheep. I can give you the details, but her boss says that doesn't prove anything. Did you find anything when you were at the farm?'

'Did you ever meet Brodie's friend Emil?' I asked, avoiding the question because I wasn't ready to reveal all my cards yet.

'No, Brodie talked about him and their travels, I think he saw him as sort of an adoptive brother, why?'

'Because Emil is also missing, he came to Scotland to see

Brodie, and no one has seen him in weeks and his brother says he's not responding to his texts.'

Chris was getting pissed off with me, I could see her scowl from the corner of my eye and I was sure she'd have no hesitation in giving me a piece of her mind later, but that was future Rowan's problem, right now I wanted to make doubly, triply sure that my gut feeling about Grant's innocence was right.

'Do you think he's involved in the drugs or that he's in trouble?'

'I think he's in danger,' I paused, 'In fact I think he's being held somewhere on the farm.'

'What makes you think that?' Chris interrupted.

'Because when I was at the farmhouse earlier today I saw his backpack in the boot room.'

'Interview suspended,' Chris said before taking me by the arm and almost dragging me into the corridor where Don was waiting.

'Why the bloody hell didn't you mention that when you got here?' Don asked. 'You've given him all the ammunition he needs now to create reasonable doubt.'

'He hasn't even been formally charged yet, so I think you're getting ahead of yourself, I needed to talk to him,' I turned to Chris. 'I did try to tell you earlier, but you said you were tied up today, but Grant Fraser came to see me this morning to say that it was his brother that I should be looking into not him.'

'Well, he would say that wouldn't he?' Don said before Chris had a chance. 'What was I thinking letting you get involved.'

My phone buzzed, it was a text from George:

Car registered to Aileen Fraser Whiney Farm, Strathcarron. George

Thacker was still talking but I had stopped listening. 'What was Henry Frasers first wife called?'

'What?' Don said mid tirade.

'Henry Fraser was married for a brief period to his current wife's sister, she died and then he later married his once sister-in-law, what was his first wife called?'

'Who cares!' The DCI ran his hands angrily through his hair.

'Why do you need to know?' Chris asked.

'Can you please trust me and ask someone to check.'

She nodded and disappeared back down the corridor leaving me with an angry faced DCI Thacker who'd now begun pacing the corridor.

'I'm sorry, I didn't mean to blind side you, I thought if I mentioned it to you, you'd want to tell me how to lead the conversation and I needed it to be more organic than that.'

'Are you always this infuriating?'

'Probably,' I answered.

'It was meant to be a rhetorical question,' Don said but he was smiling now. 'Amadeus did say you had your own way of doing things, I should've listened to him.'

Part of me wanted to know how much Amadeus had shared with his former colleague, the other part preferred to be in ignorance.

Chris came back through the swing doors at the far end of the hallway, 'Aileen, her name was Aileen Fraser.'

'And the car that followed me yesterday?' I asked.

'Registered to an Aileen Fraser,' Chris replied.

'Aileen Fraser not Eileen Fraser,' I said. 'He must never have changed the registered keeper.'

'It was an easy mistake to make,' Chris said, no doubt knowing whoever had made that mistake was going to be torn a new one very soon.

'Details,' The DCI shouted in the hallway. 'It's the details that count in a murder investigation.' He put his hands on his hips and hung his head slightly, then he looked up at me. 'You were right, we have arrested the wrong bloody person. We got carried away thinking we'd found that car.'

'The important thing is that you know now,' I said.

'We'd better cut him loose, first the backpack in the boot room and now the car.'

'I think we should ask him to stay here for a bit,' I said. 'If you release him and word gets back to Henry, he might decide it's time to cut his losses, at the moment he believes that you have enough evidence to have arrested his brother and that suits him fine and gives us the upper hand. I think he'd always had this as a back-up plan, that's why the shepherd's hut was on the boundary of their land, he could say he knew nothing about it and everyone would believe him, after all it's Grant that has the rather more interesting past, everyone thinks Henry Fraser is a good upstanding member of the community.'

'I can't see Grant Fraser being interested in helping us out,' Chris said.

'Let me speak to him,' I replied. Don nodded and I went back into the room.

'Good news, you're no longer under arrest,' I said.

'Thank you…how…why…'

I smiled, 'I managed to help DCI Thacker see that you had nothing to do with Brodie's disappearance.'

'How can I thank you?'

'Well, you could do me a favour.' I explained to him that

we needed him to stay here for a while to help us close in on Henry, and as I had expected he was happy to help.

Chapter 35

Sitting in DCI Thacker's makeshift office I shared everything I'd discovered so far with him and Chris.

'I have a few contacts in Interpol, I'll reach out to them to see if they have anything on this Andreas bloke and I'll send someone in to have another chat with your bouncer, don't worry I'll have them be discreet,' he said seeing the look of concern on my face. 'We need to find the bothy and get inside without drawing attention to ourselves,' he continued.

'I could ask Michael to show me around the farm, I've got a container to return to his mum and we seemed to get on alright before,' I suggested.

'Could be risky,' Chris said, 'how do we know he isn't in on it with his dad? For all you know the smiles and good manners could be fake to keep you off the scent.'

'That's true, I'll be careful and I'll keep my wits about me.'

'I'm not sure, I don't like the idea of you being up there

with no way of me knowing if you're alright or if you're in danger.'

'I'll message you when I head up there, and if you haven't heard from me in a couple of hours then you'll know there's been a problem, I always send a location tag to Sonya anyway.'

'Okay if you're sure,' DCI Thacker said.

'I'm sure, worst case scenario he doesn't fall for it and we find out nothing, best case scenario he does and leads me right to where the lads are being held.'

'Or worst case scenario you end up kidnapped too,' Chris muttered.

'I don't think so, taking me when I could so easily be traced directly to them would be madness, I can't see Henry taking that kind of risk.'

The next morning Alana was already up and in the kitchen when I came downstairs, she poured me a mug of coffee, 'are you sure this is a good idea?' She asked.

'Yeah, it'll be fine.' I took a big swig from the mug, grateful for the fact she'd made it extra strong. 'I know you're worried, but Chris and DCI Thacker know where I'm going to be and Sonya will have my location as always, if they don't hear from me, they'll know where to find me.'

'They'll know where to find your phone, doesn't mean to say it'll be with you,' she replied.

'You're right, it's not without risks, but it's the best plan for trying to find Brodie and Emil.'

'Fine. But try not to put yourself in more danger than is really necessary.'

I smiled.

'I'm not joking mum, I know this is "all in a day's work" stuff for you, but these people have already killed dozens of people that we know about, and probably more as well.'

'I'll be careful.' I gave her a big hug.

I ate a full breakfast before I got in the car and headed up to the farm. Michael was just leaving the main house when I pulled into the courtyard area. He stood and watched as I got out.

'I wasn't expecting you back so soon,' he said smiling and striding towards me.

'I thought I'd better return this to your mum,' I held out the container, 'I know my Gran is particular about getting these sorts of things back.'

'Oh, thanks, hold on I'll just stick it in the kitchen.'

I waited for a few moments until he came back out, 'all done.'

'Right, well, I'd better get on my way, don't want to disturb you,' I said hoping that he would ask me to stay.

'Umm, do you want to stay for a wee bit, you could help me feed the horses, I'm on my way over there now.'

'Are you sure?'

'Yeah, it's a much nicer day than it was yesterday.'

I walked beside him round to the stables where the horses already seemed to be getting taken care of by two teenage girls. Michael saw me looking at them.

'We stable their horses here, and in return they come and help with mucking out and generally looking after all the horses, otherwise stabling can be prohibitively expensive. They don't have to do everything of course, they wouldn't have time for that, we have farm workers who do the lion's share of the work.'

I walked towards a speckled grey horse and gently stroked its nose.

'This is Smoky, he's getting on a bit now, he used to be mum's horse, but she doesn't ride as much these days and Smoky is really just enjoying his retirement, being regularly spoilt because everyone loves him and brings him carrots and apples.

'I can see why, he's lovely,'

'Excuse me a minute,' Michael said, and I stayed with Smoky as he strode off to talk to one of the farm labourers. 'Sorry about that,' he said when he came back. 'I was just checking everything was all good. Anything else you'd like to see?'

'I don't know, you're in charge of the tour,' I replied, so far this was going well but I wanted to be careful not to make it obvious that I wanted to find the bothy.

If we go back to the yard and pick up one of the quad bikes I'll give you the full guided tour, never know, might change you into a farm girl before you head home.'

I could have punched the air in satisfaction, if he was going to give me the big tour that had to include the bothy and with a bit of luck we'd find Brodie and Emil this morning.

I wasn't sure if Michael was taking it a bit easier than usual on the throttle, but being on the back of the quad didn't feel as much like an out of control fairground ride this morning as it had done yesterday. So far I'd seen the sheep in their field, the space that he wanted to build Yurts for glamping when he was finally in charge of the farm and a lot of empty fields, I'd heard all about his idea for a farm shop, but that his dad thought it was nonsense, but not once had he mentioned or had we come close to seeing the stone built bothy boarding house that he'd mentioned to me before.

Now stopped on the highest point of the farm Michael was busy pointing how far you could see from this vantage point.

'It's amazing,' I said. 'It's a shame you're not able to put some of your ideas into place now.'

'Dad says the farm is doing well and we don't need the extra hassle, he doesn't want tourists tramping all over the place, getting lost and ending up in the fields with the lambs, that kind of thing and I see his point, but I think it would be possible to have both, but there's no point arguing. I even suggested putting a few statics in the field down there for the labourers and use the bothy for events, because it's big enough, do you want to have a look?'

'Yeah, what sort of events were you thinking?'

'Weddings, parties, evening walking group things, it's really big, more of a barn than a bothy to be honest.'

Michael started the engine and my heart pounded. How would he react when he discovered Brodie and Emil being held hostage on his farm? Was I bringing this innocent man unknowingly into danger? I tried not to think about what would happen when we came face to face with Andreas.

The path to the bothy looked torn up with tyre tracks and I noticed Michael slowing down to look at them. The building itself was long and narrow and almost set back into the trees, which gave it good camouflage. We stopped a short distance from the door.

'What do you think? I was imagining this outside bit tidied up and maybe some decking or gravel area, I don't know, something where people could sit outside in the summer,' Michael said.

I was barely taking in his words, my hearing tuned into the buzz and thud of blue bottle flies smacking into the bothy windows. He hadn't noticed.

'I've got the keys, I'll show you my plans for inside.'

I hurried across next to him, the door was stiff and as

soon as he cracked it open the smell of death rushed out to meet us.

Michael gagged, 'what the hell is that?' He made a move to go in, I grabbed hold of his arm pulling him back.

'Trust me, you're going to want to let me do this.'

He frowned, 'what are you talking about?'

'Please Michael, let me go in and then if I'm wrong about what's causing the smell, I'll let you know.' I wasn't going to be wrong, I'd smelt this before. I pulled up the neck gaiter I was wearing to cover my nose and mouth, took a deep breath and walked into the bothy. The door to the shared bedroom area was propped open with a chair, I followed the stench.

The body of Karl Weber was sprawled on the ground, the massive wound on the back of his head had seeped blood into a thick gloopy pool under his body, it would have been this that had attracted the flies. It was hard to tell how long he'd been dead, his skin was yellow and waxy looking and the blood had congealed.

I looked around the room, empty Pot Noodle cartons and crisp packets were strewn on the table at the other end. I stepped around Karl's body and made my way to it, I pulled on my latex gloves and rummaged around in the debris, my fingers catching on something cold and metal, I cleared a space and saw a St Christopher, I picked it up, the clasp was elongated and broken, I'd seen this kind of damage before, it had occurred when a necklace had been ripped off someone's neck. Next to the table were two chairs, discarded zip ties and faint blood spatter on the floor and walls.

I took my phone out of my bag and dialled Chris.

'You need to get a team up to the bothy at Henry Fraser's farm right now,' I said as soon as she answered.

'Have you found them?'

'No, I've found Karl Weber, he's dead, but this is definitely where Brodie and Emil have been kept. I'll call Sonya as well.'

'Do you think Michael is in on it with his dad?'

'I don't think so, he seemed genuinely shocked by it all.'

'Okay, don't do anything stupid,' Chris said. 'I'll be there as soon as I can.'

I sent my GPS coordinates from my phone to hers and walked back outside. Michael was hovering at the door.

'What's going on, what's that smell?'

I came out into the open, closing the door firmly behind me, glad to take huge deep breaths to clear out my nostrils.

'There's a dead body in there.'

Michael made a move to push past me to the door, I blocked him. 'It's my bloody bothy, I've got a right to see,' he said.

'I promise you this is not something you want to see.'

'But it's okay for *you* to see it?' He turned and walked a few paces away rubbing his hands through his hair.

'It's not the first one I've seen,' I replied, very grateful that I had been alone the first time I'd stumbled across a corpse and that no one had witnessed me rushing from the room to throw up in the garden.

Michael looked at me confused.

'Occupational hazard,' I continued. 'I've called the police, they're on their way.'

Michael pushed passed me and into the bothy, I didn't try and stop him this time. He knew what he was going to see. Moments later a pale looking Michael reappeared, he closed the barn door and stood almost frozen, one hand propping up his weight against the wall of the barn. He looked over his shoulder and then staggered back towards me sitting down on his quad bike, silent.

I needed to call Sonya. The conversation was short and to the point, I knew that even whilst I was still describing what I'd seen she was gathering her things and heading to her car.

'I need to phone dad,' Michael muttered finally and then fumbled getting his mobile phone out of his jacket pocket.

I leant forward and took it from him, 'I'm sorry you can't, the police don't want anyone else to know until they've had a look at the crime scene.'

'It's not a crime scene, it's a bothy,' he shouted at me.

'You've had a huge shock,' I said opening my bag and taking out a bar of tablet I'd picked up from one of the many croft boxes that I'd seen dotted around. I broke off a section of the sugary treat and held it out to him. 'Here eat this.'

He tried to push my hand away, 'I'm not hungry, I feel sick.'

'I know, but the sugar will help, eat it.'

He took it from me and obediently put it in his mouth. After a few moments he said, 'how can you be so calm about all of this?'

'Like I said, it comes with the territory of being a private detective.'

'I thought that would've been all cheating spouses, finding runaway kids, that sort of thing.'

'It can be those things, but a lot of my cases have involved murder, that's how I've come to work with the police so many times.'

'Dad was wrong,' Michael glanced at me. 'He said you were out of your depth looking for Brodie, Mum said that was rude, but he was adamant, what would a woman know about investigating anything. I'm sorry I didn't stand up for you more, most people I know wouldn't be standing out here with their wits together after coming across a dead body like that...' he stared at me for a minute. 'It wasn't Brodie, was it?'

I shook my head, 'no, it wasn't.' I didn't elaborate on the identity of the body.

'Dad will go mental, he hates it when anything interferes with his routines. God that sounded awful, I don't mean that he won't care about the body, it's just...' he trailed off.

'That's okay, the police will deal with all of that, nothing for you to worry about.'

'Will they want to question us?'

'They'll need a statement from us both and if you feel up to it, they'll likely do it when they arrive.'

All of a sudden Michael rushed towards the nearby bushes and vomited, he stayed bent over and retching for a few moments, then he spat out a glob of thick saliva and stood up. When he turned back to face me a little of his colour had returned.

'That was embarrassing,' he said.

'It's okay, it's the shock.' I handed a bottle of water to him, he took it taking a tentative sip.

Our conversation was cut short by the arrival of Sonya, 'you both okay?' she asked looking more in Michael's direction than mine.

'Yeah, we'll be fine, the body is in the room to the left, I've been in, but I didn't touch him or anything, it was pretty obvious it was too late.'

She nodded and pulled a paper cover all out of her bag and suited up before going inside. A few moments later

Chris and DCI Thacker arrived followed by the forensic team and three uniformed officers.

Chris and Don walked across to me leaving Michael with a uniformed officer. 'Are you okay?' DCI Thacker asked.

'Fine.'

'No sign of the others?'

I shook my head, 'no and there was already mould growing on the half-eaten sandwich on the table, I think they probably left in a hurry though, otherwise surely they would've made an effort to hide the body and tidy up after themselves?'

'Is there any evidence that Brodie or his friend Emil were even there?'

'Someone's been cable tidied to chairs and there's some blood spatter so if you've anything to compare it to then you should know for sure, also Brodie's Saint Christopher was in there, it looked like it had been ripped off his neck.'

'I thought the Saint Christopher was something you made up to get another look at his room?' Chris asked.

'It was, but I must've seen it on him in the pictures and not realised because he really does wear one.'

'What the fuck is going on here, get off my land, all of you, get out of here immediately,' an angry voice bellowed from behind us.

Chapter 36

We all turned quickly to see Henry Fraser, shotgun in hand marching towards us. 'Get off my land,' he said looking directly at me. He raised the gun and pointed it in my direction.

'I strongly suggest you put that down Mr Fraser,' DCI Thacker said stepping towards him calmly.

'Don't tell me what to do on my land, you're not welcome either.'

DCI Thacker grabbed the barrel of the gun pulling it in the direction of the sky whilst simultaneously thrusting his shoulder against the man causing him to lose his balance. As Henry struggled he fell to the ground and DCI Thacker took possession of the gun, before calling for a uniformed officer to come and take it away. Turning his attention to Henry, he pulled his hands behind his back and cuffed him.

'Never a wise move to point a gun at a police officer,' he yanked on the man's arm and brought him to his feet.

Michael ran across to his father, 'what are you doing to him, he's an old man…'

'Your father can't point a gun at people without there being consequences,' DCI Thacker said. 'He'll have an opportunity to explain himself later.'

'But…' Michael said and then stood open mouthed as he watched his father being put in the back of a police car. 'This can't be happening,' he said. 'You can't think my father would hurt anyone.'

'I think that when someone points a gun at you all bets are off, this being his farm doesn't give him the right to threaten people like that.'

Michael looked like he was on the brink of collapse, and for a moment I felt guilty that I had engineered this situation without really thinking about the implication on him. But it was hard to feel too sorry for the him when Brodie and Emil were somewhere, terrified, and very possibly injured.

Sonya came back out of the bothy and walked towards us.

'What's the verdict Doc?' DCI Thacker asked.

'Cause of death was blunt force trauma to the back of the skull, it's hard to say what the weapon was at this stage, but if I was going to give an educated guess I'd say you're looking for a metal mallet of some description. As always, I'll know more after the post mortem, which if we can get him to the morgue I'll do immediately.'

'Thanks Doc,' DCI Thacker said. 'Any read on time of death.'

'It's always hard to say at this time of year, I've taken some of the insect life and I'll send it away to get a better idea, but I think at least forty eight hours but could be nearer to seventy two.' Sonya turned to me, 'I could do with a second pair of hands at the lab for photographing etc, how do you feel about me taking Alana?'

'No problem.'

'Assuming she wants to, obviously,' Sonya continued.

'Hold on, isn't Alana your daughter,' Don said. 'I don't feel comfortable having a minor in the morgue.'

'Good job she's an adult then,' I smiled.

He frowned.

'Second year forensic anthropology student, top of her class.' Sonya added.

'Oh right, whatever you think's best Doc.' DCI Thacker added and then very wisely chose not to say anything else on the matter.

'What's the plan of action now then?' I asked.

'We'll question Henry down at HQ, see if he's willing to give up this Andreas bloke or tell us where the other lads are,' Chris said.

'I'll get more uniformed officers up here to look for the weapon and comb through the area, he looked around, 'but it might be a bit of a needle in a haystack.'

'What about Michael?' I asked.

'I'll take him back to the farmhouse when we inform Mrs Fraser of what's happened, see if we can get anything out of either of them, even if they're not involved, they might've seen something that will help,' Chris said.

'Why don't I do that? I got on really well with her when I met her yesterday and she might respond differently to me than you, especially if I can lay it on thick that I've been looking out for her boy.'

DCI Thacker raised his eyebrows in thought, 'might be worth a try, we're already thin on the ground with the area we have to search, it wouldn't hurt for you to have first crack of the whip, mind you share anything you find out though, I don't want to hear you've gone off on your own investigating a lead that ends up with you in a body bag.'

'You're all heart,' I said.

'I don't want that on my file. Do terrible things to my career progress don't you know,' Don responded matching my level of sarcasm.

DCI Thacker instructed one of the uniformed officers to take Michael and me back up to the farmhouse. Martha Fraser came to the doorway as soon as she saw the police car draw up in the courtyard. I got out the front passenger side door and walked round to help Michael out the back.

Martha rushed forward seeing her son looking pale, 'what's happened?' She gasped.

'I think it's best if we get Michael inside and then I'll explain everything,' I said.

'I'm fine, I can walk,' Michael protested although he still looked very shaky.

In the kitchen Martha sat her son in a tattered leather armchair near the AGA and forced a cup of extremely sweet tea on him, 'drink this,' she said. Then she looked to me.

'I came to drop your container back this morning and Michael offered to give me a tour of the farm, but when we got to the bothy, I could tell something was wrong…'

'Wrong? What do you mean, wrong?' She interrupted.

'I found the body of a young man inside.' I said deciding it was best to get it out in the open right away, no beating around the bush.

Martha looked at her son and then back at me.

'It's been the shock of that and then seeing his father being arrested.'

'Henry's been arrested?'

It was interesting that she hadn't asked what for, did she think her husband was capable of murder? 'Yes, unfortunately there was a bit of a scene when Henry came down to

250

see why the police were at the bothy, I'm afraid he threatened me and two police officers with his shotgun.'

Martha shook her head, 'bloody fool.'

'I think I could do with a lie down,' Michael said from the chair.

'I'll come and check on you in a bit,' Martha said as she watched her son walk out of the room.

Should I have asked Michael to stay so that I could ask him about Karl Weber? He didn't look like he was in any fit state to be answering questions and his response seemed genuine to me.

'Did you know there were people staying in the bothy?' I asked.

Martha looked down at the mug she was resting on her lap. She looked back up at me, 'Something's not been right for a while,' she said.

'What makes you say that?'

'Four years ago we got into some bother, financially that is, Henry invested in stocks and shares, but he didn't take advice, typical, always thought he knew everything about everything and it was a bad investment, we lost a lot of money and were at the point of thinking that we were going to need to sell the farm or at least some of the land. I tried to make Henry see that was going to be the only way to keep our heads above water, but he wouldn't hear of it. Then it seemed like our luck was about to change, a German film company wanted to do some filming here for a documentary and they reached out to all the local farmers etc because they needed space to put their people up, it was off season and the hotel had to shut for some major repairs, we rented out the bothy and they even had some statics brought in for the couple of months they were staying and they paid a good figure for it. It helped keep us afloat and I said then to Henry that there was something in this tourist accommodation stuff and we should seriously consider doing it on a permanent basis.'

'Michael said he had the same idea, but that Henry wasn't keen,' I said.

'He wasn't, he said that one of the investments he'd made had come good and that topped up the bank accounts and from then on the farm went from strength to strength, only…'

'Only what?'

'It felt wrong, we were making *too* much money, now I know that sounds daft, who complains about making too much, but I have friends who are farmers wives and whilst they were struggling, we were flourishing, then during the pandemic everything started to dip again and that made no sense to me.'

'Did Henry ever go across to Germany on business?'

'He got friendly with one of the directors and he visited with him a couple of times.'

'If you didn't think the extra income was coming from farming, where did you think it was coming from?'

'I don't know, I thought maybe he was doing something illegal, selling red diesel, I don't know.'

I paused wondering if she really thought there was that sort of money to be made in selling fuel, perhaps there was, it wasn't something I knew a lot about. 'Did it ever cross your mind that it might have something to do with drugs?' I asked realising there was no delicate way of asking.

'No. Dirty, filthy things, they destroy lives.'

'What about when you heard about the shepherd's hut going on fire?'

'Henry said it must've belonged to Grant.'

'Henry didn't seem to have a lot of time for his brother,' I said.

'No, Grant was bitter that his father left the farm to Henry and not him, as the oldest he thought it should've come his way.'

'The way I heard it was that Henry demanded the farm and threatened Eileen if Grant didn't agree.'

'No, surely not, I know he doesn't do much for his own image, but threatening people, women, that's not how he is.'

'He didn't seem to have any issue sticking a shotgun in my face earlier,' I replied.

'He's changed, maybe you can't see it, but he used to be a kind, loving man.'

I found it hard to believe that Henry Fraser had ever been either of those things, but perhaps to Martha he had been, after all she'd stepped in at his hour of need and looked after him.

'Did he ever introduce you to a man named Andreas?' I asked.

'Do you mean Andreas Wagner?'

'Yes.' I had no idea what Andreas' last name was, but the likelihood of their being multiple Andreas' in Henry's friend group had to be slim.

'Of course, he's one of the directors that stayed here, I have his card somewhere if you want it.' She stood up and rummaged through a kitchen door, she came back holding out a business card for me to take.

'Has Henry been acting strangely lately?' I asked putting the card into my pocket.

Martha went to open her mouth and then closed it and tilted her head to one side, 'I wouldn't say strangely, but he has seemed to be more stressed than usual.'

'Any idea why he would be stressed?'

'It's a small place, I think everyone's been on edge since Brodie went missing.'

'Michael told me that he and Brodie got on well, did you know him at all?'

'Nothing more than to wave hello to, but then he's a young man, can't imagine he'd have a lot to talk to an old dear like me about.'

I was thinking about our conversation, she never had answered my question about the bothy, instead she'd given me a potted history of their finances, had she been trying to avoid talking about it?

'The people in the bothy, how long have they been there?'

'Are you married?' Martha asked.

'No…'

'Then you won't understand.'

'What won't I understand?'

She didn't reply.

'This isn't the time to be coy, two young men are dead, another two are missing, hundreds of thousands of pounds worth of drugs were recovered from a shepherd's hut I very much suspect you know belonged to your husband, unless you want to risk you and Michael taking the blame, I would suggest you tell me everything you know.'

'Michael has never had anything to do with his father's business.'

The door to the kitchen opened, Michael stood in the doorway looking at us both, for a moment I thought he was about to do something stupid, there was bound to be another gun in the house, and it was entirely possible that Michael could've been working with his father. My heartbeat quickened, I shouldn't have let him out of my sight.

'I knew they were there, at least I knew that someone had been staying in the bothy,' Michael said.

'Then why take me there today?' I asked.

'Dad said they were gone now, that it was over.'

'That what was over?'

Michael shrugged, 'do you think my dad killed that man?'

'Do you?'

'I don't know anymore, what's going to happen to him?'

'It depends what he's done, but whether he killed Karl and Ben Weber or not he'll still be going to prison for the drugs offences.'

'You can't prove that he had anything to do with that, everyone in the village is saying that it was Uncle Grant that was trafficking the drugs.'

'That's what your father wanted everyone to think, but your uncle's just another victim in all of this.'

'You need to leave,' Michael said, his tone turning from meek, hurt boy to angry man in the flick of a switch, he strode across to me and grasped hold of my shoulder and tried to yank me out of the chair. I thrust my elbow backwards connecting with his bollocks and causing him to let go of me and crumple forward.

'You need to sit down, and don't you *ever* put your hands on me again,' I said as I directed him to a seat next to his mother.

'If you hadn't gone sticking…'

I slapped him hard across the face, his head jerked round and he stopped talking, my palm stung from the impact. 'Shut up. Your father and his drugs are responsible for the deaths of countless people, including one of your neighbours Lauren Davidson and you know what I've always wanted to know, was it coincidence that her drink got spiked? Did Ben do it to get back at Brodie because he got the girl or did someone ask him to target her, knowing that with her medical condition that she would be sure to die?'

'What the…' Michael stood up, looking as though he was readying himself to square up to me again.

'Sit down,' Martha instructed in a way that surprised us both. Michael was stunned but complied. 'What's Lauren got to do with any of this?' Martha asked.

'The drugs that Henry stores and helps distribute across Scotland and beyond are the same ones that killed Lauren. I'm going to give you both one final opportunity to tell me what you know or I will call DI Hampton and tell her you are both as guilty as Henry and she will send some officers up here to arrest you, now is that what you really want?'

Chapter 37

'I knew someone was staying in the bothy,' Martha said breaking the silence that had been hanging between us for the last few moments. 'At first, I thought maybe Brodie was hiding out there, that perhaps he was in some sort of trouble. I told Henry if the police found him there he could get into trouble, but he told me to stay out of it and to trust him and that's what I meant when I asked about you being married, because when you've been with someone as long as I have with Henry then you have to trust them sometimes.'

'What about you?' I said to Michael, who was sulking and still nursing his cheek, even though it was only a little pink.

'I'd seen some people going in when I was out looking for a couple of lost sheep, I asked dad about it and he said it was probably a couple of walkers that had got lost and were taking shelter, but I knew that couldn't be true because the place is kept locked.' He paused for a moment, 'so I followed him one evening, I saw him there with Andreas, they were carrying something to the car and then a couple of days later that lad's body was found and I worried that might've been what I'd seen them carrying.'

'Did you ever go back?'

'No but I saw dad go there most days, if I'm being honest I didn't want to know what was going on, I assumed it had something to do with Uncle Grant because I'd seen dad go down the hill with a jerry can of petrol and the next thing I know the shepherd's hut is up in flames, I thought Grant had done something and this was dad getting his own back.'

'Why not tell the police what you'd seen?' I asked, even though I was pretty sure I already knew the answer.

'Because he's my dad and besides what good would it have done,' Michael replied.

'For starters I'd say it would have saved Karl Weber's life and perhaps now Brodie and Emil would be in the process of reuniting with their families instead of being god knows where.'

'That's not fair, to put that on the boy,' Martha said'

'It's not fair that the Weber's are going to be burying their sons, it's not fair that Brodie's family are out of their mind with worry or that Emil's brother doesn't think he'll ever see him again,' I said angrily. 'And it's not fair that the Davidsons, your neighbours, lost their only child to a drug that your husband trafficked, so if you want to discuss the moralities of hiding your husband's activities, I suggest you decide how you'd like to break the news to those families first.'

'I didn't mean it like that,' Martha looked at her hands.

'I accept that neither of you wanted anyone to get hurt, but the sad truth is they *have* but that doesn't mean that you can't do anything to help put the situation right.'

'What could we possibly do?' Michael asked.

'Andreas must've taken Brodie and Emil somewhere; he doesn't know this area like Henry does and my guess is that he's trying to lie low at least until he knows whether Henry is being charged with anything. Where would he go?'

They both mumbled that they didn't know.

'You're going to have to do better than that, where would Henry have gone if he wanted to lay low?' I was looking at Martha, they'd been together for decades and both of them had lived their whole life in the area, she was the most likely to know her husband's hiding places.

'There's only one place I can think of, but it's hard to get to and I'm not sure Andreas could find it without Henry,' Martha said.

I said nothing, hoping that the silence would be awkward enough to induce her into giving up the location.

Michael got up and pushed his chair under the table causing the legs to scratch across the kitchen floor. 'I'm not staying here to help you get my dad into trouble.'

'Sit down,' I said pointing back at the chair. 'I can arrange to get you picked up by the police as well if you like.'

He sat back down, 'I can't believe this is happening. I liked you, I thought you were cool.'

'I'm flattered,' I said dryly, 'I think we should get one thing clear though, Henry's actions are on him, I didn't get him "into trouble" he did that all by himself, and now he has to face the consequences of his actions.'

'There's an underground shelter in the woods about a mile away from here, Henry's dad dug it in case of nuclear war back in the day. When Henry and Grant were little they used to play there, he took me a few times years ago, but I don't think I could remember how to find it.'

'Do you know where it is?' I asked Michael.

'No, this is the first I'm hearing of it.'

'He's telling you the truth, we never took him there, it wasn't well maintained and it had started to get dangerous by the last time I was there and we didn't want him going up there on his own and the walls to collapse onto him.'

'Stay here,' I instructed as I walked into the hallway to call Chris.

'How's it going there?' She asked.

'Okay, I think I've got a lead.'

'That's good, you need my help?'

'Not just yet, do you think you could send someone over to the farm though to keep an eye on this pair.'

'Do you think they're involved?'

'No, they both knew something was going on and it's possible that Michael saw his father and Andreas moving Ben Weber's body, without really knowing what they were carrying. I don't think they're entirely blameless, mainly because they did nothing.'

'Then why do you need someone to come up?'

'I need to go and check out this lead and Michael has been a bit volatile, not violent or anything, just unpre-dictable and I think that if he's left to his own devices he might end up doing something stupid.'

'Okay if you can wait twenty minutes then I'll have an officer up there to relieve you.'

I thanked her and hung up. Before going back to the kitchen I took the opportunity to go back to the boot room, but Emil's bag was gone. Had Henry realised that I might've seen it when Michael took me that way the day before?

'A police officer will be here shortly to stay with you until further notice,' I said as I re-joined Martha and Michael.

'We don't need babysat,' Michael said.

'Them being with you is as much for your safety as

anything else, after all until we have Andreas in custody there's no guarantee that he wouldn't come back here, and you wouldn't want anything to happen to your mum would you.' I looked at Michael and he held eye contact with me for a few moments before looking away.

We sat in silence for the next ten minutes until the uniformed officer arrived. Back out in the courtyard I was glad to be able to jump in my own car. I made the short drive from the farm to Grant Fraser's small holding.

I knocked on the door hoping that he wasn't still with the Police.

'I wasn't expecting to see you again so soon,' he said as he answered the door

'I'm glad you're here, I wasn't sure if you still be helping DCI Thacker.'

'No, he didn't need me anymore – not with everything that happened this afternoon, they say you found the body of another young man.'

'Yeah, but that's not why I'm here, I actually was hoping that you might help me.'

'Help you?' He looked confused.

'I need you to take me to the underground bunker your dad built.'

'Why?'

'Because Martha said she didn't know the way and I figured as you played there as a kid there was a chance you would.'

'No, I meant why do you want to go there?'

'I think it's possible that's where Brodie and Emil are being held.'

'Wouldn't we be better letting the police handle this,' he said.

'There's not the time and besides they're already spread

pretty thin with the crime scene and dealing with Henry, if we see anything suspicious we'll let them know. You can take me there and then leave if you're worried.'

'Wait, something happened with Henry?' Grant asked.

'He's been arrested for threatening a police officer with a shotgun.' I said, 'I can tell you the whole story another time, but we need to get a move on.'

'Give me a minute to get my boots.'

I stood on the doorstep and waited, a few moments later Grant reappeared. 'Come on then,' he said and I got into the Land Rover passenger seat.

'We can only get so far in the car and then we'll need to go the rest of the way on foot.'

'Okay.'

After a few minutes of driving Grant pulled off the main road and took a farm road towards the woods, after a while it became nothing more than a mud track and I was glad we'd come in his car not mine.

He slowed to a stop next to a copse of trees, 'it's on foot from here,' he jumped out of the car and waited for me to join him on the path.

A few days ago I wouldn't have trusted Grant Fraser as far as I could throw him and now I was in the middle of the woods letting him lead me to an underground bunker. If I was wrong then this could end very badly, but my gut told me that he wasn't the villain that he'd been labelled as. Not the most upstanding citizen perhaps, but not a drug dealer and a murderer.

'Michael said he saw his dad take a petrol can down to the shepherd's hut just before the fire, by the way.'

'I thought it would've been him.'

'I think he was trying to set you up by having it on the border of both your land.'

'I didn't really help myself either, I'm sure if I'd spoken to Brodie and explained that those drugs had nothing to do with me that we might not be in this situation now.'

'It's unfortunate that Brodie jumped to the wrong conclusion, but the rest is not your fault.'

'I can't get over the fact that he thought I was responsible for Lauren's death. I know she wasn't interested in me and that I was wrong having a fling with her, but that doesn't take away from me caring about her.'

'I know. How far is it from here?'

'About another ten minutes walk.'

The ground under our feet was hard from the cold, there were little patches of black ice, that if you weren't careful could land you on your arse. 'So, you used to play here when you were kids?' I asked.

'Yeah, we used to drive the quad bikes over and spend the day here, it was a great place to get away from the world.'

'When was the last time you were here?'

'I dunno, I'd have been in my early twenties I think.'

Grant put his hand up to indicate for me to stop and then put his finger to his lips. He pointed ahead where we could see the tracks of a quad bike on the verge of the path where the mud had softened. Quietly we walked on before we came into a clearing, a quad bike had been parked as far into the trees as possible and there were signs that someone had been dragged through the undergrowth, was that because one of the men refused to walk, or because they couldn't?

I was just about to ask Grant where the entrance was when the ground crumbled beneath my feet.

Chapter 38

Grant grabbed hold of my wrist and yanked me towards him as the earth under my feet gave way slumping into a dip.

'What the hell.,' I said.

'I think one of the interior cavities must've collapsed, it happened once when I was a kid, luckily dad was with us at the time, he dug us out and we helped him rebuild it.'

'How big is this bunker?'

'It's pretty large, a bit like a rabbit warren for people, it's under a large part of this clearing, the walls were propped up by fence timbers back then, but if they've not been maintained they'll probably have rotted away.'

'Shh,' I said, listening intently.

'What is it?' Grant whispered to me.

'I thought I heard someone shouting.'

'We need to get in there and see if anyone's trapped in the fall.' He walked across to what had looked to me like a moss covered boulder and lifted it away as if it weighed nothing. 'It's fake,' he said seeing my confused expression.

I moved to go through the opening first, Grant held up his arm in front of me as a barrier, 'I'll go in first and this isn't one of those I should go in first because I'm a man things, it's just because I know where to go.'

I accepted his explanation and held back to follow him, he took a torch out of his pocket and shone it into an otherwise pitch-black chasm.

'Hello,' Grant called out.

Then two voices in unison shouted, 'help.'

'Brodie?' I called into the space.

'Yes,'

'Brodie it's Grant, I'm here to help you.'

'Grant?' Brodie's voice sounded questioning.

'Yeah pal, did you get stuck in the collapse?'

We rounded a small bend and came face to face with Brodie, he looked gaunt and ill, his face covered in cuts and bruises.

'Grant I'm sorry,' he mumbled.

'That's alright, I would've thought the same if I were you, are you alright, can you walk?'

'I can, but Emil can't, I think he's got a broken leg.'

I looked to where Emil was lying on the ground, his jeans leg dark with leaked blood. 'When did it happen?' I asked.

'Emil's trousers got caught in the quad, it threw him from the bike, and Andreas went over his leg.'

That explained the drag marks at least. 'Where is Andreas?' I asked.

Brodie pointed to the huge mound of earth next to him, 'he's the other side of that.'

Clumps of mud fell down on us, rolling to the ground, coming to a stop next to our feet. 'We need to get out of here,' Grant said. 'This whole thing could collapse any moment and we'll be trapped.'

He was right, I cursed myself for not telling Chris where I was going, even if the locator of my phone was still attached to hers, she wasn't likely to look for me underground.

'Come on,' I held my arm out to Brodie to give him something to lean on to help him up.' He stumbled but made it to his feet, wobbling like a baby deer.

'I'm not leaving Emil, it's my fault he's here.'

Emil looked up at us, 'it's okay Brodie, you get out of here, I'll be okay.'

The earth moved again, 'that collapse must have desta-bilised the whole thing,' Grant said to me quietly.

'We have to get them both out,' I replied.

'Emil, I'm going to get you out of here, but it's going to hurt, nothing I can do about that, but once we're out I can get you help,' Grant said.

Emil nodded, Grant bent down scooping the young man up into his arms, Emil let out a scream before his head lolled to one side as he passed out. I wanted to run out of the tunnel, but each footstep had to be carefully placed so as not to aggravate the already dangerous construction.

We made it to the side of the clearing moments before the entrance to the bunker collapsed leaving little more than a muddy crater in its wake.

'We need to get him to the hospital,' Grant said motioning towards Emil.

'How did you know where to find us,' Brodie asked.

'You've got Rowan to thank for that,' Grant said.

Brodie looked confused and I realised that he had no idea who I was, or that I'd spent what should've been a relaxing holiday looking for him.

I pulled my phone out of my pocket, one bar of reception, hopefully it would be enough. 'Where the bloody hell are you,' Chris' voice sounded like a cross parent, somewhere between relief and anger.

'It's a long story and you and DCI Thacker can shout at me later, but right now I need an ambulance…'

I paused to look at Grant who was mouthing 'air ambulance' at me.

'an air ambulance,' I added.

'Are you hurt?'

'It's not for me, it's for Brodie and Emil.'

'You found them?'

'We found them, but Emil is in a bad way, he has a broken leg and Brodie looks like he needs checking over.'

'We?' Chris asked.

'I'm with Grant Fraser.' I replied holding the phone slightly further away from my ear waiting for her response.

'What the hell were you thinking…'

'You can yell at me later, right now we need that ambulance.' I interrupted.

'Where are you?'

'Um, hold on a second.' I handed the phone to Grant, 'Chris wants to know where we are,' I said as he took it.

Grant explained our location and that it wouldn't be safe to land here, but that he knew there was another clearing not far that he could carry Emil to.

Now that Grant could stand up, he put Emil over his shoulder in a fireman's lift, Brodie wrapped his arm around my neck, and we walked slowly behind. Thankfully there wasn't long to wait for the helicopter to lower in front of us. Two paramedics headed out of the side towards us with a stretcher.

With Brodie and Emil safely whisked away to a hospital

Grant and I made our way back to the clearing. 'Thanks for today,' I said.

'You're welcome, do you think they'll find Andreas down there?'

'I hope so.' We stood waiting for Chris and DCI Thacker to arrive with a team to try to excavate the bunker, it was cold and even in thick socks and walking boots my toes were starting to go numb. I stamped my feet into the ground.

'I wouldn't do that if I were you,' Grant said. 'That bunker hollowed out a good portion of this clearing and now it's started to collapse I don't think it would take much to make the whole thing go.'

'I'm surprised it hasn't happened before now,' I said looking into the clearing.

'I don't think anyone has been here much, although I could be wrong, I've no idea what Henry has been up to, and I guess he must've taken Andreas here at least once.'

'Did you have any idea your brother was involved in something illegal?'

'Henry's always been a bit shady, but I wouldn't have expected him to get involved in drugs, our dad will be turning in his grave over all of this.'

The distant sound of quad bikes came into range and a few moments later DCI Thacker and Chris appeared followed by a team of mountain rescue volunteers.

'What the hell were you thinking coming up here by yourself,' Chris said.

'I wasn't by myself, Grant was here.'

'Great, because that makes it *so* much better,' she shook her head, 'I'm supposed to be happy to learn you just jumped in the car with someone only a couple of days ago you thought was a kidnapper and murderer?'

'And then I found out he wasn't, no point holding a grudge, and besides no one would have found this place without his help. It was a bloody good job we got here when we did otherwise Brodie and Emil would be trapped under there as well.'

DCI Thacker walked tentatively around the edge of the clearing to join us, 'this your idea of being careful?'

'That's what I said,' Chris looked at him and they exchanged a look of frustration.

'Is this how you behave in Fife?' Don asked.

I thought of all the times I'd gone off following a lead without telling George what I was doing, 'sometimes, less these days.'

'I feel sorry for the team down there in that case.'

'But just think you'll be able to get on the telly tonight and tell everyone that you've found two missing men and brought down a huge drug ring, at least part of one.'

'There's an officer on their way from Interpol as we speak, I described Andreas to them and he's wanted all across mainland Europe, they'd been tracking his movements but lost him when the pandemic started, and lock downs made it harder to keep tabs on him.'

'Will they take him back to Germany to be tried?' I asked.

'If we find him alive, there's a string of offences he's wanted for in Germany, Belgium and the Netherlands.'

'What about Henry?' Grant asked.

'I'm sorry I can't discuss him with you at this stage,' DCI Thacker said. Then he turned to Chris, 'will you make sure this pair get home safely, I'll stay here and manage things.'

We walked back to Grant's Land Rover. 'My car's at Grant's house,' I said.

'In that case I'll come with you both and then you and I can go for a wee chat,' Chris said to me.

My feet were frozen and the tips of my fingers had gone that horrible way that your extremities do when you're so cold that they hurt when touched. I tried sitting on them in the hopes that my butt would thaw them out slightly. There were no mod cons in the Land Rover, but at least it kept the cold air from whipping in.

It was properly dark by the time Grant pulled into the small holding. I said goodbye and Chris followed me to my car. I was glad of the heating, we had to sit and wait as the ice melted off the windscreen.

'What were you thinking? If I'd known that the lead you were following up was so dangerous you know I'd have said to wait to get a team in,' Chris said.

'I know, I also knew those lads were running out of time, I don't think Andreas was taking them there to hide it out with them, I think he intended to kill them and leave their bodies in the one place he believed they'd never be found.'

'You were lucky.'

'It wasn't luck, it was following the leads and solid investigating.'

'I meant you were lucky nothing bad happened to you, I'm not questioning your ability, I think you've more than proved yourself capable.'

Chapter 39

Back at Ellie's cottage I let Alana fuss over me, 'you look like you've been underground,' she said brushing peat out of my hair.

'She has,' Chris said as she sat back and drank the coffee Ellie had provided whilst I told the others how my afternoon had turned out.

'So, Brodie is going to be okay?' Ellie asked.

I looked at Chris, I'd heard nothing since he was airlifted to hospital. 'He's being treated for dehydration, mild hypothermia, he's got a couple of broken ribs and some general cuts and bruises, they'll be keeping him in for observation for at least a few days.'

'I suspect he'll have traces of Blue42 in his system as well,' Sonya said.

'We made the hospital aware to run the tests, I suppose it depends on how much they'd managed to salvage from the haul in the shepherd's hut.' Chris said.

'I need to speak to his family,' I said to Chris.

'Technically it should be a police officer that lets them know, but in the circumstances, I think it will be okay.'

'You should probably have a shower first,' Alana said.

'It's only a bit of mud.'

'Well that's as maybe, but you don't smell great so you'd be doing the rest of us a favour if you did,' she laughed.

I gave her a playful push.

'Well before you do any of that can I grab a word in private,' Chris said to me.

'Sure,' I replied, and we went through to the living room. 'Is everything okay?' I asked perching on the arm of the chair.

'Everything's fine, I just wanted to fill you in on how things went with Henry Fraser, but I can't really talk about it in front of everyone.'

'Has he at least admitted to his part in it all?' I asked.

'He's admitted that Brodie and the others were, what he termed as "staying' in the bothy, when I asked him why they were there he said he was helping out an old friend, this Andreas bloke, he said that Brodie owed Andreas money and he knew that Andreas had "invited" him up to the bothy to sort it out.'

'Is he really trying to say that Brodie was there of his own free will, and if that was the case why not come forward?'

'That's what I said and eventually he admitted being party to kidnapping Brodie, he wasn't at home all night on Hogmanay as he originally said...'

'Well, we knew that he'd dropped Michael off at the hotel,' I interrupted.

'What we didn't know though was that he didn't go home, he parked his car around the corner and then a bit later he came back and that's when he'd spiked Brodie's drink with the Blue42.'

'How come no one saw him then?'

'He came back to the hotel and hung around near the toilets and when he saw Brodie out there taking a phone call, that was from Ben Weber by the way, he stopped him to wish him happy New Year and ask how he was getting on at the small holding. Brodie wasn't at all suspicious of Henry and that made it easy for him to distract him long enough to administer the drugs.'

'Brodie must've realised that he'd been drugged, I wonder if he had any clue that it was Henry.'

'Andreas drove Brodie off the road, Henry was driving behind in case Andreas' car got messed up in the process. When Brodie's tyre gave out Andreas pulled up behind him and Brodie tried to make a run for it. Henry said he had no idea that Andreas had a knife, but that Andreas and Brodie got into a fight, Brodie fell to the ground and tried to crawl away, he took off his jacket to check on where he was hurt. Andreas bundled him into Henry's car, they intended to go back for the jacket but they could see what they thought was another car in the distance so they left it behind and drove off.'

'Did Henry say anything about who killed Ben and Karl?'

She shook her head, 'he keeps saying that had nothing to do with him, all he wanted was for Brodie to tell him what he'd done with the drugs, he says that he believed Andreas when he said if he got the drugs back then he'd let the boys go.'

'I doubt that very much,' I replied.

'Me too, but perhaps he was naive enough to think Andreas would be true to his word.'

'No. I don't buy it, especially not after Ben was murdered, he must've realised what sort of man his friend was then.'

'If he did he wasn't ready to admit that a few hours ago.'

'Do you think there's any chance that DCI Thacker would let me talk to Henry?'

'Ordinarily I'd say no, but I think he quite admires you so you never know, you might be in with a chance. Why would you want to though?'

'I want to find out if he had Lauren Davidson killed or if was just some very weird coincidence that she died that night in 2020.'

Chris' phone rang interrupting our conversation, 'It's Thacker, I need to take this.'

'Alive?' She said.

I tried to listen in and catch the other side of the phone call, but Chris had the phone pressed tightly against her face and Don's voice was too muffled to make out.

'Okay will do, yes I'll meet you there, but can you get someone to pick me up because I came here in Rowan's car.' There was a pause as Don spoke, 'okay sir, see you there,' she hung up and turned back to me. 'They've found Andreas in the collapsed bunker, he's alive but in a bad way, he'd got trapped under quite a mound of earth and was barely breathing when they discovered him, he's being air lifted to hospital now. I've to go back to the hotel to speak to Henry Fraser with the DCI. Andreas is unlikely to be able to talk to us until tomorrow.'

'Will they take him to the same place Brodie and Emil are?' I asked.

'We're a bit short on hospitals around here so there's not another option, the lads will be guarded, and I don't think there's much chance of Andreas posing a threat to them at the moment, not with what the DCI said about his injuries anyway.'

'I was planning on going to see Brodie tomorrow,' I said.

'I'm not sure if he'll be up to face-to-face visitors by then, why don't you phone him instead, I can set it up with the hospital for you, if you like?'

I thought about how I might feel if some random stranger wanted to come see me in hospital after what was probably the scariest experience of my life, it was hard to remember that he didn't know me, I'd spent the last week delving into his life. 'Okay that works.'

There was a knock at the door and a uniformed officer stood in the doorway ready to pick Chris up, she was just about to leave when she turned back and said, 'I forgot to tell you Callum is getting out of hospital tomorrow, he'll still be off work for a bit but at least he can rest up in his own bed.'

Chapter 40

It was mid-afternoon in Canada when I FaceTimed Lilly, I hadn't spoken to her in a couple of days, I'd been putting it off because I wanted to have a proper update for her. Now I was sitting in the bedroom, looking forward to being able to tell them that Brodie was okay.

Lilly's face appeared on my screen, 'Rowan, did we have something scheduled for today?'

'No, but I wanted to chat to you as face to face as possible, are your parents home as well?'' I asked.

The colour drained from her already pale face, 'Oh my God is he dead?' tears welled up in her eyes.

'It's not that,' I said quickly.

'You promise?'

'Yes, so are they there?' I didn't have to wait long for my answer, I could hear her father's voice in the background and a few moments later all three of them were on my screen.

'Have you got an update for us?'

'I do, I'm happy to let you know that this afternoon I

found Brodie, he's been taken to hospital, but he's going to be okay.'

There was a moment of stunned silence before Mrs Cullen started to cry, an uncontrollable weep that left her almost gasping for air.

'You've really found him?' Lilly asked.

'Yes.'

'How can we ever repay you?' Mr Cullen said. 'Obviously we'll cover your fee and expenses, but you understand we'll forever be indebted to you.'

'What had happened to him, where was he?' Lilly asked.

That was a long story, and I wasn't sure how much of it I could tell them without breaching confidentiality. 'It's complicated,' I said, 'and the police will be in touch soon to make the information official, all I can tell you at this point is that he'd been held captive since he went missing on Hogmanay and when we found him he was with his friend Emil, who is also in the hospital. I haven't informed his family though, so I'd appreciate it if you kept that information to yourselves for now.'

'Of course,' Mr Cullen said.

His wife had recovered from her overwhelming emotions. 'I'm sorry about that, I think mentally I had prepared myself for the other outcome, made myself accept I'd never see my boy again,' her voice cracked and tears rolled down her face, but this time she held her composure. 'When can we see him?'

'DI Hampton will contact you in a little while and she'll give you all the details for that, he's a bit battered and bruised, but all things considered he's doing alright.'

'What about his other friends?' Lilly asked.

This wasn't the time to explain that the Weber brothers had been anything but friends to Brodie, better that they heard that from Brodie himself, when he was ready to talk about it. 'They didn't make it I'm afraid.'

Lilly looked sad, I wished she wasn't wasting any sympathy on them. 'Do you know who kidnapped Brodie?'

'Yes, the men responsible have been found, one of them is also in the hospital and the police will need to wait until they get the all clear from the doctors before they interview him.'

'Have they given any indication as to why they took Brodie? Surely it must be a case of mistaken identity,' Mrs Cullen said.

Did I tell them everything I knew; how would they feel if they discovered their son had put himself in such grave danger to avenge a woman they never even met. 'He discovered people trying to traffic drugs and he tried to stop them.' I responded and hoped that it would be enough to satisfy their curiosity, even if it was only for the time being.

We chatted for a bit longer before I said I needed to go, promising to ensure that someone from the police would get in touch with them and arrange for them to talk to their son. I sat for a couple of moments in silence on the bed, it had been amazing to be the bearer of such good news, but their emotions had been a lot and I felt worn out from our conversation.

I pushed my laptop over on to the side Alana had been sleeping on and lay down closing my eyes, we'd been due to leave and go back home in two days, I would need to ask Ellie if we could stay on a little while, to tie everything up and perhaps take some of those trips we'd planned before we came. I was almost dozing when the vibration of my phone disturbed me.

'Hello,' I said stifling a yawn.

'Did I wake you?' DCI Thacker sounded amused by the prospect.

'No, I've not long finished talking to the Cullens and it's been a long day.'

'I was just calling to check that you're alright,' he cleared his throat.

'I'm fine, just tired and very glad that the lads have been found, how are they doing by the way?' I really needed to phone Emil's brother, I thought.

'Brodie is doing well,' there was a pause, 'but Emil's leg is badly broken, they've put it in a cast but how much use he'll get back is something we'll have to wait and see, other than that he's going to be alright.'

'Bloody hell, that's rough, have you spoken to his family yet?'

'No, have you?'

'Not yet, I was planning on phoning his brother soon.'

'Okay let them know we'll be making all the official calls shortly.'

'Great, I told the Cullens that you'd help them arrange to speak to Brodie tomorrow.'

'No problem.'

'What about Andreas, any idea when he'll be in a fit state to interview?' I asked.

'He has concussion and a head wound the doctor was a bit worried about, as well as some broken ribs and he'd got mud in his lungs, so they think it will be a couple of days before he'll be up to it.'

'Any chance I could sit in on that one?'

'No danger, the Interpol officers will be joining me, and I don't think they'd take too kindly to your presence, but DI Hampton did tell me you'd like to talk to Henry Fraser?'

'If that's okay,' I said.

'It'll need to wait until tomorrow, and as long as the interview is recorded and DI Hampton or I am present I've no issues with that.'

'How about tomorrow morning?' Ideally I wanted to talk to him before I spoke to Brodie.'

'You want to head over to the station for about 10am?' DCI Thacker said.

'Perfect.' I was glad he hadn't said an earlier time.

There was an awkward silence

'Is there anything else you need?' I asked.

'No, no I don't suppose there is. I'll see you in the morning.'

I said goodbye and then called Emil's brother immediately after, who was elated. He promised to tell his parents to expect the call from the police and thanked me for letting him know. He was, he explained, going to get the first flight here to be with Emil as he recovered.

Chapter 41

I went to sleep knackered and now that it was morning, and I was awake I didn't feel any less knackered. I stood in the shower hoping that the less than hot water would help to wake me up. When that didn't work, I resolved to drink a gallon of coffee before heading over to the station to talk to Henry Fraser.

I was buttering some toast when Ellie came into the kitchen. 'I'm so glad Brodie and his friend are safe, I think I slept soundly for the first time since all of this happened,' she paused for a minute, 'it's weird to think that was the best night's sleep I've had all year.'

'Lucky you,' I said.

'You still not sleeping?' She replied.

'Sleeping, just not very soundly, luckily this one sleeps through anything,' I said waving my thumb in Alana's direction.

After breakfast I drove into the village, I wanted to have the chance to catch up with Chris before the interview.

Henry's Land Rover was in the car park, I wondered if Martha had come to check on her husband.

I heard raised voices as I entered the building, 'what do you mean I can't talk to him?' It was Michael.

'I'm sorry but your dad's under arrest and the only people allowed to visit with him are his lawyers.' The uniformed officer looked exasperated.

I was hoping to sneak past without Michael seeing me, but I wasn't so fortunate.

'What are you doing here?' He shouted at me and then turning back to the officer he said, 'how come she gets to go through there, but I don't.'

'You need to leave, we'll contact you when we have any news,' the officer had his hand on Michael's elbow trying to guide him to the door.

Michael shook the man off and charged after me catching hold of my shoulder, I turned to look at him. 'I want to see my dad, this is all bullshit, he's got nothing to do with any of this and you know it,' he said.

I could feel drops of his spittle hit my face and it made me feel moderately sick, 'get out of my face,' I said quietly and much more politely than I wanted to.

'No, you're not going anywhere until you take me to see my dad,' he stood in front of me blocking my path.

I took a step sideways and went to walk by him, he lashed his hand out grabbing hold of a handful of my hair and lurched my neck backwards. I balled my hand into a fist, I'd stopped listening to what he was saying, I was vaguely aware of the police officer trying to get him to release me. I pulled back my arm and thrust a punch into his gut, momentarily winding him and making him release my hair.

I stood up and rubbed the back of my head leaving the

officer to manoeuvre Michael to the ground. I caught sight of DCI Thacker coming through the double doors towards me.

'What the hell happened here?' He asked.

'Michael was just getting a bit carried away,' I said.

'Are you okay?'

'Yeah, it's the downside to having long hair,' I replied. I had thought about having it cut a couple of years ago, but had decided against it, I liked my long hair and I'd be buggered if I was going to let a few thugs make me wear it in a way I didn't want to.

'I take it PC Scott saw everything?'

'I think so.'

'Excellent I'll need you to give me a statement as well.'

'Okay.' Once I would've felt sympathy for Michael and thought about not pressing charges but these days I believed that letting that sort of behaviour slide was in a way telling people like Michael that lashing out was okay.

Chris was waiting for us just beyond the double doors, 'I only caught the end of that,' she said, 'does this sort of thing happen to you a lot?'

I tilted my head to one side and thought, 'not a lot, a lot, but more often than I'd like. That wasn't too bad, I didn't even lose any hair, I've had much worse. Does Henry know that I'm going to be interviewing him?'

'No, we thought it would make a nice surprise,' Don said.

I agreed, I looked in my bag and pulled out my brush and tidied up my hair. 'Right, shall we get this show on the road?'

'I thought it would be best if you and Chris went in.'

Henry Fraser looked tired and dishevelled, he glared at me, 'what's *she* doing here?'

'Rowan has been helping us with our investigation and she has some questions she'd like to ask you,' Chris said.

Henry folded his arms and continued glaring. I half thought he was going to refuse to talk to me.

'Emil may never walk again; did you know that?

He shrugged.

'Because your friend Andreas ran over him in your quad bike.'

Still nothing.

'How did you meet Andreas?' I asked.

'He rented out the bothy for his documentary, he's a legitimate professional,' Henry said.

'I've never known a documentary maker taking two young men captive before, why did he do that?'

'They could've left any time they wanted to,' Henry said.

'It's pretty hard to leave when your wrists and ankles are cable tied to a chair, I saw inside the bothy Henry, I saw the blood where you and Andreas beat them. Was it you or Andreas that murdered Ben and Karl?'

'I've never hurt anyone.'

'That's a lie, you help distribute drugs all through Scotland, dozens of people have died from taking those drugs.'

'Not my fault if they choose to put that filth in their bodies.'

'They didn't all choose though, did they, Jackie Smith didn't choose to take drugs, she was just out with her friends, wasn't even drinking because she had a little baby at home, Emily Paterson didn't choose to take them either, she had an Olympic career in front of her.'

'That's very sad and all but what's it got to do with me?'

'You know what I think?'

'What?'

'I think that you and Andreas thought it would be a good idea to test out your new drug, you got Ben to spike club goers drinks, you wanted to see what would happen, I'm guessing that even you weren't all that sure of how strong it was.'

Henry looked away.

'There's one thing I'd like to know, was killing Lauren Davidson just a by-product of your plans or did you have Ben do it deliberately?'

'What happened to Lauren was an unfortunate accident.'

'No, it wasn't, her drink was spiked and that caused her heart to stop, but you would've known that taking drugs would be lethal for her, she grew up around here, you knew her parents, they were neighbours, friends even, and you knew that she had a heart condition, you'd have seen the lengths they went to in order to protect Lauren. So why did you want her dead?'

'I didn't want *anyone* to die,' Henry said looking at his knees.

'Did you have some sort of falling out with the David-sons?' I paused looking at him, 'no this wasn't about them was it, this was about you finding another way to punish your brother, not enough that you bullied him into giving up the farmhouse, or that you watched him grieve the loss of his child, you wanted to take everything and everyone he ever loved from him, didn't you.'

'Do you know how humiliating it was everyone talking about him having an affair with her? He was old enough to be her father, and even after she called it off he couldn't take no for an answer, fawning all over her, trying to scare off anyone that she dated. I heard he still carries a photo-graph of her around in his wallet, our father would turn in his grave if he knew the shame Grant brought to the Fraser name.'

I scoffed, 'because drug dealing, kidnap and murder all make you an upstanding citizen. No, this wasn't about your family name, otherwise you'd have taken it out on Grant directly, you saw an opportunity to make your big brother hurt even more. What happened, did you see the photos that Ben took and realise that he was hanging out with Lauren, was it too good an opportunity for you?'

'I saw the pictures on his social media and of course I recognised her, Ben had a crush on her, but she turned him down several times for Brodie, he was already pissed off, him spiking her drink had nothing to do with me.'

'You see I don't believe you; I think you told him that he should drug her, teach the snooty cow a lesson or some such thing, Ben wouldn't have known the risk, but you did, you knew that there was every probability that she would die. And perhaps you thought if she died then it would be written off as someone taking drugs when they shouldn't have, but I doubt you expected so many people to die or get sick, that must've been a shock to you and Andreas.'

'She'd lived longer than her parents expected, she should've picked her friends more carefully.'

I wanted to lean over the table, grab his collar and punch him repeatedly in the face, he was goading me, I knew that, so I ignored him. 'Are you proud of yourself for killing her?'

'You know I saw Grant cry when he heard about it,' Henry smiled.

'Can you hear yourself; you murdered a young woman to upset your brother, you sound like a dick.' I thought about the day I'd met Lauren's parents; they were nice people and their neighbour had ripped their lives apart, using her as a pawn in some stupid sibling rivalry.

'How did Andreas feel about what happened in Glasgow, not the glowing endorsement he would've wanted for his product, I'm sure.'

'He was pissed off, but then the pandemic interrupted our business, and he used the time to make Blue42 safer, we didn't want to draw attention to our operation and punters dying isn't good for business, we just wanted them hooked that's all.'

'But then Brodie found out, didn't he.' I intended to ask Brodie how he discovered that Ben had been the one to spike Lauren's drink and how he'd joined the dots.

'I found him at the shepherd's hut, the place was cleared out and I thought it might've been him, I'd seen him there a couple of times. He had no idea that I was involved. I asked him what he was doing, and he told me that he thought Grant was involved in something illegal, didn't want to tell me what at first, but then he admitted that it was drugs. He said he'd taken the stash and that it was hidden, and he was going to hand it over to the police. I tried to get him to tell me where it was, offered to help him bring down Grant, but he wouldn't tell me.'

'Was that when you decided to kidnap him?'

'I had to tell Andreas what had happened, he came over, we came up with the plan together, we'd drug Brodie, take him up to the bothy and persuade him to tell us where the drugs were and then let him go.'

'What went wrong?'

'He wouldn't give up their location.'

'What did Andreas do?'

'He told Ben it was his mess and he needed to clean it up, he wanted Ben to torture Brodie, but he wouldn't do it, and then to make matters worse Ben got this other boy Emil involved.'

'So, Emil wasn't one of your drug runners?' I asked.

'No, I'd never seen him before, he'd come up to see Brodie and then ran into Ben and Karl, they brought him to the bothy, he went mental when he saw Brodie tied up so we had no choice, Andreas was mad that Ben had fucked up like that so he killed him.'

'What about Karl? Why did he have to die?'

'We've all got to die at some point,' Henry said.

'That's true, but natural causes didn't smash his head in, did it.'

'He'd been difficult ever since Ben died…'

'Funny that,' Chris said.

'I wasn't there when it happened, you'll need to ask Andreas.'

'You knew he was dead though, you knew his body was slowly decomposing in your bothy, that's why you threatened us with your gun, you thought you could prevent him from being discovered, but it was too late.'

'I'd intended to get rid of it yesterday, but you were sniffing around, and I knew I couldn't risk it.'

'When did Andreas take the others to the bunker?'

'He called me after Karl died, saying he needed somewhere else to hide, it was the only place I could think of that he'd be safe.'

'How did he know where to find it?'

'He didn't, I took him up there to show him, then he came back for the boys and took them up overnight, so there was less likelihood of being seen. It was clear the whole thing had gone tits up, your lot had the drugs,' he nodded his head towards Chris. 'we couldn't let them go and the bunker was an ideal place to leave the bodies, only me and Grant knew of its existence and if they were ever discovered it made it easy to blame on him.'

'Like you planned to do with the shepherd's hut,' I said.

'It worked didn't it, everyone thought he was guilty. Even you suspected him in the beginning.'

'You were meant to take Karl's body to the bunker, weren't you?'

Henry didn't reply and I considered how close we'd been to finding Brodie and Emil's bodies, when Henry didn't turn up with Karl's body Andreas would have suspected that something had gone wrong.

'What was the plan then? You kill Brodie and Emil, leave them in the bunker to rot and then what? You go back to the farm and carry on as if nothing ever happened and Andreas, was he supposed to be going back to Germany?'

'Do you know the value of the product that little shite stole?' Henry said, beads of spit flew out of the corners of his mouth and landed on the table.

'Hundreds of thousands,' I replied.

'Do you have any idea what they'd do to Andreas back in Germany if he had to go back there and say he'd lost that much product?'

I thought he'd get what he deserved, a painful, torturous death at the hands of people he'd chosen to get into business with, the outcome he was facing now seemed a cushy option by comparison.

'Like you said, everyone's got to die sometime,' I said smiling.

'He's got a family, two young kids…'

'I guess he should have thought about that, you didn't seem to give a shit about Jackie and her family, you can hardly expect me to worry about Andreas' children.'

The thing is, though, I did worry about them, whatever

their father had done I would hate to see the anger of some drug king pin taken out on them, with a bit of luck Interpol would have taken that into consideration. I stood up.

'You done now, are you?' Henry asked.

I didn't reply, instead I headed for the door whilst Chris gave the time and turned off the recording.

Chapter 42

'Interpol are here,' DCI Thacker said when we re-joined him, they've sent an officer straight to the hospital, so they are there when Andreas wakes up.' He looked at me.

'In that case I'd better be off, don't want to make things complicated here,' I said.

'What are you going to do for the rest of the day?'

'I'm going to drive up to see the Davidsons, there's a possibility this will come out and I think they deserve to hear it from someone like me, rather than read about it in the newspaper and then this afternoon I'm speaking to Brodie.'

'Try to stay out of trouble for the next twenty-four hours at least,' Don smiled at me

'I'll do my best, but I can't make any promises,'

Chris walked with me to the front door, 'I think the DCI might have a bit of a thing for you, you know.'

I frowned, 'I don't think so.'

'Would it be so bad if he did?'

'Never mix business and pleasure,' I'd crossed the line

once before and decided straight away that it had been a mistake, besides there were only so many DCIs I could have in my life.

She laughed and waved me goodbye as I walked back out into the cold air and across the car park to my car.

By the time I'd left the Davidsons home I was exhausted. They'd cried, and raged, and eventually become numb. They'd seemed crushed, the realisation that their daughter had been deliberately targeted by one of their own neighbours had seemed too much of an enormity for them to fully take in. I felt guilty, being the bearer of bad news was not a task I ever relished. I'd slipped out of their home leaving them to comfort one another. I was grateful that there was a break between now and talking to Brodie. I wanted to go home and give Alana a huge hug.

By the time I got back at the cottage I discovered that Callum had come to visit, and Alana was busy chatting with him in the living room. I stuck my head into the room to let her know I was back and to tell Callum I was glad to see he was on the mend.

Sonya and Ellie were in the kitchen. 'I was just about to make some sandwiches if you're hungry,' Ellie said.

'Ravenous,' I replied, being emotional always left me with an appetite.

'I think I'm going to head home tomorrow,' Sonya said. 'There's not much left for me to do here, Karl's post mortem is done, and the local pathologist is due back in a couple of days so I doubt they really have need of my services.'

I wanted to ask her to stay, there was something very comforting about having her around, but I'd never be so openly needy.

'You should stay for a couple of extra days,' Ellie said as

though she'd read my mind. 'You'd have the chance to relax for a while at least.'

'Maybe you're right,' Sonya said. 'It would be nice to put my feet up, even if was just for a day or so. I guess it depends if Alana wants her bed back.'

'I think she'd rather have you here,' I said. The door to the kitchen opened and Alana walked in, looking super cosy in a fluffy Christmas jumper. She came over to me and put her arms around me, resting her head on my shoulder. 'You okay?' I asked looking at her.

'I'm fine, it just felt like you might need this when you popped into the living room earlier,' Alana said.

I kissed her cheek, 'I did, thanks. We were just trying to persuade Sonya to stay here for a couple of extra days.'

'You totally should,' Alana said, 'Callum was telling me that the police are going to be clearing out of the hotel today and tomorrow as they don't need to be out here and the landlord thought it might be nice to have a bit of a do after, something to bring the village together, live music and a bit of food, so you should at least stay for that.'

'You've twisted my arm,' Sonya said.

Alana collected the sandwiches that Ellie had made for her and Callum and went back to the living room with them.

'Do you think that might be the start of a budding romance?' Ellie asked nodding in the direction Alana had just gone.

I thought about it, she did seem to like his company, he was related to DS Hargreaves and seemed like a decent young man, but who knew. 'Hard to say, she's a sensible young woman though, so I'm sure she'll do whatever makes her happy.' I took a bite out of my sandwich.

'You never know, long distance might work quite well for

Alana, no one around to distract her whilst she's studying,' Sonya said.

We finished our lunch trying to discuss things that weren't murder and kidnaping, which resulted in Sonya and me listening to Ellie talk us through her plans for the next term working with schools and their drama projects. It was nice, and by the time I was sitting in the bedroom ready to video chat with Brodie my brain felt refreshed.

He was propped up in bed, his face still looked sore, a couple of paper stitches were holding the cut in his eyebrow together, the bruises were still angry and purple but it would probably take a few days, if not weeks for them to go away completely.

'Hi Brodie, how are you doing' I asked.

'Better, thank you for finding us. I spoke to my family earlier and they told me how much you did for me.'

'That's okay, I'm just glad we got to you in time.'

'I still can't believe it was Henry Fraser, I feel so bad for thinking it was Grant, I can't imagine he'll be too pleased to see me again.'

'I think you'll find he doesn't hold a grudge against you, for a while I thought it was Grant too. He's definitely done his share of poor decision making but he's not a bad person,' I said.

'Is it bad that I wish I'd killed Henry and Andreas? Or does that just make me as bad as them?'

'It's not bad, you were angry, they took someone you love from you, I understand that feeling. In time though you'll probably feel better about yourself that you didn't.' I wasn't sure that I believed the last part of what I'd said, in Brodie's shoes I'd have been fairly satisfied if I'd killed the people who conspired to kill the love of my life.

'Thanks, DI Hampton said the police found Andreas.'

'Yeah, he was trapped when the bunker collapsed, but it's likely that he'll make a full recovery, I understand Interpol are going to take him back to Germany.'

'What about Henry?'

'He's been arrested and charged.'

'That's good, at least.'

'How did you find out about Ben being involved in what happened in Glasgow?' I asked.

'Ben and Karl were friends with Emil really, not me, but I knew that he'd stayed in contact with them since we'd all gone home in 2020. I actually never really liked Ben, I know it sounds bad to say because he's dead, but he was an arrogant asshole, always playing the hard man. We'd had a couple of arguments because he kept trying to hit on Lauren and he made her feel really uncomfortable.' Brodie stopped talking and seemed to be lost in the past for a moment.

'How did you feel when Emil told you that Ben and Karl would be travelling through Europe with you?' I asked.

'I told him I'd been hoping it was just the two of us, but he persuaded me that Ben had settled down. He hadn't though, and he kept going off places everywhere we went and then coming up with weird excuses for where he'd been, Karl was always having to go and find him and bring him back. Anyway, one day we're getting ready to leave the hostel we're staying at and I'm looking for the train tickets and Karl says they're in Ben's backpack. I went to go get them and found a bag containing little bags of pills, I recognised them as the ones that had been all over the news after Lauren died, so I confronted him.'

'What did he say?'

'He didn't try and deny it, he said it was his job, that's why he'd been in Scotland when I first met him, he'd been picking up product from the north. I asked him outright if he'd spiked Lauren's drink and he laughed in my face and said that it was just meant to be a laugh and he didn't expect her to die, he actually thought it was funny, her having a heart condition. I'll admit that I lost it and I started to hit him until Karl came in and pulled me away, by then he'd told me where he picked up the drugs from. I couldn't believe it was the same village Lauren came from.'

'And then Ben followed you here?' I asked.

'He'd been trying to get in touch with me, he was threatening me to stay out of it, I don't know if he came here to find me or if he was just on one of his routine stops.'

'And then you followed him and found the shepherd's hut.'

'That's right, and then I thought I'd teach him a lesson and I took all the drugs and Archie, Lauren's granddad, helped me hide them, I guess Ben figured out that it was me that had taken them, then he wouldn't stop calling, trying to bump into me in the shop and things,' he paused, 'then on Hogmanay, he phoned me and said I needed to promise to return the drugs by the end of the next day – I told him he'd have to wait, I had no intention of giving him back the drugs. He told me if I didn't then I'd be sorry.'

'Did you know you'd been drugged that night?'

He nodded, 'I knew something wasn't right, I'd had one whisky to see in the New Year, there was no way I should've felt how I did and thinking back I should never have got in my car, but at that point I just didn't know who I could trust. I don't remember much of that evening though, the next thing I remember is waking up tied to a chair and realising that I'd suspected the wrong Fraser brother.'

'Had you ever seen Andreas before then?' I asked.

'No.'

'What about Emil, how did he get involved in all this?'

'When Ben and Karl had come across to Scotland, Emil had come with them, but he decided to visit some friends in Edinburgh before heading North. I don't know what he was thinking, but Karl brought him to the bothy and when he saw me tied up and my face all beaten up, he tried to get Karl to let me go. Andreas and Henry came back and were mad with Karl for bringing Emil there, Karl said he thought that Emil could've taken Ben's place, but Emil tried to free me, and Andreas and Henry held him down whilst Karl zip tied him to the chair.'

'Did DI Hampton tell you how Emil is doing?' I asked.

'Yeah, I got the nurse to take me to see him, he was surprisingly okay about breaking his leg, his brother is flying over to stay with him until he's well enough to go home.'

'That's good,'

'I just feel so incredibly guilty though, you know, if Lauren hadn't been with me then maybe Ben wouldn't have tried to hurt her.'

'That didn't really have as much to do with Ben as you think, it was Henry's idea for Ben to spike her drink, he knew about her heart condition, he knew that spiking her drink was going to kill her and he told Ben to do it.'

'Why though?'

'To hurt Grant, he'd been in love with Lauren, maybe even still was a bit in love with her, and Henry saw another opportunity to hurt his brother.'

'That's twisted,' Brodie said.

'I spoke to Lauren's parents this morning; they'd really like to meet you before you go back to Canada.'

'After I met Archie, I liked him so much and he already knew about me and Lauren, he told me I should introduce myself, but the more time passed the harder that became to do.'

'Lauren's mum told me she was so grateful to learn that her daughter wasn't alone when she died, Lilly told me that you held her as she slipped away. Her parents say it means the world to them knowing that as she died she was with someone who loved her.'

'They don't blame me?' Brodie asked.

'No, they don't, not at all.'

Brodie began to cry, 'I know everyone says I'll get over her and maybe I will, but even after all this time it feels like my heart will never mend.'

'I don't know much about the affairs of the heart…' I said, I'd rather have been talking about death than love, well this sort of love, because I was pretty certain that I'd never been in love with anyone, lust, sure, but not love. '…but I do know that your family are so relieved that you're alive and I can imagine they're not going to stop fussing over you for quite some time.'

Brodie smiled and then he yawned. 'Excuse me,' he said.

'I'll go now and let you get some rest, you've got my contact details if you want to talk to me about anything.'

Chapter 43

The next two days passed without anything very much happening and it was nice to finally be relaxing on our holiday. Alana and I were getting ready for the night at the hotel, I'd not really brought anything fancy to wear with me so ended up going for a casual look of jeans and a dark green V-neck jumper.

I drove us all to the hotel, it had been raining most of the day but thankfully it was a couple of degrees warmer now than it had been earlier in the week. Once inside we made our way across to a table situated perfectly between the log fire, the band and the bar. Chris and Don joined us, the DCI looking more relaxed now than I'd ever seen him.

'Interpol say that Andreas will be well enough to transport at the beginning of next week,' Don said. 'And Henry is on remand waiting for his court date.'

Looking around the room there was no sign of Martha or Michael, no great surprise there, I doubt that either of them would feel comfortable. Michael was waiting for a court date after he assaulted me.

'I saw a for sale sign on the farm when I was driving that way yesterday,' Callum said as he sat down next to Alana.

'Can't say I blame them; not sure I'd be comfortable staying here after what Henry did.'

'No more shop talk,' Ellie said, 'surely for once you lot can find something else to discuss.'

There were a couple of moments of silence whilst we all tried to find a new topic, which resulted in us laughing at our ridiculousness, but we soon found other things to chat about, Ellie's drama plans and Alana's studies.

'What about you, what will you do when you're back home and Alana is back at uni?' Don asked me.

'More work probably, I like to keep busy, I was checking my inbox before we came out, there's an email from a very angry wife who found a receipt for a very expensive necklace a few days before Christmas, but when she unwrapped her present it was a fifty quid Amazon gift card.'

'She got any idea who got the necklace?'

'That's what she wants me to find out.'

'Is that your bread and butter work, then?'

'Actually, not as much as you'd think, I do more corporate fraud work than cheating spouses, but I like to mix it up, keeps my days interesting and you never know what else you might uncover.'

Don took a sip of his drink and then stared into the half empty glass, 'I was wondering if you fancied meeting up for a drink some time, I live in Falkirk so I'm not that far from you.'

'Do you mean as friends or on a date?' I asked.

'I was hoping date,' Don looked up at me. He was a good looking man, he obviously took care of himself and he seemed like he was one of the good guys.

'I'm flattered, but I just don't think it would work out,

my lifestyle isn't conducive to healthy relationships and someone in your position, who's also ambitious would more than likely get frustrated having a partner with a job like mine.'

He looked disappointed, maybe even a little hurt, I speculated that he wasn't used to being turned down, but maybe I was being too harsh, and he really liked me.

'What about as friends?' He asked.

I smiled, at one time my standard response would've been that I didn't need any more friends, these days I was learning that adding in a new friend now and then was okay. 'Friends would be nice,' I said.

'Friends it is then,' Don said.

'I told you he liked you,' Chris leant across and whispered to me.

'I smiled, 'if you're ever down my way give me a shout, won't you?'

I'd enjoyed working with Chris and I was going to be sorry to leave her behind, but I'd also missed George. I'd missed our banter and the comfort of knowing that he respected me and understood how I worked.

Alana and Callum looked deep in conversation, there was the subtle touching of fingers, the brush of her hand on his leg, this was definitely more than a friendship. She caught my eye and her cheeks flushed a deep shade of crimson. I smiled and she stuck out her tongue, knowing that I would be grilling her for information on the drive back home. I wondered what Jack would make of all this, how far we'd come in the last four years, but I knew the answer, he'd have been beyond proud, of me, of Alana, of everything we'd achieved and the people we'd developed into.

I sat back in my chair and observed the room, thinking back to Hogmanay when I'd done a very similar thing, except now I didn't feel like an outsider. Throughout the evening nearly everyone had come up to me to shake my hand or pat me on the shoulder and say thanks. Now this felt like a home from home, and I was going to be sad to leave it behind.

Also By Angela C Nurse

Rowan McFarlane Detective Mysteries

Jack In A Box

Sally In The Woods

What She Didn't See

Lies She Didn't Tell

Novella - Discarded

Novella - Bloody Snow

DI Ravenscroft & Professor Laing Thrillers

A Killer Conversation

About the Author

Angela C Nurse was born in the Kingdom of Fife and spent her teenage years in Penzance before returning to Scotland. With a career spanning from Nursery Nurse to Bank Manager, before becoming a full-time writer.

Now living in the Scottish countryside with her husband, Angela finds inspiration in woodland walks and road trips in her campervan. A character-driven crime fiction writer, she crafts intelligent, independent, and often sarcastic female protagonists who lead gripping investigations.

In addition to writing, Angela is a dedicated creative writing coach. Her students have gone on to win competitions, secure publishing contracts, and become bestselling authors.

For more information
please visit her website:
www.angelacnurse.com